HARBOUR VIEW

GM Wilson

Harbour View
Copyright © 2019 GM Wilson. All rights reserved.

ISBN(13): 978-1-9161953-1-8

First published 2019

Credits
Cover Design: Jenny Masters

Acknowledgements

Firstly, I must thank the Writer's Block writing group from Sydney, especially Elaine and Martin, whose writing tasks set a high standard. Secondly, I thank the adult education system of Australia, which has a varied selection of affordable writing classes for inspiration and learning. Importantly, to all the authors I have loved reading, whose characters and stories have kept me absorbed for hours, often until dawn; and, very importantly, the lesbian authors who wrote story lines that I could relate to and described a culture I could recognise and be a part of, you have my deep and lasting gratitude.

Lastly, and by no means least, my wife Lynn. Her belief in me has been inspirational. Her support, interest in my story, and trust in me, along with her knowledge of grammar rules and editing skills has been invaluable.

Chapter One

"The trouble is," Jane said, turning the photo slowly around, "you'd get confused and end up not knowing what bit of who you had."

Although probably illegal, and definitely immoral, having a friend with a camera store who developed photos for a living and kept copies of some of the results was hard to resist at times. This was one of those times. Liz had bought over some photos a client had asked her to develop. This offering was either an orgy or a new indoor group game for adults. Jane was amazed at what people asked Liz to develop. Why not buy a printer?

Liz didn't share Jane's moral dilemma. She believed those involved wanted someone to see them, to be shocked or aroused, it was part of their fantasy. Besides, what was the difference between the beautiful scenery shots that Jane had kept and framed, and these? It was an old argument between them. Jane always floundered on that point so usually remained silent, refusing to look. Liz had been very insistent with this lot, arguing the skill of the photographer warranted analysis.

Jane continued to watch Liz as she concentrated on a photo. Liz was totally focussed, and Jane had time to consider their friendship. They were an unlikely pair. Liz was tall and slender with an extrovert nature. Jane was shorter, more rounded (or sporty as she preferred) and more reserved.

Jane had never enjoyed the party scene, preferring gatherings at friends' houses. Since her breakup with Sally, Jane had withdrawn further, being alone was easier than faking happiness for the benefit of others or answering intrusive questions about her personal life.

Liz, on the other hand, was a party girl who loved the bar scene, and was still pulling all-nighters. Recently however, she was keeping very quiet about a new woman and Jane was determined to find out more. She had already discovered that the mystery woman was called Bronwyn. This woman had lasted much longer than any of the others and friends were hoping it would continue. Bronwyn seemed to anchor Liz in a way no one else had.

Liz looked up from the photo she was examining.

"The photography student, Ross, who took these photos is really very good." She mused. "Look at how he uses the unusual angle and position of the subject in this one. I'm having trouble working out what part of the body this is; let alone that amazing tattoo design! Imagine taking the time, let alone having the inclination, to take photos at a party like this!" Liz paused in her artistic critique to pass Jane the photo.

Jane studied the photo and nodded her agreement, the composition was very good, but returned to her original point,

"No matter how good the composition is, it's still a mess of body bits. You'd be hard pressed to work out who's doing what to you."

Liz passed over another photo,

"You're probably right, but you could switch to fantasy or just concentrate on the sensations."

"Then why bother? Fantasy can be used solo - and it's safe."

Jane was annoyed, her shoulders tensed as she turned away from Liz. All thought of investigating Liz's personal life was lost as Jane experienced a sudden downturn of mood. Why did everything come down to sex for Liz? Jane worried Liz would never settle. She worried even more that she herself would never find a new love.

Liz rolled her eyes in frustration. How long was it since someone had made a sexual move on Jane? Liz didn't understand her friend's withdrawal from life since the breakup with Sally. Jane was good looking, intelligent and quick-witted. She worried Jane was far too reserved to take the risks needed to find new love.

Liz had always admired Jane's fuller figure and her brown hair that behaved itself. Her own darker hair was wavy on a good day; uncontrollable in wind; and, in humidity, seemed to have a life of its own. She thought her own figure was too thin, though she did like the eccentric-artist appearance her figure and hair gave her.

There had been a time when the two of them might have got together. When they first met there was some sexual tension, but Jane had just met Sally. It was rarely spoken of now, but both had acknowledged they were much better as friends. There was still a great deal of closeness and affection between the two, despite their differences.

Jane had seen the eye rolling as Liz turned. She guessed its meaning, got upset then checked her retort. They had argued a lot since Sally left. Liz urging Jane to have a fling and 'get over it', it was what she would do. It was what she did -- regularly. Liz was infamous for moving in and out of relationships. Until Bronwyn came on the scene, she had picked up new girlfriends like she took on new fads.

It was Liz's impatience with Jane's social withdrawal that had led her to an attempt to help Jane's love life. It had nearly ended the friendship when Liz had set up a blind date without Jane's knowledge. The night was a disaster. Liz blamed Jane for wanting to wallow in self-pity and Jane felt Liz was totally insensitive. It was their worst fight. There were still wounds needing to be healed so Jane chose not to respond, and they sat in an uncomfortable silence.

They had met in a photography class as a part of their fine arts degree. They shared a passion for the subject and became firm friends. On graduating, Liz had decided her talents lay more in sales than in the art of photography, so she went into big debt with both her parents and the bank to open a store. She had shown an unexpected flair for business and quickly developed a reputation for excellent advice, equipment and repairs. As a result, business was good. 'Snapshot' was one of the few camera stores still printing in its own darkrooms. It had developed a loyal customer base amongst photography enthusiasts.

Jane had also taken the plunge and set up business as a freelance photographer. She worked at Snapshot with little pay for free use of the darkroom. It was now increasingly difficult to book time there as more people turned from digital to film photography, preferring to do things 'the old way'.

Jane's first jobs were friends' weddings and portraits. She gradually built a good reputation, especially for portraits, as people felt she captured the spirit and personality of the subject. Most of her work came from word of mouth. Initially she had focussed on the photography alone but, more recently, was adding stories to the pictures. She had achieved some success publishing her articles online and her first commissioned piece was about to be published in a print magazine. If it was well received, the magazine had indicated they would want more articles from her. Liz's visit was to celebrate the news, but Jane was increasingly feeling it was more an intrusion, so the visit was becoming awkward.

Not wanting to break the silence, but finding it difficult to endure, Jane watched Liz move to the balcony and look out over the harbour. Jane could tell Liz was uncomfortable, and felt guilty as she hoped Liz might leave, but Liz stepped forward and leaned over the balcony. Something had grabbed her attention.

Jane smiled. Liz was infamous for her distractibility. She could drop something and move onto whatever next took her interest without so much as a look back. It was one of Liz's most infuriating, yet endearing, traits. She couldn't hold a grudge, as she couldn't keep focussed on any one thing for long. How Snapshot was such a success amazed all who knew her.

Jane leant on the balcony next to Liz. The harbour was not at its best. It was early summer and the wind that chopped the surface of the water was cool. The iconic Sydney Harbour Bridge and the water had the same grey look to them; the sails of the yachts and dinghies providing the only colour. Jane always tried to appreciate the view whenever she came out on the balcony. No matter what the weather, it was too wonderful to take for granted. She lived in the house she had inherited from her aunt, much to friends' envy, close to the harbour in Balmain. The two-storey terrace was placed towards the bottom of the Darling Street hill that ran down to the ferry wharf. Jane loved her view and the fact she looked out on a working harbour.

Opposite the ferry wharf, the big container ships docked with tugboats pushing and pulling at them and huge cranes lifted the cargo onto the docks. Sometimes the noises from across the water would disturb her but mostly she viewed the thumps, bumps and clangs with affection. Those houses on the hill behind the terminal may have a less favourable opinion of the noises but what a position they occupied! So close to the city with a view of marinas and islands; and beyond to the

Parramatta River.

Jane preferred the working noises to that of the party boats that came so close to shore with their thumping music and annoying squeals and calls from the numerous drunks on board. She found them especially irritating in summer when she wanted the windows open.

Jane followed Liz's gaze to check what had captured her attention. As usual the harbour was busy with ferries, water taxis and tourist vessels but, despite her years of familiarity with the view, Jane could not recall having seen police boats flanking one of the harbour ferries before.

"Have you got some binoculars? Maybe it's a drug bust!" Liz was intrigued.

The binoculars were readily found, being kept on the bookcase next to the balcony doors. The dust that had gathered on them caused a disapproving frown from Liz and Jane tried not to look guilty. Liz started a familiar recitation on the delicate nature of lenses and the need for greater care, but Jane headed her off by asking what was happening on the water. Liz recognised the deflection but was happy to go along with it. This was a comforting return of their old, teasing friendship. She settled for a muffled plea for the case to be found. Hopefully the awkwardness of the past few months could be forgotten.

Even with binoculars they were unable to make out any reason for the police presence and had to settle for an unsatisfactory view of three men in the nearest police boat. The boat was slowly moving in a small circle. Two men were standing together, one pointing towards Darling Harbour then at Jane's place, the Darling St. Wharf, while the third leant over the back.

"Maybe he's vomiting. It is rough out there!" The idea of the water police succumbing to seasickness amused Liz and she returned, grinning, to the photos.

Jane took the glasses and watched while the two men continued their discussion. She panned over to the man in the back, to see him talking into a phone. It appeared the conditions were worsening as the standing men were being forced to brace against the waves. The discussion broke up with one going inside the cabin while the other went to the back and sat next to the man on the phone. The conversation ended as he appeared to get angry and hung up. He then turned to the man who had just sat down and shook his head. Both got up and went into the cabin.

Jane was no longer interested in the photos. She couldn't see the wharf and wondered if there were police there too. She would walk down there later. If something were happening in her area, she wanted to know. Between the much loved, but infrequent, visits to her aunt as she grew up and now living here, she was very attached to the neighbourhood. She was intending to do a project of the photographic history of the area at some stage.

"Oh, really! Hey Jane, have a look at this!" Liz's sudden laugh called Jane back to the photos.

Liz had finally worked out which body part was pictured, its position and the tattoo design she had been puzzling over. Jane reluctantly left the balcony to look again at the photo. Once Liz pointed it out to her, she could now see the edges of a skull made of... petals? The photographer was entering a collage of the photos for a 'rising star' youth arts award. He, like Jane, was working in the shop in return for darkroom time. Liz must have held the young man in some regard to give him such access.

Liz left an hour later, and Jane returned to the balcony, but the police boat and ferry were gone. Only a couple of small runabouts and a hardy canoeist remained in the area, moving in circles as if they were searching as well. The sun was setting behind the clouds and the light was fading.

Jane listened with amusement to noisy fights as pigeons, parrots and starlings squabbled over the best roosting spots for the night and the first few of the thousands of fruit bats flew overhead heading for the botanical gardens and the fig trees growing there. She loved the antics of the birds that lived nearby, and they were being joined in increasing numbers by cockatoos escaping from the arid drought-affected inland areas to find food and water along the coast. Their screeching cries and thuggish behaviour added to the pandemonium. Sitting on the balcony with a cup of tea watching humans, animals and the changing harbour scene was a favourite pastime for Jane. It was like checking in with an old friend -

comforting.

Jane reluctantly gave up watching and listening to the sounds of nature changing from day to night and started thinking about clothes to wear for a dinner party that night. Despite being very curious about what she had seen earlier, she'd have to wait until tomorrow when she went for her morning walk. Heading to her bedroom she promised herself an early start.

Chapter Two

Jane sighed as she opened the wardrobe door. Dressing to go out was an activity she disliked intensely. She felt that she never quite managed to get the right outfit together and the weight she had put on over the past year did not help. She returned yet again to speculate about Sally: the affair, the fights, the final parting and felt a wave of self-pity welling up. Taking a deep breath, which also aided her struggle with her jeans, Jane went over the reasons she was better off single, allowed herself some bitchy thoughts, and focused on the evening to come.

The mystery on the harbour passed from her mind as she struggled with her jeans and the choice between looking slimmer or being comfortable. As she suspected she would, she soon gave up the struggle with the jeans and reached for her looser trousers.

Since the breakup, Jane had lived alone. It was both her nature and her choice. She found it easier to deal with her sadness by herself. She had considered renting a room out but quickly dismissed it. She had buried herself in work and the reward was the commissioned article. Early on she had accepted party invitations from close friends, only to be crushed by the sight of Sally holding her new love and so had increasingly declined. She stayed at home worrying about being pathetic and losing friends.

There were only a few friends who had persevered with her. They continued inviting her out, understanding the invitation refusals and sudden retreats when her emotions got the better of her. As was usually the case, there were many mutual friends, some had taken sides, but most had wisely said they would continue to invite both Jane and Sally. It was up to them to decide whether to attend or not. While Jane understood the wish to remain neutral, she felt it was unfair. Sally had left her for someone else. She would find it easy to attend these functions; she had someone to go with. Jane only had herself and she struggled.

Things were improving of late, she was coping more often than not, and dinner tonight was with two long-time friends.

Jane had known Jo and Marion long before she met Sally and, while not taking sides, they let Jane know she was special to them. They had made the effort to keep in contact, even when Jane was hibernating. They were friends she loved, trusted and felt comfortable with.

It was a Friday night; her article had been accepted for publication and she was determined to enjoy herself!

Driving along Balmain Road twenty minutes later, Jane almost ran into the back of a van at some traffic lights. The large rusted dent in the rear bumper suggested she wasn't the first to be caught out by it stopping suddenly. She berated herself. Her concentration as well as her self-confidence had suffered since the split. It really annoyed her. Enough that she had been seen too often with red, puffy eyes, but to be red, puffy-eyed and vague was too much. She resolved to focus more on her surroundings.

"Attention all brain cells! Report to the front office. All hands on deck!"

She shook her head. She was talking to herself as well. Vague, red and puffy-eyed woman who talked to herself! It was time to start a new life; this one was getting weird.

A good-looking woman was walking along the hospital side of the road and Jane looked at her with appreciation, concentrating had its benefits. Jane turned her head to look up one of the many small streets on the other side of the road. Traffic slowed to a halt, allowing her the time to fully take in the sight of a young man relieving himself against the wall of the corner house. She quickly returned her gaze to the hospital, being aware of her surrounds may have benefits but it came with potential downsides. Selective awareness was what she needed.

The majority of the hospital was actually the new College of the Arts but its long history as a psychiatric hospital meant it was still 'The Hospital' to the locals. It might be known as 'The College' one day but not yet. Up until recently there were still some wards open for chronic psychiatric patients, but those functions were closing down.

The blue van she had nearly rear-ended turned into the hospital and travelled on a road parallel to Jane. She pondered on whether or not it was a visitor or employee.

'Probably a resident being returned by family after a day out,' she thought.

Although feeling silly, Jane enjoyed the distraction of creating the story. Jane's route meant she turned right, down a road to the side of the hospital, and continued to parallel the van's path. She watched it drive ahead of her; past the turn off to the wards to eventually park next to an overgrown cottage down near the water: a hospital employee she surmised.

She drove a short distance further then turned left and immediately parked. Jo and Marion's house was on the corner. She got out of the car and checked her watch. Thankfully, she was on time. Time was one of Marion's sore points: she was always complaining about 'Lesbian Time' being at least an hour behind real time. Jane smiled at the memory of a berating she and Sally had received when they were once late. It had been delivered in good fun, but they had never been late for Marion again. Jane was knocking on the door when she realized the thought of Sally hadn't hurt. Her smile widened. She could look forward to a night with good friends.

That good feeling was short-lived.

Her smile of anticipation had faded as Jo opened the door to Jane with an apprehensive look on her face. Her expression then progressed to a grimace as Jo whispered that Sarah was there, and, worse, was looking forward to meeting Jane. Jane had never formally met Sarah, but her reputation was fearsome. She reportedly had the tenacity of a terrier once she set her sights on a potential partner.

"Sorry, but she wouldn't leave." Jo explained and didn't try to hide her annoyance as she turned back to the room to lead Jane in. There was silence as Jane entered and Sarah stood to greet her. The description of a terrier suited Sarah – small stature, wiry hair and lean body – Sarah positively oozed nervous energy. Jo ignored the implied request for an introduction, and Jane stood awkwardly before Marion moved to smooth over the moment and start a conversation. Sarah pushed Marion to one side to sit next to Jane on the couch. It was a wide three-seat couch, but Sarah moved so close that Jane was pressed up into the arm of the couch to get some separation from her.

In a bid to get away from Sarah a short time later, Jane announced she had forgotten to bring something to drink. Jo started to protest but stopped at the look on Jane's face and instead offered to walk to the Bottle Shop with her. Marion assisted their escape by asking Sarah to stay and help her prepare the salad.

Jo had hardly shut the door before launching into an apology. Jane could guess what had happened but wanted Jo to suffer through the explanation. Sarah was one of those people who never knew when to go. She left silences for others to fill and relied on their reluctance to ask her to leave. She was never directly rude but her inability, or unwillingness, to take hints often incited rudeness from reluctant hosts who were unable to move her in any polite manner.

Sarah had arrived mid-afternoon, catching Jo and Marion off-guard. Jane started to laugh but she wasn't ready to let Jo off the hook immediately so coughed instead. Jo gave her a suspicious look but continued with the story. Sarah had continued sitting after they had announced that they couldn't chat anymore as they had to prepare for dinner.

"Don't mind me!" she had stated and had stayed... and stayed... until they felt forced to invite her to dinner.

What amazed Jane was that Marion, who she believed so forthright, was as stumped by Sarah as everyone else. The really alarming aspect of Jo's story, however, was her recounting of Sarah's line of questioning once she knew Jane was the dinner guest. Was she still single? Was she available? Was she into flings?

"Oh God!" Jane looked up in desperation and saw a look of amusement cross Jo's face. "You're joking, aren't you?" She was horrified.

Jo raised her hands in protest.

"Well, maybe not quite those words but she's definitely interested."

Jane knew of no one who had tactfully thwarted Sarah. Despite her small stature and feminine look, Sarah was a force to be reckoned with. One of her targets, Judy had moved interstate. Jane was told it was work related but now she was wondering. Others had tried frank statements of disinterest, but Sarah was rumoured to take these as challenges. When people became rude, Sarah had the uncanny knack of looking like the victim… until you'd seen the situation repeat itself a few times.

Jane was going to require a lot of determination and strength in the next few hours. Her earlier good mood faded. She felt overwhelmed at the thought of coping with the rest of the evening.

By the time they reached the Bottle Shop they had decided that more alcohol was a bad idea, so they bought mineral water and headed back. Jo was concerned by Jane's silence.

"Sorry, but I thought you'd better know that you're about to be stalked by 'She of the Endless Visit'."

They plotted increasingly impossible strategies to get Sarah off the couch and out the door. Jo offered to collapse from food poisoning, but both agreed Marion would be eternally insulted.

Jane started doubting the wisdom of returning for dinner as they passed by her parked car.

"Maybe the best way to get us all off the hook is my going home. I wouldn't have to deal with her, and she'd have no reason to stay on."

Jo was now desperate. "No way! This is our night! And besides she might stay, and we'd be alone with her! Damn it, we were going to celebrate you getting published! We think you've turned a corner. You seem much stronger in yourself. Happier. We've almost got our old Jane back."

Jane felt her eyes stinging at the obvious affection in Jo's voice and gave her a hug.

Chapter Three

Marion looked at Jane in concern, and Jo in reproach, when the two appeared. Jane was crying and Jo was alternating between apologising and trying to make her laugh. It was after Jo recalled a funny story involving Sally, producing renewed crying from Jane, that an angry Marion stepped in and sternly told Jo to shut up. Jo started to say something but turned and went into the kitchen instead.

Marion's temper was not often seen but was legendary when fired up. People thought Jo was the more assertive in the partnership since she was more extrovert in social situations; but theirs was a balanced relationship, they both made it work. It was a relationship that Jane admired a great deal.

Marion had never seen Jane so openly distressed. Jo was not known for her tact so Marion was sure Jo must be at fault. She put her arm around Jane and steered her towards the sofa. Jane was grateful to sit with her head turned into Marion's shoulder.

Sarah started towards Jane with a comment about how she too knew what it was like to be lonely, Jane's shoulders shook all the harder. Marion spared a fleeting thought for the silk blouse that Jane had buried her head in. She suggested that considering Jane's state it was probably better if dinner were cancelled and Sarah leave.

Sarah argued that she too should offer consolation to Jane but at this a strangled cry could be heard from the kitchen. In a muffled voice Jane called out,

"Oh, Jo. Don't cry, it's not your fault!" and nestled further down into Marion's shoulder.

Marion gave Sarah a firm look and motioned towards the door. Sarah reluctantly nodded and left with a comment about 'bloody dyke dramas'. There was silence for a moment after the door closed. Marion leant back and took Jane's chin in her hand gently asking,

"What did Jo say?"

At this point Jo came through the kitchen door with a bottle of champagne and three glasses. Smiling broadly, she sidled up to the window to furtively watch Sarah driving off.

"Well done, honey! I knew you could do it!"

Marion's initial look of confusion was quickly being replaced by one of anger.

Jane rushed in, "We figured if you had the motivation, you'd be able to move her, we just had to... um... work up your motivation..." Jane's words slowly dried up under Marion's gaze.

"Oh, come on, Marion, don't get shitty, you were wonderful. You're just upset we thought of it and you didn't."

Jo wasn't as daunted by Marion's ominous silence as Jane was. Jo sat down, putting the bottle and glasses on the table so her hands were free, and she could join the conversation. She gave Marion her biggest smile, turned to Jane then started to giggle,

"And you! You were great! I thought I'd stuffed it when I started laughing but you called out to reassure me!"

She returned to Marion, "Look, sorry if you're angry, but there was no time to fill you in and we needed you to be really pissed off and protective..."

Finally, Jo faltered under Marion's continued silence.

Marion moved forward without comment and took hold of the bottle.

"Well then, let's drink to our success. You were both amazing, you bastards! God Jane, when did you take up acting?" She looked reflective for a moment, "I did move her though, didn't I?"

Jo was quick to Marion's side and gave her a kiss. "You were wonderful. So strong, so brave, you're my heroine!"

Marion finally laughed but Jo frowned. "'Damn it though, we'll never be able to tell anyone of our triumph!" She smiled slyly, "Well, maybe a few."

After a few toasts to their success, Marion asked,

"How did you do it? You really looked like you'd been crying."

Jane hesitated, so Jo answered,

"It was easy actually, we stood outside while I told her how much we loved her; how stupid Sally was; and how she'd better find someone we approved of, or there'd be trouble."

Marion raised her eyebrows and commented dryly,

"So, news of our regard for you is that distressing?"

Jane got up to propose a toast to friends, but Marion suddenly jumped up cursing and rushed to the kitchen; coming back to announce dinner was not totally ruined, just nearly.

A short while later, as they sat over a rather chewy lasagne, Jane announced that thoughts of Sally were upsetting her less and that Jo had been unsuccessful in raising tears by talking about the breakup. There was agreement that this was the first time that any of them could recall Jane having a good laugh since Sally left. Jane had a sense of relief, mixed with some surprise that she had needed to fake upset. It felt like some boundary, a significant one, had been passed.

This realisation set off a more sobering line of thought. Could Sarah's unwelcome interest be the result of some unconscious move to being sexually available? Did Sarah sense something? No one had approached her in the year since Sally left. Was she now giving off different vibes? Had she passed some unspoken point in time after which you could be hit upon?

Even more worrying, could Sarah sense a new availability? Was it like a scent? Would it get stronger? Would she have a conga line of lesbians following her down King Street? She stifled a nervous giggle. All this meant one thing. She would be starting the whole dating business again. Awkward silences, clumsy conversation, introducing a new 'HER' to family and friends! And what if she didn't find anyone or, worse, no one fancied her? No conga line…

Jane's despairing loud groan got Marion's attention and Jane hastened to assure them she wasn't dwelling on Sally. Jo laughed as Jane outlined her fears, "You haven't even met her and you're panicking."

"I'm not panicking, I'm just... well, okay, I am panicking! It's... God, it's six years since I dated!"

This brought both Jo and Marion to her side with hugs and reassurances. Marion went to get dessert saying,

"I am glad it's you and not me though," while throwing a smile at Jo.

The next hour or so was spent reliving past dating disasters with quick reminders to Jane that they were all older now and things would be different. Jane laughed at their stories and told her own but the business of finding a new partner was extremely daunting.

Toward the end of the evening Marion asked Jane if she felt safe going home alone after 'today's news'. Jane looked blank.

Jo prompted, "you must have heard. It was right off your wharf!"

Marion wondered aloud if Jane had gone into religious retreat, adding,

"There was a body found in the water just off the wharf. It's not been identified, but they say it was execution style, probably a drug hit."

Jo quickly added that if it were drugs, Jane would be safe as it would likely be a gang hit or something, nothing to do with the general public.

Jane recalled the police boat and felt a bit sick. She filled Jo and Marion in on what she and Liz had seen that afternoon. Marion detailed the news she had heard about how the body was found. A tourist on the ferry had been filming the ferry manoeuvring to dock. The body had suddenly surfaced, possibly raised by a combination of decomposition and the turbulence of the ferry engines.

Jane started to express concern for the poor tourist when Jo cut her off and reported the 'poor tourist' was not upset about seeing the body but by having the clip copied then deleted by the police before he thought to post it online. Marion and Jo exchanged a few comments and joked together about possible TV programs - 'World's Wackiest Body Videos'.

Jane felt unable to laugh at something so macabre, and so close to home. Literally. Jo picked up Jane's mood and changed the topic back to the earlier excitement of the evening. They stayed on this topic until Jo announced the time and a general clean up was started.

Jane left feeling happier than she had for a long time and noted with amusement that the van she had seen on her way to dinner was also on the move. It seemed to be leading the way home, but it left her behind at a set of lights.

Once home, Jane opened the door, welcomed the sense of familiarity, but looked anew at the furniture. It was time to make decisions about clearing some of it out, too many items were connected to Sally. She needed space for herself. It was only on going upstairs and looking out over the harbour that she remembered the news of the body. She turned on a few more lights than normal as she got ready for bed.

Chapter Four

Jane was woken by the sound of hushed but persistent noises. Assuming it was time to get up, she checked the clock. It was 3.15 a.m. - only a few hours after she had gone to bed. The police must be still searching, she thought. Curiosity got the better of her and she jumped out of bed and headed to the balcony. Besides being curious, she knew her friends would want her to take any opportunity she had for news.

Jane had felt a sense of intrusion on learning about the body. This was her area, her home. She felt safe here and someone had violated that. Not that they would care, she mused; anyone who could kill in cold blood wouldn't think about the effects on the people where the body was dumped.

She walked onto the balcony, silently welcoming the police and being reassured by their presence. But it didn't look like the police, in fact it didn't look like anyone. There were no lights, no police cars, no one to be seen. Just the occasional muffled splash and hushed voice. Nothing like the sounds Jane was so used to hearing on the water.

Jane quickly moved back into the darkened doorway. If it wasn't the police, then it must be the murderers - who else could it be? With her heart pounding, Jane crept back to the edge of the balcony and looked over again. There was definitely no indication of police activity down there, but equally there was nothing sinister either. There was nothing to be seen. At three in the morning that wasn't unusual, but the noises were.

Leaning back through the doorway Jane grabbed the binoculars but everything was far too dark. She sat down on the lounge and wished she had someone to talk this over with. Sally would have been no good. She was so grumpy when woken up. Liz would probably have the two of them down there taking photos and number plate details.

Caught between these two extremes Jane decided she should ring the police and let them sort it out. Never having rung the police before, Jane found herself getting nervous. The act of ringing meant it was serious. By the time she had found and dialled the number for the local police, she was starting to question the wisdom of the call and had decided to hang up when a recorded message informed her of the times the local station was staffed and gave her the numbers for police headquarters, the police assistance call centre and emergencies. Jane looked at the handset in annoyance.

"Oh great! I could be getting murdered and there's a recorded message."

She recalled the fuss about the downgrading of the local station a few months before. More annoyed than nervous now, she dialled the call centre. A woman answered and asked how she could help. Jane felt her annoyance fading as she came to the reason for the call and stumbled over the first few words. She could hear the controlled sigh in the woman's voice as she asked Jane to repeat herself, slowly. As she explained, Jane began to feel foolish; even to her ears this was sounding lame. The woman politely explained that while she wasn't aware if police were there or not, she doubted any officers would want a lot of noise and light disturbing the local residents. She reminded Jane that current police policy was very community oriented.

Jane was becoming increasingly desperate to end the call and her own related feelings of stupidity. The woman further added to them by suggesting it could be maintenance work by Sydney Ferries.

"I... I didn't think of that."

Jane was dismayed at the meek tone in her voice. The woman then thanked Jane for her concern, told her not to worry and suggested she return to bed to get a good night's sleep. Jane hung up; trying to work out if she was more annoyed at the patronising tone of the woman or herself for not thinking things through.

She remained sitting a short while then headed for her bedroom. She would go out, get cold, lose sleep and find out who it was out there. Jane knew she was being silly and stubborn, but she had started thinking the act would somehow counter the embarrassment of the phone call.

The suggestion of maintenance work had reassured her. Jane decided the outing was just an early morning walk. She had wanted to go on one anyway. It was just early... very, very early.

Pulling on her track pants, Jane was surprised at how excited she felt. As a child, she had often pretended to be a spy. Long forgotten memories and even smells came back to her, lying under a bed or chair, climbing fences, hiding in garden beds and sneaking unseen across neighbour's backyards. To be honest, she had snuck around the neighbourhood until well into her teens. She was still proud she had never been caught. She had not been like her peers. The thrills they sought were easy and mundane to Jane's thinking - smoking, drinking, boys and occasional shoplifting. While they boasted of their adventures, Jane kept hers secret. She enjoyed the thrill and craft of stealthy movement. She smiled as she checked over her outfit, the same as all those years ago, close fitting and dark colours. It was missing one piece. Her smile widened as she searched out a black beanie to wear.

She grabbed a small bag and headed to the back door. Her front door opened directly onto Darling Street, which lead down to the wharf. No discreet exit there. She checked the bag and removed a few items including her wallet but left her pocketknife, tissues, keys, pen and paper in the bag. She decided against the binoculars *(too heavy)* and her mobile *(needed charging)* and, shaking her head at her own behaviour, she closed the kitchen door behind her and headed for the back fence and rear lane.

A few moments later, Jane found herself stuck on top of the fence, a leg on either side, and very aware of how she had aged and how her confidence in her climbing ability had gone. She dimly recalled that the trick was to tackle the fence at speed, swinging one leg over, with the body and other leg following. She hadn't done that.

Her hands felt as if they were being cut in half, and Jane was aware that if she slipped it wouldn't only be her hands cut in half. That would definitely end any conga line fantasy! She gathered courage, swung the leg from inside the fence as hard and high as she could and pushed off.

She was still turning as she landed and ended facing the way she wanted to go. The pride at actually getting over her first fence in over ten years made up for the gouges in her palms and a pain in her foot. She hadn't even made much noise. She smiled to herself at what the maintenance workers would think if they saw a woman hiding behind trees watching them. No, they wouldn't see her; she would watch without being seen; like she had as a child. She had been very good at hiding and moving unseen. She was determined she would be again.

Chapter Five

The laneway was the old access path the Nightman had used when emptying the backyard toilets that had been at the rear of every property. For some in Balmain, this practice had only ceased in the 1970s or so. The laneway was now the domain of foxes, cats, rats and the occasional human, usually with illegal intentions. That thought took a little of the excitement away and Jane started walking cautiously.

At the end of the lane, residents had allowed tall weeds to grow, hoping to hide the rear access to their properties. All in all, it had seemed to work with only a couple of break-ins from the laneway before Jane moved in. Jane pushed through as quietly and carefully as she could; made sure no-one was watching and ran across the side street that ended on Darling Street.

She leant against wall of the corner house nearest the wharf. A quick look towards the wharf revealed an empty street but no view of the wharf. She started to congratulate herself on how well she had done so far, despite this setback. She needed to get further down Darling Street, maybe to that small park. She quickly checked up the hill towards the shops and stopped, frozen; all thoughts of moving ceased. There were two men standing at the top of the hill in the middle of the road. She moved back into the shadow of the house.

Jane was angry at herself for not expecting lookouts and wondered whether she would have expected them at the age of ten. She decided yes; at ten she would've been pretending they were bad guys, not maintenance men. At the end of this logical process Jane felt her stomach knot; a cold sensation crawled along her arms, leaving goose bumps. Why would maintenance men have lookouts? The men were wearing suits. Her heart raced, if they weren't police or maintenance workers, they must be the bad guys.

Initially Jane was immobilised and just stood staring at the corner, expecting someone to come around it. She finally persuaded herself to move back towards the corner and peered up the hill to see the two lookouts standing boldly in the middle of the road facing the other direction. There was only the one road to the wharf, and they were obviously there to ensure there was no interruption.

She was torn between going home and ringing the police again or trying to get close enough to get some details. She knew the most sensible thing to do would be to ring and try to convince the police to investigate but Jane felt she couldn't ring that condescending woman without more evidence.

She was trying to decide whether to go on or not when two thoughts occurred to her. The first was that she couldn't go home now: there was no way she could get over the back fence again without the rails to help her. The second was that the cliché was true, villains really do return to the scene of the crime! Although not helpful, it did make the situation seem less scary. She decided the best thing to do was to wait to get car number plates as the bad guys left, then she could pass proper evidence onto the police.

Jane was congratulating herself on the decision when disaster struck. The anxiety of the last few moments had its effect. She had to go to the toilet. It was the familiar sensation that she recognised as her 'two-minute warning'. In her excitement she hadn't done the most basic of all preparations. She hadn't gone to the toilet before she left the house.

Jane started to jiggle around in the universal manner which signalled urgent need. She couldn't return home. Opposite her and down the hill a bit was a small park with bushes in the middle and trees along the fences; she would head there. She had tissues with her; and she could even get a view of the wharf if she climbed the trees.

The road looked wide, very wide. She would be exposed while crossing it… She was planning on being exposed afterwards as well. The thought bought a small tight smile.

The lookouts were still in the road. Jane looked down towards the wharf; no one could be seen. In desperation she jiggled around on the spot; another thing she'd not done in years. The lookouts were moving off the road. Soon they would be behind a bus shelter. Another quick look back towards the wharf, still no one could be seen.

Jane took a deep breath and moved off with the determined thought that they could shoot her when she finished. It was now or never; and never was something her bladder could not consider.

Running whilst crouched over didn't assist speedy movement and compressed her bladder, but she made it. She crossed the path in one stride and threw herself over the fence. She registered somewhere that she would hurt tomorrow but landed more or less safely, rolled and dashed to the bushes, hands grabbing at the waist of her track pants. Thankfully she had not worn the jeans with the button fly.

It was a short while later, when able to concentrate again, that Jane realised there were no sounds of pursuit. She hadn't been seen. She cautiously moved to check up the road as far as she dared. The men were back standing on the road. She curtailed any self-congratulatory thoughts. She had still to gather evidence if she hoped to persuade the police to take her seriously.

There was no way she wanted to repeat the road crossing; so she hoped it was just a case of climbing a tree and sitting tight for a few hours. Jane chose a tall jacaranda tree that she hoped would offer the best view of the wharf and, despite its purple flowers being on the wane, there was still some cover to protect her if she got up high enough. It was a tree she often admired from her balcony, the rich and vibrant purple flowers were the highlight of her springtime view. She headed towards the tree, past the sign proclaiming the 'Marjorie Gillis Reserve'. She sent Marjorie a silent blessing, and a quick apology - whoever and wherever she was.

Jane found the climbing relatively easy and was rather pleased with her decision. It was going quite well. She was lucky not to be worried about heights, she realised she'd have to climb quite a bit higher than anticipated to see the wharf, if she could.

She had climbed four or five metres and was grabbing another branch when the dog from the house next to the reserve startled her by barking.

"Good boy. Shut up!"

Jane hissed, then jumped again as she heard someone running down the footpath toward the park. Hurriedly climbing another two branches, Jane continued making what she hoped were soft calming noises at the dog. She froze as she turned to see two men entering the reserve. They did a quick scout around as Jane searched higher, even one more branch would make her less conspicuous. She reached up with her right hand, took careful hold of the next branch and raised herself up yet again. She was high off the ground at this stage, near the top of the tree with nowhere to go. She hoped she could find the way down as easily as her fear had found the way up.

As Jane was sitting quietly and out of its sight, the dog had quietened down, only giving the occasional warning bark. The men continued their search, heading for the bushes where Jane had first taken refuge and relief. One silently indicated that the other should go in to check. The area the bushes covered wasn't large, so it wasn't long before Jane heard a muffled curse. The man waiting moved quickly to the bushes,

"Brian?"

"I just stepped on a tissue. It's wet! Someone's pissed here and recently!"

The waiting man swore quietly and asked, "Are you sure?"

Brian was certain, "It hasn't rained in days, it's been hot and everything else is dry."

Jane's heart dropped. She had decided to collect the tissue later. Her punishment for littering could be harsh.

The guy nearest Jane didn't reply but took a small object from his pocket and spoke quietly into what was obviously a radio. Jane couldn't make out much of what was said but someone called Paul was being told there was a problem.

The man put the radio back in his pocket and took something out from under his jacket. As he swung around checking the area, Jane got a clear look at what he held so casually. She had never seen one before in real life, but it was definitely a gun. Her knees went weak and she tightened her grasp on the tree.

Brian came out from the bushes wiping his shoe on the grass. His partner touched his arm and motioned towards the back of the park. They moved off, but it was obvious they'd return soon.

Jane forced her arms and legs to stop shaking. She was unlikely to be seen, especially from a distance; but someone looking up the tree couldn't miss her.

She moved closer to the trunk and wedged herself in a

position where she would stay wedged even if shot. She was surprised at how calmly that idea came to her. If they saw her, they were likely to shoot. The noise would wake someone who would ring the police. The bad guys would leave and, if she was still alive, she'd be saved. She briefly thought of silencers but the sound of the men returning froze all thought. It seemed to stop all breathing as well.

The men halted a short distance from Jane's tree. She could hear them talking but she couldn't see them. The man, Brian, wanted to continue searching but the other was unsure. They agreed Paul could decide and the radio was brought out again. Brian started moving towards Jane's tree whilst the other asked Paul what he wanted them to do.

Jane clung-on way above them and looked over the fence, calculating the distance she'd fall if she jumped that way. The dog had wandered off but it now returned to the fence pricking its ears at the men's voices. Jane could hear dead grass and twigs crunching as the man moved under the tree to her right.

She had decided to risk moving to a position better to jump from when she looked down to see an older woman standing under her tree looking up at her. Jane was stunned for a second and then urgently motioned the woman to move away, leave, anything - just not look up!

The woman's mouth opened but the soft voice was right beside Jane.

'Don't move. They won't see you. Stay still.'

Jane stared as the woman faded from sight underneath her and started appearing on a nearby branch. Jane was dimly aware of her own jaw dropping as she watched the last part of the woman on the ground fade to reappear and complete the form more solidly on the slender branch in front of her.

"What fun! I haven't been in a tree for years, well, decades." The woman looked around with obvious delight. *"Oh, the view! I'd forgotten how lovely it was... My, it's changed so."*

Jane was stunned at what was happening; confused by the way the woman's voice sounded inside her head; but also surprised at some level that the woman was wearing pants. She seemed the age where a knitted cardigan and a sensible wool skirt would be more appropriate. The woman was wiry and so Jane could easily imagine her climbing trees. However, it was her eyes that held Jane's attention. They seemed to reflect a great deal of sadness, despite the ready smile.

Jane was astounded at how much she was taking in about the woman, given the situation. At the back of her mind she thought fear and shock were contributing to a hallucination. Another factor holding her attention was the woman's obvious delight and interest in what was happening. It was hard to miss.

Jane was still staring, speechless, when the woman finally seemed to remember her presence.

"Don't worry, you'll see I'm right! Just what are those men after? I must admit I wasn't happy at you using my house as a toilet, but you apologised and sent those lovely thoughts," she gave Jane a big smile.

Jane's embarrassment overcame her amazement.

"You watched me! I... I was desperate! I've never... What thoughts?" Jane stammered and then remembered the men below and hissed, "Quiet! They have guns. They're murderers!"

The woman looked down.

"Those murderers are right below you."

Jane followed the woman's gaze and stopped breathing. She locked eyes with Brian and they stared at each other, neither moving.

Chapter Six

Something was different though. Jane felt as if she were watching him through thick glass; his movements were distorted, jerky and blurry.

The woman's voice gently encouraged her. *"They won't see you if you stay still. If you must move, move very slowly. I can only do so much you know!"*

Brian was complaining.

"I know I heard something. Must've been a possum. Maybe the old derelict we saw yesterday pissed in the bushes, I don't know but it's weird. They better finish down on the wharf soon. This is giving me the creeps. Got that dog going too."

His partner nodded with the same jerky movement and pointed his thumb towards the road. Jane slowly turned her head to see the dog moving in the same disjointed way while it started barking.

A voice called out, "Shut up, Tosca! Go to bed!"

The dog gave one last bark and moved back to the house. Jane slowly turned away from the dog and saw the men reaching the front of the reserve. Another man was waiting for them; pointing to the top of the hill. She was starting to feel a little queasy from the distorted movement when it suddenly returned to normal.

The two men started to walk quickly up the hill and moved from sight. The new man stood for a moment staring into the park, his face lit by the streetlight. Jane watched him carefully until he turned and walked down the hill.

Her companion was still sitting as before, watching Jane with a slight smile on her face, head cocked to one side. Jane had no idea what to say so she fell back on social custom and introduced herself. The older woman smiled and said her name was Marjorie, Marjorie Gillis.

Jane knew the name.

"Do I know you? Well, I mean, should I know you?"

"I live here, this was my house until it burnt down."

The woman looked around with moist eyes and, with a shock, Jane recalled the sign on the reserve. What did she know about Marjorie Gillis?

"That was many years ago. Didn't Marjorie Gillis... you... die in that fire?"

Any other words Jane intended stuck in her throat. The woman looked at Jane.

"Yes."

That simple reply bought Jane the closest to panic she had been all night. She closed her eyes, hugged the tree even tighter and tried not to fall.

When Jane opened her eyes again, it felt like hours had passed, but she knew it was only a few minutes; waking up in her bedroom seemed like days ago, certainly not only an hour or so.

Marjorie Gillis was no longer there, which was a relief. There seemed no way to rationally consider Marjorie and the implications of both her presence and her intervention. None of it bore thinking about for too long. Jane couldn't grasp what she had seen; what had happened. It wasn't logical or rational, but she knew it had happened.

Jane had always believed in the existence of a spirit world but to experience it like this was another thing entirely. She questioned her own mental state. Stress, anxiety, fear, can all do strange things to perceptions... can't they?

With an effort Jane made herself focus on her more immediate problems. It was easier to think about murderers and guns. She had no idea how long she'd been in the tree but the creeping ache in her right buttock suggested it was too long.

The view from the tree was far more limited than she had hoped. She couldn't see the wharf, let alone cars or any other details. She realised that she had a decision to make. Did she sit and wait for dawn; find a safer place to wait; or get closer? Whatever she decided, she had to move, at least to a more comfortable branch.

Jane decided to move closer. A better, and safer, view might be had from the park to the right of the wharf. Beneath her fear, there was still anger at this intrusion into her part of the world. How dare they scare her up a tree! It was, however, no surprise to Jane that her hand was shaking as she took hold of the first branch to make her way down.

She'd have to cross the road again, Jane thought glumly as

she reached the ground. Why hadn't she thought about the park next to the wharf earlier? She had seen the bushes, the privacy they offered, and just run.

She would make her way down the side lanes to the park and move to where there was a clear view of the wharf. As she walked toward the road, she passed the sign bearing Marjorie's name.

Jane smiled to herself.

"Great, I'm on first name terms with a dead woman."

Nevertheless, she reached out and touched the lettering of the woman's name. She got a sense of steadiness and comfort in doing it. Imagination or not, she felt better and smiled again at the thought of Marjorie watching over her.

Jane felt far more vulnerable as she crouched outside the reserve on the road curb, contemplating the second crossing. She reflected how much easier the crossing had been when she was focussed only on reaching the bushes. This time the risk was taken with a clear head and with the knowledge that the men had guns.

She wondered how far Marjorie's ability to look after her extended. Only within the bounds of Marjorie's home? Or would it reach out and into the harbour side park? It was a park that Marjorie would have known well, probably walked in on a daily basis.

Jane hardened herself to the idea she would have to look after herself. Help from anyone else would be welcome, but unlikely. She promised herself she'd go and hide in the little lane behind her house at the first sign of any more watchmen. No one was visible on the road, but that didn't stop her heart pounding. She took a calming breath and then didn't stop running until she was in a side lane, well away from Darling Street.

Once stopped, Jane visualised the area of the park she was heading for. It would be best to move along the tree line to where she thought there might be a view of the bus stop and turning area. It was the most likely place any cars would be parked. She might be able to see some details from there.

Jane stopped again in a recessed doorway in the road above the park and stepped into its shadow to listen for any patrol. She didn't have to wait long before hearing steps and a man appeared ahead of her. He walked along with no apparent purpose but paused to look up the road. Jane remained unseen as she stood still, deep in the doorway's shadow.

She felt more in control than when she was in the tree and so put off ideas of retreating to the back lane just yet. After her return crossing of Darling Street, what was a small side lane? She waited until his steps faded, waited even longer, and then peered out onto the roadway.

The man was still walking away from her and Jane reasoned he would turn and retrace his route from the end of the street. She had to move quickly or wait for him to pass again.

She had discovered that the waiting was far harder than the action, so she ran the short distance to the sandstone wall and hopped over it as quietly as possible. She knew it was only a few feet high, so she swung over it without hesitation. Her landing made little noise as she landed on soft dirt.

Listening for any pursuit she then quickly moved along the wall into some bushes. There was a small cleared space between the wall and the bushes. Litter showed it was a secret spot for thousands of children across the years, and like the countless children before her, she sat still in the dirt and listened to the sound of footsteps passing on the roadway above. Unlike those children, Jane mused, she didn't fit easily in the small space and she didn't feel any urge to giggle with excitement.

Once the footsteps had faded, Jane moved out of the bushes and edged toward a thick copse of trees above the playground. She'd just reached the first tree when another man walked into the playground to her left. Moving quickly behind the tree, Jane wondered if he could hear her heart pounding as loudly as she could.

He continued on his way, oblivious to the sound of her thudding heart, and passing just metres from where she stood. Once he had gone, she realised she was frozen rigid against the tree. It took a while to unlock her knees and move. She shakily moved to the darkest area within the trees and sat down heavily with her back to the thickest tree trunk she could find.

A part of her, she realised, regarded this as an adventure or a game. A challenge she'd set herself and was unwilling to give up. What a way to express a personal crisis! What was she trying to prove? That she was still exciting? Young? That she was over Sally? Why not just go on a date, or join a gym? Even Sarah seemed a good alternative to this!

Jane calmed her thoughts. Whatever the reason, it was stupid, dangerous and it was over. She was lucky to have avoided being caught... so far. There were a lot of armed men on watch, more than she had expected. She reminded herself that nothing was worth her life and it was only just dawning on her that it really was her life that was at stake. These men would deal with a meddling woman quickly and permanently. She should have thought this through earlier. Jane shook her head yet again and decided to stay just where she was and not risk being caught. She could return home when they'd gone.

She wouldn't tell Liz; she wouldn't ring the police. The decision to investigate was a mistake, she was stumbling from one near disaster to another. It was dangerous and, she realised, embarrassing as well. Some stealthy spy she had turned out to be! She would just forget the whole stupid thing. Whatever was going on was big, too big for her.

Jane felt happy now she had made the decision. If she didn't continue, they'd not look for her and she would be safe. In her heart, she knew this rationale was rubbish, but it made her feel better. She rested with this thought for a time and felt calmer, until she heard the steps of the watchman approaching.

He had varied his route and moved into the edges of the trees. She stayed on the ground with the trunk between them, fearing she might make a noise getting up. That was if she could get up. Jane felt so sick with anxiety that she doubted she could stand.

The man was so close she could hear him breathing. Luckily for Jane he was concentrating on the area below him. Jane's legs started shaking and the dry twigs and grass around her rustled. He turned his head to listen, but seemingly dismissed the sound and moved on. She realised she had started to cry with the anxiety and roughly dried her face with her sleeve.

It was clear she couldn't handle much more of this. She needed to find a safe place to see out the rest of the night. The men on watch were varying their routes. The next pass might bring them further into the trees. She thought about returning to the space between the wall and bushes but going back would be more risky than moving elsewhere. She certainly wasn't going up a tree again.

She mentally pictured the park. The only suitable area she could think of was by the water's edge. There was an old, small maintenance hut there that was soon to be demolished. They had probably already checked it, and, if she could get down there unseen, she could stay there until morning.

If necessary, she could even go over the seawall and stand in the water on the narrow ledge she knew was there from watching bold water rats on it. She tried to visualise the ledge and how much cover it would give. It wasn't a good option, but she felt unable to go back.

Jane felt like some crazy sadistic force was driving her forward. Each time she had to move, the only option seemed to take her closer to the source of the danger. Why hadn't she stayed in bed?

Chapter Seven

Jane left the shelter of the trees once both watchers were out of sight. She had a vague plan to jump into the water and swim away, if seen, but quickly pushed that thought away. She would be fine, she reassured herself.

Despite her situation, the shaking had stopped. Action had helped. She moved from the trees and squatted next to some play equipment. She was starting to feel drained by the constant swings between fear, adrenalin, the relief of action and the physical slump that followed. She would have to harness any calm detachment she could and ignore her nerves, if she was going to succeed.

Her goal was a small wall leading down to the walkway around the water's edge. If necessary, this could be used as cover as she moved around to the hut. Jane looked around carefully and saw the blurry outline of the watchman patrolling the far end of his route before turning back. Jane broke cover and ran as fast as she could toward her goal.

The sudden hard footsteps that came in pursuit were from behind her. Not wanting, or able, to look behind, Jane changed direction to head for the nearest part of the wall. She could hear his breath as he closed the gap on her.

He must have been just behind her as she jumped down the half metre or so to the walkway. She quickly veered off to the right and her pursuer was caught off-guard by the drop and fell heavily, letting out a loud groan.

Jane took the opportunity to jump straight back up behind the sprawled man and ran for the hut. Jane felt her heart pounding once again at a dangerous rate and made a mental note to have a cardiogram. It seemed unlikely her heart could survive much more of this. Leaning against the hut wall she gasped for breath as quietly as she could.

Once she could hear past her own breathing, Jane heard muffled, but intense, conversation. She could hear snatches of what was said and realised that luck, or Marjorie, had been on her side. Her pursuer had fallen onto his radio, which had both broken and winded him. He had looked for her when he got up, but he had needed to wait for the other man to come over before they could radio for backup. The boss was obviously angry from some of their defensive comments on the radio

The man hadn't noticed her doubling back behind him, so Jane had some extra time to catch her breath and decide on her next move. That proved easy. There was no option about what her next move had to be. It just didn't look very inviting. Jane sat on the seawall on the opposite side of the hut from the men. The harbour water was black with bits of rubbish and the shine of oil reflecting in the moonlight. She hoped her pursuers would find it less inviting than she did and let herself down onto the narrow ledge.

The ledge was slippery, and Jane had to hold onto the top of the seawall to keep her balance. She accepted she would probably end up in the water, willingly or unwillingly, and put her bag around her neck.

The men were searching to her left but higher, possibly in the bushes where she had been earlier. The top of the wall was level with her chest, which meant moving to her right was easy to start with. However, ahead, the ledge dipped, and the top of the seawall would be very awkward to use. There were thick wooden piles beyond that point which supported a small fishing pier off the main ferry wharf, and Jane intended to place herself between the seawall and these piles if she could. The occasional broken oyster shell on the ledge were going to be difficult but the approaching voices from above reminded her that cuts were the least of her worries. Cuts could heal, but a gunshot wound may not!

Jane grew more desperate, as the voices grew closer. The hoped-for cover from above wasn't there. She was squatting down as low as she could with just her fingertips gripping onto the top of the wall. All the men needed to do was to look down and they would see her. Jane watched the piles moving with the waves and realised how little cover they offered, and how difficult they would be to hold on to.

As well the sounds of the men searching around the hut, voices were now coming from the other side of the small fishing pier. Jane stopped breathing – she was surrounded.

Jane accepted that her only option was the harbour itself. She would have to get into the water and swim - either to the yard owned by the Ferry Services Board or out to the maintenance pontoon.

Jane took the opportunity to move when she started to hear raised voices from near the hut, hoping the noise would cover any splashes she made. She put one leg in the water with great trepidation, hoping to feel solid ground. There was none.

Jane put her bag on the side and lowered herself into the water as gently as she could. She was immediately up to her neck in cold, black water and had to fight the impulse to gasp. She took hold of her bag and hesitated. There was a crash from the hut and she pushed off.

She affected a less than stylish sidestroke with one arm as the other held her bag above the water. There was a sudden memory of the only other time she had swum in her clothes, many years before. Those dreaded, bronze medallion swimming lessons were paying off. If only her P.E. teacher could see her now!

Her wry smile suddenly froze as she also recalled that the harbour was a shark nursery and that people and dogs had been attacked a little further up than where she was now. This made the decision of where to swim easier. The pontoon was nearby, and she could see the silhouette of a ladder standing out against the lights of the dock opposite.

It proved a good decision on two counts. Firstly, the pontoon had two levels so Jane could shelter from the wind and see the park and the wharf with little chance of being seen. Secondly, once she was on the pontoon, Jane could see someone searching through the yard that was her other choice.

It seemed she was safe. The men in the park were visible as they walked away from the hut and returned to patrolling the park. No one was following her that she could see. Although welcoming the sudden lack of interest, it puzzled her. Why did they give up the search for her? Maybe someone else had been found in the hut and Jane hoped she hadn't caused a homeless person any grief. She tried to analyse all possible angles but soon gave up. Now the tension was relieved, she was cold, tired and starting to feel her many aches and pains. She had, however, rather ironically achieved her initial goal of getting a good vantage point from which to view the wharf.

Taking out her damp pen and paper, Jane tried to see if there were any identifying details she could jot down. She was too far away to make out number plates, but she did note that there were two cars in the bus turning area above the wharf; a van lower down as far as it could get on the road; and two men actually on the wharf.

If you added two watchers on the road and another three in the park... Not for the first time this night Jane shook her head and contemplated how foolish and lucky she had been. With this in mind she painfully stirred herself to look carefully at the waters surrounding the pontoon. No boats, swimmers or trail of air bubbles coming toward her refuge that she could see. She refocused her tired eyes on the wharf.

The wharf had three levels. The top level which consisted of a covered area for waiting passengers was next to the narrow road where the van was parked; steps led to a middle level, for boarding the ferry; and the third was at water level and, in the daytime, usually contained people fishing. On this lowest level the two men were standing, watching the water.

Two divers appeared, one threw the waiting men a rope and started getting out of the water. The other stayed in the water guiding the rope from below the wharf until something broke the water surface. The two watchers and the diver all pulled on the rope and dragged the obviously heavy object onto the wharf. The second diver then started hauling himself out with the help his diving partner. The two suited men were busy wrapping the lump in something. When they finished one then tied it up, like a parcel. Another body? It certainly made sense. They must have dumped another body and wanted to recover it before the police did a more thorough search.

This gave Jane more questions: Why weren't the police there now? What was so important that these men were willing to stage a dangerous night recovery? And why on earth dump bodies off one of the most populated areas on the harbour? They must have been in a huge hurry to get rid of the bodies. Maybe a boat was coming to pick up the bodies later to better dispose of them? Jane soon gave up trying to list all the questions she had. They were unlikely to be answered, at least not by her, and not that she'd ever know.

The two men were now struggling with the lump, trying to

carry it up the steps to where the cars were parked. The divers were gathering their gear and following. The men from the park moved to help carry the load.

Jane recalled the suits the watchers were wearing and thought of the dry-cleaning bill. The dry cleaners in the main shopping area were having a special this week. Could they claim the money as tax deductions for work-related expenses?

With some effort she brought her head back to the current situation. Wary of the effect of tiredness and shock, Jane shook her head to clear it. She needed to focus.

Looking closer, Jane could see the men with the body were heading for the van. She could hear the door slide open from across the water and made a note of the colour, blue, and make of the van and the two cars. The van was the same colour as the one in the hospital grounds she'd seen that night, just a few hours ago. Dinner and laughs with her friends seemed a lifetime ago.

It couldn't be the same van, could it? She strained her eyes to look but the rear door was open so couldn't see if there was any damage to it. There were probably plenty of blue vans in Sydney, but even so, Jane could feel herself getting excited. This would be something to tell the police. She even knew where the van had been parked in the hospital.

This train of thought was broken when the sound of the side door closing brought her back to her watching duties. She'd lost focus again. She wouldn't be ringing anyone when she got home. She'd go home and sleep until she was able to tell a coherent story. Jane moved position again to try to force herself to stick to the job of watching. The sudden scream of sore muscles blew away any tiredness for the moment.

The operation on the wharf was winding up and there was still no search for her. This continued to be both a relief and a concern. They must have found someone in the hut. What had happened to them?

She pushed her speculations aside to concentrate on what was happening now. She'd just have to deal with any problems as they arose, if they arose.

The two men from the road arrived and joined others around the van. Some pushing and shoving started but no words reached Jane. She wondered if it had anything to do with her. The fight soon finished when a third came over and separated the fighters. He pushed one towards the van, the other towards a car. Jane had the distinct impression he must be the boss since neither man resisted. The first man pointed aggressively towards the other and slammed shut the rear door on the van. The wharf light revealed a damaged area. It had been rear-ended. Jane almost cried out aloud. It was the same van! This might just make all the fear and pain worthwhile - she may have cracked the case! Jane hoped the same woman would still be on duty when she rang the police call centre back.

The 'boss' stood alone looking down into the waters off the wharf, as the others drove off. Jane thought it must be Paul, the one who had been called to Marjorie's property earlier. He moved back to his car, looked around a last time as if checking nothing had been left, and then and drove off.

Chapter Eight

Despite wanting to get home as soon as possible, Jane decided to wait half an hour before swimming back to shore. She only lasted ten minutes before the cold became too much and she got down into the water again.

It was a relief to discover she was warmer in the water than on the pontoon. After brief consideration, Jane decided to head back to the park as it was closer. She wasn't happy with the idea of returning to the park but that felt more comfortable than heading for the wharf. She shivered at the thought of swimming over the place from where the lump had been retrieved then having to climb up on the wharf where it had been laid. Thinking of it as a lump was far easier than thinking about a body. A body was, had been, someone. Someone who died too young, possibly terrified, possibly horribly, possibly alive when they entered the water. The shiver became a shudder and she desperately cast around for something else to concentrate on. She swam on and the thought of sharks hovered uncomfortably in her head. Despite her tiredness, her speed picked up.

She aimed for the area of the seawall near the wharf where she could get herself onto the ledge and could stand with the top of the wall level with her shoulders.

Her bag was damp but not wet as Jane threw it on top of the wall. She searched for cracks in the wall to haul herself out of the water and then hung onto the top of the wall, grateful for a few moments rest before trying to get up.

Looking at her position, it was obvious she couldn't lift herself up from where she was. She moved so she was between the wall and the pile nearest to it so she could put her feet against the pile for extra help. This was only partially successful and resulted with Jane being stretched between the wall and the pile. She rested with her hands and chest on top of the wall and the rest of her angling down to her feet on the pile.

Resisting a strange urge to giggle, Jane walked her feet up the pile a little and pushed off it with as much energy as she had left. She threw her legs to the side and let out a cry as her hip crunched against the top of the wall.

She rolled onto her back and lay still, again reminded that she might well be too sore to move tomorrow. When was tomorrow? It was today, wasn't it? Jane looked at the sky after giving up on pushing the small light button on her watch. It would soon be light, and she'd be safe. She put a child-like faith in the rising of the sun and started feeling better.

Although tempted to remain lying down, Jane struggled painfully to her knees and from there to her feet. As she rose, her eyes fixed on a ladder attached to the seawall only a few metres from where she had been struggling. She'd not noticed it as she lowered herself into the water earlier, nor as she swum back to the wall. In a fit of pique Jane limped over and kicked the ladder as hard as she could and turned to head home.

"Gawd! The monster from the black lagoon strikes out!"

Jane froze but the wheezing voice continued.

"Don't worry about me, love! Marjorie said you'd be along. Mind you if I'd known they was gonna thump me, I'd have bloody well thought bloody twice! Not that Marjorie would have let me. She's a right bloody nag when she gets stuck on something..."

Jane looked around to discover the source of the verbal wanderings was sitting next to the hut. A small dishevelled woman was studying her with keen eyes; eyes that were swollen from a recent beating.

Jane hesitantly moved closer and saw the woman's face was bruised as well. Jane could see more bruises on the woman's arms but as she moved closer, she realised some were tattoos. Other possible bruises or tattoos were lost in the voluminous skirt that she wore.

"Shit! Did those bastards do this to you? What do you mean 'Marjorie' said I'd be along? We have to get you to a hospital! Do you know Marjorie?"

The woman laughed, coughed, and patted the ground beside her. It took a few slow breaths before she could speak again.

"You just sit here, and I'll answer some of your questions. I don't need no hospital. Just time and a brew or two. I'll fix meself up thanks. Bloody doctors likely to do more harm than what's wrong with ya!"

Jane's head was spinning. She felt more in need of a hospital than the old woman.

The woman continued,

"No. You'll not get me into one of those places but we're not here to discuss the medical system. I'm here to give you something."

Jane sat up, tentatively touching the woman's worn skirt as she did so.

"Ah! I am real you know! Marjorie insisted I come down here, find something important and give it to a young woman. 'What young woman?' I stupidly asked. 'You'll know her when you see her' was the reply. As usual, Marjorie's right. It's you - wet, miserable and thick - but it is you!"

Jane turned to the woman, interest taking over from her aches and fear.

"What do you have to give me? Who are you? Tell me about Marjorie. Did you know her?"

"I'm Alice. Been around here all me life. You've probably seen me but not noticed. Most do that, but I've noticed you. I knew your aunt, she was a kind woman, you look a lot like her. English, wasn't she? She used to give me any vegetables she had spare and always had time to give me cat a pat and a chat. Anyway, Marjorie and I were friends. She lived down the road a bit. We'd walk to the shops, talk about life and things. She was a good woman. After she died, I mostly stayed at home, still do. Go out to buy food and pay bills, but not much else. Only had one kid and he moved somewhere years ago. Fred died many years ago. Anyway, a while after Marjorie died, she starts talking to me again as I walked to the shops. I worried about meself for a while, but she said I was okay. That was enough for me. Marjorie wouldn't lie. It was good to have her back. She told me I should get out more! We have some beaut fights about politics and art..."

"Art!" Jane was incredulous.

"Yes, art! Don't judge from looks, my girl!"

Alice rolled her eyes and looked up,

"Are you sure?" she asked the heavens, then nodded and sighed. "Marjorie was a member of the Art Gallery and we'd go for outings to look at the expotitions. She thought I had a good eye and wanted me to see proper art. I started painting… gave up after the fire but started again when Marjorie returned."

They both sat in silence, Alice reflecting while Jane remained stunned.

"Anyway," Alice dragged herself back to the present. "Marjorie told me I had to get meself down here. Real insistent she was, so I hurried down and sat by the hut as she said and waited. Marjorie made sure the men didn't see me."

Jane nodded remembering Marjorie's intervention on her own behalf.

Alice continued,

"I watched you running around with the man just behind you." She nodded to Jane. "You did well. They found me as you got in the water. They were scared of the boss man and told him a little old nutcase was the intruder they had chased."

Alice laughed hard.

"Stupid man didn't check, if he'd seen me, he'd know I couldn't outrun anyone! While they were hitting me, I was able to do some looking and came up with this!"

Alice pulled out a cigarette case from under her skirt.

"I could've grabbed a few other things, but Marjorie was certain this was it."

Alice pushed the case at Jane who took it and turned it over in her hand.

"You mean while they were beating you up, you were picking their pockets?"

Jane asked amazed and looked closely at the woman. Were her bruises starting to fade? Jane was sure the bruises on Alice's face had gone from dark purple to a lighter shade. It was if they were cycling through the life span of a bruise at speed. Jane shook her head vigorously to clear it, a move that Alice took to indicate disbelief.

"It's true! I've been practising at the shops and in the supermarket!" she said proudly. "I wanted to try pick pocketing both men at once, but Marjorie was sure the smaller guy had what we wanted. I'm sure I could've done both, but she wouldn't let me try. Bloody spoil sport!"

Jane was staring at the cigarette case wondering why it

was so important and why she was being given it when Alice suddenly jumped up,

"We should go now. Marjorie says it's time."

Jane scrambled painfully up.

"What happened to Marjorie? Why is she still hanging around?"

Alice cocked her head to one side and thought before answering.

"There's things she needs to do."

"But what about the fire?" Jane persisted.

Alice was turning to walk around the water's edge.

"Oh that. It was murder. Deliberately lit, she was locked in and couldn't get out. Bye Jane, we'll be meeting again soon I think!"

Alice moved remarkably quickly for an injured old lady and, in the time it took for Jane to realise Alice had actually used her name, Alice was already out of sight.

Sounds of the harbour stirring and preparing for another day roused Jane to look around. The sun had risen. Birds were starting to call out about their territories. How long had she sat there?

The first ferries were bustling on their way and tugboats were moving to push and pull at the huge boats that relied on them. Jane generally loved to look at this early morning scene but, this morning, she didn't care for, or even notice, the water traffic.

She focussed her thoughts and fixed them on the journey home and sleep. She started back up the hill. This time she'd go through the front door.

She moved slowly, telling herself it was cautious to do so, but really it was hard for her to move any faster. Every single bump, knock and bruise of the past few hours was making itself increasingly felt in every muscle of her body.

She was passing the thin case from hand to hand and stopped to look at it. The design was beautiful, very thin and slightly curved. It felt good in the hand. There were initials on the bottom left corner in cursive script: 'To my LW, with love, your MW'.

If she possessed a case like this, it would almost be a reason to smoke. She discarded that notion but kept looking at the case and the two cigarettes it contained as she'd seen a movie where secret information was hidden in a cigarette.

Her attention wandered as she continued to walk and she picked at a piece of lint stuck in the edge of the case. The lining gave way as her nails pulled at the lint and she pulled out a small folded piece of paper. She was almost too tired to care and so she went to put it in her pocket. Her clothes were still wet and her bag not much better, so she tucked the paper under her still dry beanie and pulled it down tight on her head. The cigarette case went into her bag.

There were a few early risers out jogging or off to work and she got a few curious stares. In true Sydney-style, similar to any big city, no one asked any questions of the bedraggled, sodden, limping woman trudging up the hill. Jane was surprised but smiled. Alice was right. People saw but didn't notice. She was glad no one asked any questions. What she could say to explain her condition anyway?

She had drawn level with the Marjorie Gillis Reserve and paused to look at it as if for the first time. She was pondering the whole Marjorie thing, when she was thrown to the ground from behind.

There was no time to scream as it happened, and no air in her lungs after she hit the ground. Someone was grabbing at her bag and yelling at her to let it go. The yells accompanied by blows to her head and shoulders. Jane could only think of how close to home she was and hung on grimly to the bag.

Chapter Nine

The blows suddenly stopped and the weight on her shoulders was removed. The fight seemed to move onto the ground next to her and a new voice was involved. Jane missed most of what was happening as she was lying face down on the footpath, trying not to cry.

She was too tired to fight, run or care. She was only aware of voices, yelling, the sound of running feet, then quiet with someone gently touching her and talking. It wasn't until they'd repeated themselves a few times that Jane realised the tone was friendly, the voice female and it was talking to her.

"He's gone. Are you okay?"

Yes, Jane assured herself, the voice was female.

Hands turned her over and gently moved to help her sit up. Pain flared up in the few areas that weren't already hurting, and Jane gave up on the idea of moving at all for the rest of the week.

A face came into focus. It looked at Jane with concern.

"Are you okay?"

Jane forced herself to focus on the face and managed to rasp out,

"Yes."

The face moved away, and Jane continued to concentrate on breathing and fighting off nausea and giddiness. There was more talking around her then the Face reappeared and said encouraging things while physically doing a rough check to see if arms and legs functioned.

Face's hands were strong and firm and conducted a thorough inspection of Jane's body. Jane winced a few times as Face touched the worst of the bruises – where her hip had slammed into the seawall. At Jane's sharp intake of breath and physical jolt, Face drew back and frowned enquiringly at Jane. Jane drew a couple of breaths then nodded for Face to continue.

Face assured Jane she had no broken bits as far as she could tell, but the paramedics would want to do their own examination to be sure. She then murmured something sympathetic and helped Jane to her feet.

Once up Jane managed to say, "Hang on," while she leant on Face and took some steadying deep breaths to clear her head a little.

"You a medico?" Jane asked as it gained her a few more seconds before she had to move.

"No, did a St. John's first aid course a few months ago. Lucky for you!"

While sounding light, Face's eyes were watching Jane with concern. Jane thought she'd caused Face enough trouble so straightened up and looked around. There were quite a few people watching her, neighbours and strangers. All looked friendly enough. The woman who had rescued her, Face, was an attractive woman about Jane's age. She had short blond hair, slightly taller but with a slimmer build than Jane. She was obviously fitter than Jane and displaying that for all to see in the shorts and tee shirt she was wearing. Jane's thoughts immediately turned to promises to get fitter, do a self-defence course and get back on her bike again. Face didn't look big enough to fight off whoever had attacked her, and Jane's body insisted he must have been huge.

Jane realised she knew nothing about what had occurred.

"What happened?"

Jane directed the question at Face.

Face smiled at her, "I'm not sure but it seems you've fallen into the harbour and a businessman tried to mug you, but that's just a guess."

Jane was able to smile in response, this must look very strange she thought, but said,

"A businessman? You fought him off? How big was he? He felt huge!"

"Well it's unusual, but your assailant was wearing a suit. I did fight with him but he was quite small for a guy," Face replied.

"Assailant?" Jane queried.

"Sorry," Face replied, "I'm a policewoman, it's a habit."

"Policewoman?"

Face smiled again and told Jane to stop asking so many questions. Jane couldn't help herself.

"Were you on the police call centre last night?"

"What? No, I wasn't. Why?"

Face was obviously puzzled at this sudden shift of topic. Jane just shook her head in reply.

"I need to go home and sit down."

She pointed to her house across and up the street a bit.

"Number 46?" Face asked.

Jane nodded and started to fumble with her bag.

Face gently took the bag and got the keys out. Noting the few contents she asked,

"Travelling light?"

She silently gave Jane back her bag and put her arms around Jane's shoulders to steer her toward home. Jane could hear sirens in the distance.

Rob from 48 took the keys from Face and hurried ahead to open the door. He hovered in the doorway suggesting she should take Jane into the front room, pointing where the kitchen was so Face could get some towels and water. Face thanked him and took Jane into the front room. Rob went back out, saying he'd tell the neighbours Jane was not seriously hurt. The sound of sirens was getting louder.

Jane perched on the chair's arm until Face came back with the towels, put one onto the seat and helped Jane sit down wearily on it. Soon after, Rob returned to say the ambulance and police had arrived. Face moved to leave as the paramedics came in but Jane grabbed her arm and asked her to stay.

Face thought for a while, nodded and gently detached Jane's hand and moved to the side. The paramedics brushed past Face and proceeded to give Jane a thorough check-over. During this they kept up a friendly banter and asked Jane about the various cuts and grazes she had. She felt dishonest but fended off the questions, feeling unsure about what to tell anyone just yet. She didn't think she would make much sense.

Jane was also distracted as Face had quietly gone outside. Jane's gaze followed her and returned frequently to the door where she could see Face standing outside. It felt silly, but she needed to have Face in sight – it made her feel safer, somehow.

One of the ambulance men asked Jane to help them take off her pants so they could clean up her legs. She did so but with some pain and much embarrassment. This was exactly why you were told to wear clean underwear. Jane was feeling very self-conscious in her old underwear and made a mental note to buy a new range. She was very pleased no one was there to see.

Of course, it was at that point that Face returned and cast an eye over the situation. Jane felt herself redden and Face's quick aversion of her eyes showed that she'd noticed Jane's embarrassment.

The ambulance officer finished off with advice about the cuts and bruises and the need to rest in bed for a couple of days at least. Jane wasn't going to argue with that. Face came over and said she'd phoned the station to explain that she was on duty early and why.

"Sorry," Jane mumbled.

Face laughed, "I don't think it's your fault!"

Jane suddenly realised that while she thought of this woman as 'Face', it was more polite to know her name.

"Er... My name's Jane, Jane Woods. Thank you for helping me. You're...?"

Face smiled warmly and squeezed Jane's arm.

"Hi Jane. I'm Bette Logan."

Bette leaned forward.

"There's no need to thank me, I'm just glad I was out jogging. I don't usually come this way."

The police had been taking statements from those outside but were now standing in the doorway. Apparently, there were no witnesses to what happened. Some had just heard Jane cry out (*had she?*) and had come to see what was happening. Bette walked over to join the policemen and they had a very quiet discussion.

Jane tried to move again. One part of her disagreed with the rest and she groaned aloud at the stab of pain it caused.

The police all turned to look at her, but without comment turned back to continue their discussion. Jane felt like she was outside the school principal's office awaiting a judgement on something naughty she'd done; in part that was true.

Jane made best use of the short time she had before the police approached her. She felt overwhelmed and unable to explain the events of last night, so she decided to talk only about the assault. She'd sleep and then think about what to do and who to tell. Jane had a strong feeling she should not talk about it. Although, apart from what they might make of Marjorie and Alice, there was no reason to keep silent.

Bette might be someone she could talk to; someone who would not dismiss her as foolish. Though she felt more stupid than foolish. She knew she was lucky to be just bruised and battered. She giggled at the thought of herself covered in batter ready to be fried and had to quickly regain composure as all three police turned to her again.

She hoped her behaviour suggested the idea of shock. She certainly felt she could be suffering from shock. For more reasons than the police could ever guess.

Bette squatted next to Jane's chair and smiled encouragingly but this smile was different, this smile was work-related. Jane knew that at this moment Bette was a policewoman. Bette introduced the other two officers then moved to stand to the side of them. Jane assumed this was to let them question Jane without Bette's involvement.

Jane could tell them very little about the assault. She had no idea who it was, hadn't seen him and assumed it was her bag that he was after.

She could only agree it seemed an unusual outfit for a mugger, when they commented about the man wearing a suit. As for her own wet state? She'd tripped near the water's edge while jogging and had fallen in. Yes, that's where she must have received some of her injuries, but she didn't remember specifically.

The bag and beanie staying dry? Well, she was holding it and must have thrown it away before she fell in, and her beanie had been in the bag.

The beanie... the paper! Jane clumsily felt her head and found the beanie was still on. One of the men moved to help her and she jerked away from him, then quickly apologised.

Jane felt her answers were getting more suspicious the more they questioned so she apologised again, stating that she was feeling shaky and tired, and wanted to finish the interview. All of which was true.

One of the men inspected her near empty bag and asked if the contents were the same when the assault took place. Jane was conscious of Bette nodding at the same time she did. He commented on the nice cigarette case and Jane said it was her great, great grandfather's. As the words came out, she was surprised, not knowing why she would say that.

The men said they would return if they had any further questions and asked Bette to check the mug shots to see if she recognised the assailant. She replied she already planned to.

Bette and Jane looked at each other for a few seconds in the silence that followed. Jane thought it must be difficult for Bette to be rescuer, nurse and police and so asked her to call Jo and Marion. She felt Bette should be released from all those duties, even if a large part of her wanted Bette to stay.

Jo and Marion's phones went to voice mail, so Liz was called and said she'd be over as soon as she arranged cover at the shop. Bette offered to stay until Liz arrived and Jane gratefully accepted. Bette then suggested Jane should go to bed as she was so obviously struggling to stay awake. Jane started to protest, winced, yawned and finally nodded. Bette smiled and went upstairs to go and get the bed ready. Jane briefly wondered about the state she had left the bedroom in that morning and then gave up caring. When Bette returned, Jane was asleep.

Chapter Ten

Bette didn't need to be told that Jane was a lesbian. One glance around the room had confirmed her thoughts. The women in the photos and the classic lesbian literature and music were evidence enough, but Bette was certain once Jane requested that she contact Jo and Marion. They were spoken of as a couple.

As she glanced around the room, Bette wondered what was really going on. Jane was obviously holding things back. Bette hadn't mentioned this to the other police but thought it unlikely that they were convinced by Jane's story.

This put Bette in an awkward spot. Jane seemed quite normal, certainly not a criminal type, but things just didn't add up. For example, the cigarette case; there was no evidence that Jane smoked, no ashtrays or smell, yet there were two cigarettes in it. She said it was her great, great grandfather's, but why take a treasured item to go for a jog?

The man who had attacked Jane was familiar to Bette, but she couldn't say why. She was keen to go through the mug shots as soon as possible. Maybe she could talk to Jane later to see if she was more forthcoming with information. Maybe it had been the presence of the men…? Was Jane covering for someone, or was she scared?

Bette quietly sat down opposite Jane and looked again around the room. As she had on a few other occasions, Bette wondered what would be made of her home and possessions if positions were reversed. She smiled to herself as quite a few of Jane's belongings matched her own.

As she looked, Bette could see quite a few CDs she'd like to listen to and some books she wanted to read. Jane seemed to have more time to do the things Bette never got around to. Bette sighed. Following up on the music and books was not going to happen.

Bette returned to a more professional perusal of the room. There seemed no evidence of a partner or lover, and Jane had asked for the couple to be rung.

"Pity. She seems nice enough," Bette murmured aloud, but Bette herself had no partner and chose to live like that. Her job left little time or emotional energy for anything else. Maybe that was Jane's choice too. Bette thought not, but it was a possibility.

Jane sighed and nestled down further into the chair. Bette's gaze returned to her. A glimpse of something under Jane's beanie caught Bette's attention. She sat forward and looked more closely. It was a piece of paper. That explained why Jane had reacted to the constable's attempt to help her with her beanie! She was scared the paper would fall out. Was that what the assailant was after? Why would she have it under her beanie?

Bette's eye's widened.

"Ah!" she exclaimed aloud, then mentally kicked herself for making a noise. Jane murmured and settled again. The mugger thought the paper was in her bag! What was the paper? Could she, should she, risk trying to get it now?

Bette found she had already risen from her chair and was moving toward Jane. She had her arm outstretched as she halted and considered her options. She was only a matter of inches from Jane as she tried to maintain her balance and not let her hand shake; all the while moving towards the bit of exposed paper.

The doorbell ringing made them both jump and Jane's eyes opened to see Bette standing close in front of her.

They stared at each other silently for a brief moment before Bette said, "Your beanie's falling off," and turned to go and open the door.

When Bette returned, the beanie was on the arm of the chair. The paper was nowhere to be seen. Liz entered just behind Bette and brushed past her before stopping in her tracks.

"My God! Are you okay? I hope you got a few punches in too!"

Jane started to do introductions when Bette stopped her, "Don't worry, we met at the door."

There was a noticeable awkwardness between Bette and Jane, which Liz misinterpreted and smiled broadly.

"Yes, Bette tells me she's your knight in shining armour, or should I say amore?"

Liz thought this quick jest to be extremely funny. Both Bette and Jane blushed and Liz laughed even more.

"Haven't I seen you at Millie's?" Liz's sudden question to Bette caused Jane to wince. Liz was asking if Bette frequented one of Sydney's lesbian bars, one known for its leather scene.

Bette was up to the challenge,

"Not my cup of tea, I prefer Sundays at The Club. Music you can understand, and at a volume you can talk."

Liz shrugged, "It'll close soon. No money in talking!"

Jane had sat listening to the exchange with an increasing sinking feeling. Liz was being Liz. Her directness, while sometimes admirable, made Liz legendary for outrageous statements and initiating fierce arguments. Liz would meet someone and get straight to the point, no matter what circumstances or the amount of embarrassment, especially to someone else.

Jane was angry, as well as embarrassed, at being outed by association. On looking around she realised Bette had probably picked her as a lesbian anyway. If the lesbian books and CD's in the front room and bedroom hadn't done it, then the obligatory stones, crystals and feathers on the kitchen windowsill would have been a dead giveaway.

Jane smiled at the thought of the standard lesbian decor. On reflection, it was lucky Sally had taken the dream catcher from the bedroom or she might have had the entire stereotyped lesbian ensemble.

Jane giggled, causing Bette to stop the story of her involvement and both women looked at her in concern.

"Sorry, I was miles away," Jane explained.

Bette smiled, "No wonder with all you've been through. You must be ready for bed!"

The earlier exchange between Liz and Bette caused Jane to look at Bette in a different light. It seemed obvious now, but 'she's a lesbian!' had not been the first thing Jane had thought on seeing Bette.

Jane comforted herself with the knowledge that a lot had been happening at the time. This bought back the assault and the events of the night before. Jane sighed and Bette suggested to Liz that they help Jane upstairs to bed. Liz opened her mouth and, unusually for her, shut it again at the looks she got from both Bette and Jane.

"Wise," Bette told her and winked at Jane.

Liz and Bette got either side of her and, despite Jane's protests, guided her up the stairs. By the time they reached Jane's room, she was pleased to have them there. She couldn't remember ever having felt so tired and so sore in so many places.

Not wanting Bette to disappear while she slept, Jane asked her to write down her contact details. Bette was happy to oblige, and both did their best to ignore Liz grinning during the process.

***

Bette said her farewells and, motioning Liz to stay with Jane, said that she'd let herself out. Although hating herself as she did it, her motivation for Liz to stay upstairs wasn't for Jane's benefit. She wanted to have a quick look around. Bette quietly went into the front room and checked under and around Jane's chair. There was no sign of the paper, but she hadn't really expected to find it. Bette again puzzled over the situation and wondered about Jane.

She was also struggling with her own feelings. Jane was a good-looking, single woman and Bette felt an attraction to her. Bette was, however, a police officer involved as a result of a criminal act. There could be no romantic involvement. Bette closed the door with a sigh, just her luck. A lovely woman with a sense of humour and Bette couldn't pursue anything personal.

She started running up the hill and suddenly smiled - her official role with Jane could be quite limited. Once she'd looked at the mug shots, hopefully identifying the assailant, she then had to wait until after any court case was done. She could then return to visit Jane socially. She would enjoy finding out more about this woman - police work or not.

Chapter Eleven

Liz went to speak after Bette left the bedroom, but Jane held up a hand to silence her. Liz waited impatiently as Jane listened to the noises as Bette left.

After the front door closed Liz burst out, "For heaven's sake! Are you so enamoured you have to hear her footsteps?"

Jane replied, "Did you hear how long it took her to leave? She didn't go straight out. She must have checked the front room."

Liz snorted, "You're being paranoid!" But she moved to the bedside and gently asked, "What on earth happened?"

Jane started talking about creeping through the park to get the number plate details of the murderer's cars when Liz interrupted her,

"You were what! Where? Murderers? Were you hit in the head? What are you talking about?"

It took a few confused minutes before Jane realised Liz hadn't heard about the body found off the wharf.

"Where have you been?" She laughed, "You're supposed to know everything that happens around here! Gee, Marion thought I'd withdrawn! At least got an excuse! I'm heartbroken and suffering!"

They both laughed, and Liz blushed.

"Bronwyn arrived late yesterday, and we certainly didn't watch the news! This morning I was busy at work. I had to do orders, chase up some repairs and finish off the collage with that student, Ross. You know, the one who took those photos we looked at yesterday? He is watching the shop for me."

Jane couldn't keep going; she was too tired to continue. Liz reluctantly agreed to wait until Jane had rested and Jo and Marion joined them, to hear the whole story.

Liz stood looking out through the glass balcony doors while Jane changed into pyjamas. It was while Liz was tactfully averting her eyes that Jane moved the piece of paper from under her breast to the bedside drawer. Although she didn't like it, the weight she had put on had given her a hiding place to put the paper when Bette had gone to open the door for Liz.

Liz tucked Jane in and assured her she'd be staying

downstairs. Jane's eyes had shut before Liz had even left the room. It was quite a few hours before she opened them again.

Jane woke with her dreams still vivid but any confusion about whether she was awake or still dreaming was quickly settled when she moved. The aches and pains were very real.

With a groan Jane sat up, pushed a pillow behind her and settled back into it. The dreams had been strange, seemed connected, but she couldn't grasp how. It had started in the park, her running while an old woman looked on... not Marjorie, but someone else.

Jane initially had no recollection of anyone other than the men, but the image bought back the memory of Alice... How could she have forgotten her? She would visit Alice for a chat as soon as she could move.

As soon as she could move... that thought immediately made her want to shift position again. Jane fought the need as long as possible then braced herself and pushed up the bed a little. While movement was painful, Jane knew that not moving would make it worse.

Sinking back into the pillow, Jane tried to recapture more of the dreams. She often had interesting dreams, and while they never revealed the winning lotto numbers, they often hinted at things to come.

Jane had told no one of this although she had experienced these dreams as long as she could remember. She just *knew* it wouldn't be wise to talk about them. Just like she'd *known* earlier not to tell the police what she had seen and not to hand over the piece of paper. She never dwelt on her dreams, or the less frequent but still compelling instinctive feeling that she should or shouldn't say or do something. Mostly this instinct had proved correct. She didn't know if others experienced similar things, certainly no one had ever mentioned it to her.

As usual, she left off her musings about how or why she knew things - there were never any answers. She returned to her dreams.

The main images were of running and being swallowed by something blue (*the van? water?*). People were all around her, but ignoring her; she was then somewhere dimly lit and white; and, lastly, Marjorie was shaking her finger and saying,

"I can only do so much you know," and then turning and walking into a burning house.

Jane opened her eyes and dried her tears with the bedsheet. Poor Marjorie. What a horrible way to die. Jane thought about how easily she had moved from shock and disbelief to mere surprise and, now, acceptance of Marjorie's existence.

She smiled at the new question she had posed: could you talk of ghosts as existing? To be ghosts surely they had ceased to exist?

'Only on the living plane,' came a soft voice.

Jane shot up in her bed, not noticing or caring if the movement caused pain, and frantically looked around the room for the source. Was it shock? It was so real. There was only an answering silence in her head, but a definite sense that some part of it was no longer hers alone. Suddenly she was tired, too tired to fight to stay awake. Jane dropped back onto the pillow and, despite the worry, dozed off again.

***

The next time Jane woke she heard voices downstairs. Jo and Marion had joined Liz. There was also a strange voice. Bronwyn? What a time to meet the new woman.

How long had she been asleep? She had no sense of time other than the shadows in the room indicating that it was afternoon. A quick turn of her head to check her clock confirmed the shadows' timekeeping. The room was stuffy, and Jane wanted the windows opened to catch any afternoon breeze.

It was good to hear her friends' voices; she had lots to tell and advice to ask. Jane hesitated before sitting up. She wanted to talk to them, but could she talk about Marjorie, her own dreams, and that voice in her head? She decided to start with Marjorie and see what the reactions were.

The voice was the most worrying and talking about it might get her friends concerned about her mental state. She'd better be cautious.

'Wise girl!' A woman's voice sounded clear in her head.

Jane felt tears form and she clutched at the sheet.

'Don't fuss girl. It's Marjorie!' there was a hesitation, then, *'I see I've come at a difficult time. I'll come back later.'*

Jane felt a shift and then a sensation that she was 'alone' again. She felt anger rising, "Who does she think she is? Making a bloody social visit? It's my head, not hers!" Jane found she had stood up and was pacing the floor next to her bed while talking aloud.

Downstairs she heard Jo call, "She's up!" and her friends walking towards the stairs. Desperate for time to collect her thoughts, Jane sought refuge in the toilet.

When Jane returned to her room, she found her friends there and looking eager to see her. Bronwyn apologised for meeting this way and explained that she wasn't able to stay long. Jane felt a gentle breeze flowing through the room as someone had opened the windows and, on the bed, was a tray with a cup of tea, a sandwich and a slice of cake which had her stomach rumbling. She was hungry.

All gave her careful hugs, although she felt much better than she had when she went to sleep. In fact, she was hurting a lot less than she had expected.

Marion saw her confused look and, after telling Jo to pick up the tray, gently pushed Jane back onto the bed and fussed over getting the pillows right. Jane didn't argue as her mind was spinning. She shouldn't be able to move with all the bruises and scrapes she had; yet she was hardly feeling any pain. She felt confused and a little scared, what was happening to her? Jo brought her back by asking about 'this Bette'; Liz asked about the mugging; but Marion insisted that Jane start at the beginning.

As she told her story, Jane was astonished anew at how foolish she had been and how very lucky as well. On reflection, she realised there had been a few occasions when she could have turned back and hidden in the back lane, but she had kept going.

She felt like one of those women in the B Grade horror movies walking into the crypt or dark room all alone to investigate a strange noise, knowing a crazed killer is on the loose.

She anticipated her friends' reactions would be like her own when watching those movies on late night TV – frustrated shouts of 'Don't do it, you idiot!' but their reactions to her story surprised her. Instead of being the most understanding, Liz was the most conservative. Liz couldn't believe she hadn't gone home to go to the toilet. She was horrified by the notation of toileting anywhere else! What was more important, men with guns or a full bladder? She would have gone straight to the front door!

Bronwyn and Marion were amazed at her boldness and declared they wouldn't have gone to investigate to start with. Only Jo seemed to understand the desire to recapture childhood adventure, but she too balked at how Jane pursued it. All felt they would have definitely gone home after the narrow escape in the reserve.

Her friend's reaction to Marjorie's appearance was one of silence. Jo gave Marion a surreptitious meaningful look, while Bronwyn looked questioningly from one to the other.

Liz broke the silence, "Stress?"

"No," Jane replied, "I wouldn't have come up with that, and besides the man looking up didn't see me. He was looking right at me! Marjorie is the only explanation."

Marion walked to the window and poked her head outside to look at the small reserve.

"The trees aren't good cover; looking up, he should've seen you."

Jo tried a joke.

"I believe Jane. If she were imagining it, she'd have come up with Ellen or k.d. lang!"

Marion gave a withering look to which Jo shrugged. Liz had joined Marion at the window, also craning her neck to look at the reserve.

Bronwyn reached for her phone,

"Stuff the appointment. I'm cancelling it. This is too amazing to miss!"

After she left the room with her phone, the silence was long enough for Jane to decide the dreams and the voice could wait for another day.

It was Liz who spoke first and urged Jane to tell the rest of the story. She added that there was no need to move from the reserve; Jane could have taken the details as the cars passed back up the hill.

Marion disagreed. She thought it likely the men would return; the reserve wasn't safe.

"No, the reserve was safest, if Marjorie is real, staying was best." Liz was adamant.

Jane interrupted, "You two weren't even there and you can't agree what to do."

"Thank God you didn't have a collective with you," Jo noted dryly and both she and Jane giggled.

Bronwyn had returned, shushed them all and asked that Jane be allowed to complete the story of her adventure without interruptions. Jane took a liking to her.

For the next hour that's what happened. Jane regaled them with the story of her night and morning. Despite some gasps, 'ooohs', and even expressions of shock; all thought the bravest thing she did was getting into the Harbour's water.

As for the appearance of Alice and the beating she had taken there was another silence. Jane left out the cigarette case and the way Alice's bruises seemed to fade in front of her eyes.

At the end of the story, Jane was embarrassed at how little she could tell them about the attack or Bette's rescue of her. She started getting teary at the memory of how helpless she had felt. Marion moved to her side and hugged her while she cried.

Jane recovered herself shortly and looked at Marion's shoulder.

"That's another shirt I've stuffed," she remarked ruefully.

Marion hugged her again but tighter.

"You haven't and I don't care. You're safe, that's what counts!'

Jo added, "But if the mugger wasn't after money, what was he after? The police are right, a jogger isn't a usual target and muggers don't wear suits. If he didn't get what he wanted..." Jo hesitated, "he might come back. That worries me."

Marion frowned at Jo and motioned her to be quiet.

"Maybe he thought you were someone else and once he saw you weren't who he thought..."

Bronwyn jumped in with more reassurance.

"That's the most likely. Why on earth mug a jogger or specifically target you? Just mistaken identity, I'm sure."

Jane was equally sure this wasn't the case but felt unable to confess all to her friends, especially with Bronwyn there – she didn't even know her!

Liz summed up in typical style by focussing on the new love interest.

"This just shows there's a lot of truth in clichés. Silver linings, all's well that ends well etc. You not only survived, you met Bette!"

Jane started to protest, blushed and then managed to hit Liz with a pillow despite the remaining aches.

After they had gone over aspects of the story a few more times, Jane finally came to her current problem.

"Trouble is, I don't know what to do with the information I've got. It seems pretty flimsy and far-fetched. I've got nothing the police could act on. My whole story is unbelievable, even without Marjorie, and I lied in my statement about the assault."

Jo didn't think the lie was a problem but felt that the feeling not to tell was important.

"I believe in gut reactions. There must have been something happening that triggered it. You were right to follow your instincts."

Liz added another problem.

"You also don't know if any of the police are involved. It's not as easy to get away with it now, but corruption is still there."

"I know the majority are good." Jane said, "I just don't want to risk talking to one that isn't!"

Liz smiled, "Look at their houses and cars. Isn't that where a lot of the money went? Why don't you invite yourself around to Bette's place to thank her? If her house is rented or crummy and her car's old, you'll know she's okay!"

To Jane's horror the others thought the idea had some merit. They also thought that she might help protect Jane if the mugger did return for whatever he was after.

Liz picked up the paper Bette had written on,

"Oh yes, she's keen! Not just her number; the address too!"

Marion spoke for them all.

"Go around and check out more about her. Don't ring beforehand so she can't hide anything expensive, like paintings, jewellery or whatever. You said you were going to talk to her anyway. If she seems okay then ask her what to do. You're not the criminal here, she'll realise that."

Grinning wickedly, Liz volunteered to accompany Jane.

That was enough for Jane. If she was going to do it, she'd do it alone!

Chapter Twelve

Bette had jogged home, deep in thought, after leaving Jane. She showered and got ready for work still thinking hard. She was concerned but eventually decided that she should focus first on what she could do – look at the mug shots. She was happy to concentrate on that task as it meant delaying a decision on what to do about the piece of paper. It could be important evidence, or it could be nothing.

Even if she told the investigating officers, what could she say that sounded sensible? You don't get a search warrant to look for an unknown piece of paper in a minor assault case. Yet Bette suspected it was important.

Bette thought Jane was generally a trustworthy type, and Bette wanted to trust her, but she was hiding something. She needed to talk to Jane again before taking any formal steps. But would Jane trust her? She continued to weigh her options all the way to work without making any decisions.

The duty officer told her not to worry about a report on the incident as her statement taken at the scene would be enough at this point. He wanted her to sit with the pictures and find out if the assailant had a record.

Bette was pleased to have more time on her own to continue contemplating the situation. She had never been uncertain about loyalty or professionalism before.

She knew it wasn't that Jane was a lesbian. It was more that things just didn't fit and, until they did, she wanted all her options open. She knew this was not her role. She was low on the food chain, just a Senior Constable, supposed to pass on all information and let her superiors decide whether or not things fitted or made sense.

Senior officers praised her potential and often spoke of their hopes for her. She had the same hopes but didn't want to be a poster girl for equality in the force. She wanted to work in homicide and wanted to earn the promotion through merit. She'd better not be found holding back information on a hunch. Bette inwardly winced at the likely reaction of her sergeant. It may not end her career, but it would put a very large dent in it.

The photo books were kept in a meeting room at the back of the open plan office where the uniformed police gathered. It had windows on two sides. Privacy had never been great in police stations, but since the Royal Commission into police corruption, what little chance there had been for privacy was almost all gone. Private meetings raised suspicions in many minds. However, some saw this as a joke as any meetings with secret agendas just took place elsewhere.

The only secret meetings that Bette knew about concerned illicit sexual affairs, and she didn't want to know about them. She looked at the five large volumes of mug shots, or 'Who's Who', on the table and sat down. She picked one at random and started.

Bette was tired, fed up and on her third volume when she saw the photo of the man she had tackled. A small but thickset man, he looked like he spent a lot of time at the gym. He certainly had pushed her around relatively easily when she'd wrestled him off Jane. In the photo, he had a sneer and looked ready to jump out with fists flying. Joe Small was no minor league mugger; he had a history of violent crime, with charges for drug dealing, armed robbery and assault. Why was a serious criminal mugging Jane? Again her thoughts turned to the piece of paper.

Bette's puzzling over Joe Small's actions was interrupted when the door opened and Detective Mike Grey entered. He was one of Bette's mentors and had encouraged her to stay in the job at times when she felt despairing of her ability to cope. Not just in dealing with horrible sights and people, but also when dealing with the sexism that was still present in the force.

Grey was a great source of advice and support. Bette admired him for his knowledge and also his brevity when giving advice. While other police often bragged and laughed about their exploits or cases, he said little. This didn't mean he was humourless; no, he had a very dry sense of humour - he just chose his moments to show it.

She was pretty sure he knew her preferences were for women, but it was never mentioned. It wasn't an issue. He was one of the main reasons she remained with the police. She decided to talk to him about her concerns about the paper.

Grey had not initially seen her, and when he did see her, he looked a bit surprised, then threw her a smile and waved. Grey showing surprise was an unusual thing. Bette had been amazed on more than one occasion at how well he held a lid on his feelings and kept a poker face. Bette was about to raise her arm to call him over when a memory hit her.

A few weeks ago, she'd seen the same look of surprise. She'd been sitting in traffic and had seen him walking with another man. She'd sounded her horn and waved, he'd gazed at her with a look of surprise, paused, then waved back. At the time she'd thought he was with a friend. However, the man he had been laughing with was now looking out of the picture in front of her - Joe Small.

Bette lowered her arm and sunk back into the chair. Detective Mike Grey being bent was unthinkable, yet it was a possibility. Small could be an informant, but you kept those relationships quiet, out of public gaze. You certainly didn't go for a walk with them; likewise, you wouldn't advertise you had a criminal as a friend.

Bette's head spun, everything she had believed in was turning on its head. The room, her colleagues, her work… all she took for granted was suddenly upended. She had to start to evaluate it all from a different perspective. In those few seconds her familiar surrounds were gone, there was no one she felt she could trust.

"Oh God, no!" she whispered.

One of the constables nearby came over.

"You okay? You don't look so good."

Bette took the opportunity and shut the book,

"Yeah, just feel a bit ill suddenly. I'll go outside and see if that helps."

As she stood up the door to the inner room opened and Grey headed toward her.

"Sorry, about not coming over just then. Who are you looking for? That guy you got tangled up with this morning? Heard all about it. What's with the woman? What was he after? Did she tell you anything?"

Bette tried to hide her confusion by saying that she hadn't got a good look at him, just grabbed him from behind, there was a scuffle, he broke away and ran.

"That's not what I hear. The boys say you reported getting a good look at him." Mike's eyes moved to the shut book, "Seen him yet?"

Bette was really worried now. This man knew her well and she had to get away to think carefully about things.

"I actually just realised I'd been going through this one half asleep. I'll have to go over it again. I'm not feeling well, so I was about to head outside for some fresh air."

Mike thought for a minute.

"Good idea. Go and have a sit. I'll talk to you again in a while and see how you feel about things."

Bette was sure he wasn't talking about her physical wellbeing. He knew there was more to this. Her anxiety level rose dramatically. Was Homicide interested in the mugging? Why was Grey being so pushy?

***

Bette's head was still spinning, despite sitting outside for a while. While it was only early in summer, the day was heating up and she was sitting in the only shady area available. She had decided on one thing though, that the years she had known Grey had to count for something. He had probably just gotten sloppy meeting with an informant. It wasn't unusual for police to get too friendly with their informants; it had got more than one cop in trouble.

She wouldn't tell him everything, she decided, just say that she thought the mugger was Joe Small and watch his reaction. She felt better for the decision but was still anxious about the whole situation. She was about to get up and head inside when the door opened, and Grey came out and headed toward her.

"Sorry about being so grumpy in there. I've been left off the team looking into that body off the wharf. Bit pissed off about it actually. I want to show them they made a mistake by getting information they don't have. I'm interested in anything that happens in that area."

Grey's story was plausible since the wharf murder was a high profile case. But he wasn't acting like the man she knew. He had plenty of work to do; she'd been helping him out on a couple of cases.

Why was he suddenly so interested in a case that wasn't his? Bette didn't believe his wanting to show anyone up. He'd never cared what others thought or did. It was one of the things she liked about him. This wasn't the man she had trusted in the past.

Bette quickly adjusted her strategy again. She couldn't tell him that she had recognised Joe Small. She needed more time to think, and a serious talk with Jane. If Grey was in some shady dealings, Jane could be in trouble and it may all come back to that piece of paper.

"Earth to Senior Constable Logan!" Grey waved his hand in front of Bette's face to get her attention. "You must be crook. I've been talking to myself it seems!"

Bette smiled at him, "Sorry, still not feeling well. My mind is wandering a bit. What were you saying?"

Grey grimaced.

"Did you get a good look at the guy? Who's this Jane Woods? What did she think he was after? Why was she soaking wet?"

Bette stalled for time.

"Hang on! One question at a time!"

Grey's tone was intense which was also different to his usual form. He pulled away from Bette and looked hard at her. He then seemed to make a decision and relaxed noticeably.

"Sorry, I'm just keen to follow any leads. So did you get a good look at him or not?"

Bette was torn, but her decision was quick.

"I've been through two books, was on the third when you saw me. He wasn't in the first two. As I said, I'll have to go back over the others. I got a look at him but there wasn't anything remarkable like a birthmark, scar or piercing. He was just your average Joe."

Bette stunned herself, but the intuitive use of his name got a response as Grey started but kept looking ahead. Bette didn't feel good about what was happening, so she found herself avoiding eye contact as much as possible. This wasn't hard as Grey was doing the same.

He's not happy about this either, Bette thought, and there could only be one reason why. Grey was involved but retained enough of a conscience to feel guilty.

Grey was silent for a while then turned to face her.

"So, you're not feeling well?"

"No, bit hot and feel like vomiting."

She could say this truthfully.

Grey studied her face.

"The boys said this Woods seemed genuine, but anxious, what do you think?"

Bette could answer this one honestly too and so met Grey's gaze.

"I agree; she seemed nervous, but she had apparently just hauled herself out of the harbour and then been assaulted. Not your usual morning! She just seems a normal, decent, law abiding citizen. I was with her almost two hours. I don't know... People tend to get nervous around us. Who knows? I was thinking I'd ring her tomorrow and ask her to go over the events again, after she's rested up a bit."

Grey thought about it.

"Good idea, I might come with you, ask a few questions myself. Yeah... good idea. You make a time and I'll be there."

He got up and started to move off but hesitated and turned.

"No need to tell anyone that I'll be with you. Let's leave that between us, in case we turn something up. Now go home and get to bed!"

Grey turned and went through the door without looking back again.

Bette was pleased to go home. She needed some quiet time in which to think things through.

She shouldn't have said she would ring Jane. Now she needed to talk to Jane prior to the visit with Grey and find out what Jane really did know, and what was on that paper. Depending on how that went, she could then advise Jane on what to say to Grey. She would have to keep her fears about him to herself for the present. It was bad that he would interview Jane, but good that she would be there. She still wasn't sure. Grey might be on the take, or he might not be. She had to talk to Jane and discuss what to do, all without making it seem like he was a bad cop, in case he wasn't. Now that was simple...wasn't it?

Chapter Thirteen

It was about seven that night when Jane found herself standing outside Bette's door. She had taken note of the older model car in the narrow driveway, so Bette had passed one test. They had decided that, straight after the visit, she would ring Marion and stay the night with her and Jo.

Jane had a few aches and pains but felt surprisingly good. Good physically, that was; in terms of nerves she felt dreadful. She was about to knock at a stranger's door, check out the house and decide whether or not she could trust the woman. A woman who had saved her from goodness knows what earlier and then endured teasing from a tactless Liz about a romance.

If judged trustworthy, Jane would then tell her some of the less than substantial details. Those which involved a ghost and a bag lady saving her from possible bad guys.

"Good one, Jane! Now there's an unusual pick-up routine," She thought.

Before she had time to lose her nerve and walk away Jane impulsively reached out and rang the doorbell, but no sound resulted.

Yet again, Jane was reminded of a B Grade actress about to walk into some dark room.

"I hope I scream as well as they all seemed to," she murmured.

Unconsciously, she opened her mouth to its full extent, silently rehearsing a scream. Of course, it was then that Bette opened the door.

"I thought your doorbell was broken! I was practising a scream... I mean... Oh God, you must think I'm crazy! First, I'm in the harbour, now I'm here screaming. I must look stupid!" Jane was mortified.

Although taken aback, Bette recovered. "Stupid? No, I don't see you as stupid, but unusual, definitely unusual! Come in. I thought you would be at home recovering, or was today a normal sort of day for you?"

Bette was in shorts and T-shirt again, this time with wet hair, as if just out of the shower.

Jane was unsettled on two counts: one by being caught with her mouth open and the other by just how good Bette looked.

"No, today was most unusual for me, I've never been in the harbour or been mugged before."

Jane stopped looking around at the house to find Bette watching her. She was uncomfortably aware of every gram of weight that she'd put on over the last year. Neither of them said anything as Bette led the way down the hall into the lounge.

The first room they passed was Bette's bedroom. A towel was on the bed with a large pile of clothes on both the bed and a chair. Noticing her looking in the room, Bette self-consciously mumbled she hadn't had time to put things away. The second room appeared to be a guest room/office with a sofa bed and a desk with a computer on it. The lounge was filled with old furniture, including a big old sofa with a matching chair, but there was a new sound system set up on the shelves. The pictures hanging on the wall were prints except one landscape that looked original; a watercolour of rolling hills. Jane glimpsed Bette's appraising look at her and wondered if she'd been too obvious in her examination of the house and its contents.

Bette indicated the painting, "That was painted by my grandmother. It's the view from her veranda; she lived out past Lithgow." She sounded proud.

Jane nodded. "It's lovely; well composed, and she's really captured the light on the hills. The clouds are done well too, and they can be really hard to get right. She was very talented. You have any others?"

She turned back to look across an open counter into a kitchen with a small dining area, and beyond that another door, presumably the bathroom.

"Yes, I've got two others that I'm getting framed. You seem curious about my place. Want a tour?" If it were possible, Bette's tone hovered between amusement and annoyance.

Jane surprised them both by saying yes. There wasn't much more to see. The house was a small cottage, but unusually for the area there was a small front garden with a driveway. From the front door there was a hall running down one side of the house with the two rooms coming off it. The hall opened into an open living area in the middle, leading into the kitchen and dining area. The door Jane had seen lead to a combined bathroom/laundry at the back. A quick look at the small back yard with its clothesline, barbeque, and plastic table and chairs finished the tour.

It seemed to Jane that it was the much-loved house of someone who wanted it to look nice but didn't spend much time there.

"So, to what do I owe the pleasure of this visit?" Bette had turned to face Jane.

Jane felt herself blushing and despite having rehearsed the answer managed to stumble over the first few words,

"I just wanted to thank you and ask you some questions about what happened. I bought some champagne as a thank you. I hope you like it."

Jane held out the bottle, but Bette looked flustered and left Jane holding it. "I was only doing my job. I can't accept a present…" She looked at the label of the offered bottle, and raised her eyebrows, "…no matter how nice".

Jane lowered her arm and changed tack.

"Then would you please help me drink it? And you were off duty! It's just a thank you. No other intention."

She was surprised at Bette's reaction, relieved at the honesty, but also happy to see the conflict over how nice the champagne was. This was a woman who knew her champagnes. Jane eyes wandered over Bette's athletic figure.

Bette came to a decision, "Okay, as long as we are both clear I'm just helping you. It wouldn't be good my letting you drink it alone, then drive your car home. I've got some cheese we can have with it.

Bette opened the refrigerator to get the cheese. A bottle of white wine, milk, cheese and some shrivelled vegetables were almost the only things in there.

It was Bette's turn to look uncomfortable, but they both laughed when Jane asked, "Travelling light?"

"So, I need to shop! It's cold so we'll have it first then, eh?"

Bette opened a cupboard and produced two champagne glasses.

"I was going to ring you tomorrow to see how you were and

to ask you some questions too, so your visit works out well."

It appeared Bette was a seasoned champagne drinker by the way she opened the bottle. This pleased Jane more than it should have and she pushed down the tickling feeling she was getting when she looked too long at Bette. She reminded herself of the reason for the visit and felt her delight subside.

Jane sat on the sofa and Bette placed herself in one of the big chairs. They toasted Bette's fortuitous appearance that morning and Jane's strong grip on her bag.

"Do you have any idea what he was after? I mean you were wet, in a tracksuit, and really unlikely to have any money on you."

Jane looked around the room and back at Bette.

"Do you own the house?"

Bette started to object, but realised, for some reason, this was an important point for Jane.

"Yes, my last partner bought me out of the place we jointly owned, and my grandmother left me some money when she died. It's almost entirely mine... Why?"

Jane felt unable to lie as Bette had been so open with her and it was a relief to have made the decision to talk.

"Because I need to know if I can trust you. It seems funny, but we thought if you weren't rich you were unlikely to be on the take and so safe... I need to talk to someone about this morning and it looks like you're it!"

Jane stopped and took a big gulp from her glass. Bette matched the action, then muttered it was too nice to swig and got up to refill Jane's glass. She sat down next to Jane.

"We've got lots to talk about, it seems. We should get comfortable. I think this could take a while. How about you tell me what really happened, and then I'll fill you in on my problems. Maybe together we'll make some sense of it."

'She's smart, this one. You can tell her.'

Marjorie was back and she was chuckling. Jane started at her reappearance but was relieved to have someone back her decision to confide in Bette.

The laughter was a different matter. Jane couldn't tell if Marjorie was laughing at the situation or at her reactions to Bette sitting so close to her. Jane thought the latter and silently asked Marjorie to mind her own business. This just bought more laughter that faded as Marjorie left.

A gentle cough from Bette bought Jane back and she started telling her story again. This time any interruptions were precise and purposeful. Bette made no judgements on Jane's actions, although she did shake her head more than once, and asked for clarification about the guns, descriptions of the men, the van and cars.

Jane was able to say that she thought the van had been at the hospital earlier in the evening and where it had parked. Bette had fetched a pen and pad but wrote sparingly, although she was listening intently.

Bette didn't comment about Marjorie's involvement either, just frowned slightly and asked Jane to think if there could have been any other explanation.

Jane moved to get the paper out after she described the part where Alice gave her the cigarette case and she found the paper, but Bette signalled for her to continue with the story. Jane decided not to mention Marjorie's presence in her mind.

Bette sat back. "That's amazing. No wonder you didn't want to tell us this morning."

Jane sat forward, hoping for Bette to say more, then blurted.

"Well? Do you believe me?"

Bette was slow to reply.

"Yes, against my better judgement in some ways, but yes I do. I don't know what to make of Marjorie, but I believe you believe you saw Marjorie. I want you to take me to the reserve and the park and walk me through what happened."

Jane sat back with relief and said, "Okay. Then what? We tell your boss?"

At this Bette groaned and leaned forward, putting her head in her hands. Jane sat up again.

"What's up?"

Bette looked at the floor.

"My problems, remember? I found out who assaulted you this morning but that's really strange too. He's into heavy stuff, not random muggings. There's something happening and you've, now we've, stumbled into it..." she paused, "I think the one person I could tell might be involved."

Chapter Fourteen

Bette's face showed a mix of disappointment, confusion, distress and anger.

"I don't know who to tell at the moment. I think it's just us for a while, at least until we can come up with some solid facts I can pass on. Facts that don't involve a dead woman saving your skin."

They sat in silence briefly until Jane suddenly sat bolt upright.

"The paper!"

She had to stand up to get it out of her pocket. In her vanity the tighter pants had won out in her clothing choices. Bette was amazed that Jane still hadn't read it.

"There just wasn't any time today when I was alone. I haven't told my friends about it… I thought if you were okay," Jane paused, "well, then I'd want you to read it with me in case it was something really dangerous. Then there would be two who knew and it'd be harder to kill both of us."

Bette laughed. "I think you've been reading too many detective novels; I noticed a lot on your shelves. It's usually very boring work, believe me."

Jane presented the paper with a flourish and placed it on the coffee table between them. It was a rough hand drawn map with words written on it. Bette went to pick it up but hesitated.

"We'd better treat it properly; don't touch it again."

She went to her bedroom and came back with two sets of thin rubber gloves and a plastic bag. At Jane's look she smiled,

"For work, okay? And I thought Liz was forward!"

Jane smiled again and turned her attention to the table where Bette was smoothing out the small piece of paper.

From what the two could make out it was a rough map of the area around Rozelle and Balmain, with some details enlarged. The Rozelle section seemed far older as it was more faded and in pencil. As they puzzled over it, Jane thought that the square drawn on it could be the cottage where she'd seen the van. If so, the line next to it was the road she'd been on the night before, and the large boxed area was likely the hospital. There were some other markings with arrows on the water, one pointing out in the water and the other indicating an area immediately below the cottage. The notes were hard to read but one word was 'door'.

"Door?"

Jane was sure they were reading the word wrong, but Bette thought not.

"No, it's definitely 'door' but any door there would be in the water! Maybe there's a hole in the bank with a door protecting it and they've put something in it?"

"That's as likely as anything." Jane sounded tired.

"You're tired. It's a wonder you're out of bed, let alone out visiting."

Bette went to stand but Jane shook her head.

"It's okay. I won't be able to sleep until we sort out what the map means anyway. Let's just continue for now. I'll leave later."

Bette looked dubious, so Jane reached out, placing her hand on Bette's arm. "It's true. I'm fine. Can we continue?"

Bette looked from Jane's hand on her arm to look into her eyes.

"Yes, you are looking good... er... well"

Both women blushed and quickly broke off eye contact to focus on the map.

The Balmain part was newer, in pen and showed what seemed to be Darling Street with a line with two crosses at the end where the wharf was.

"That must be the wharf." Bette pointed at the line. "So, the crosses could be bodies. The one from the ferry, and the one you saw last night!"

Bette was excited.

"This could be something I can take to one of the inspectors above Mike."

She sank back into the seat.

"But who can I trust? I hardly know their names, only met one of them more than once. Given I thought Mike was honest... well, I can't say anything until I'm sure who to tell."

Bette suddenly stood.

"You told the police call operator you heard something."

"But they said it was maintenance! They don't know I went out to check!" Jane was quickly aware of what Bette was implying.

Bette rang the call centre on her landline and identified herself to the person on the line. Jane could see Bette's tension growing as they spoke.

"So you have the number? Could you repeat it back?"

Bette wrote a number down and showed it to Jane. It was her number.

Bette was about to hang up when she quickly raised the receiver back to her ear.

"Popular? Has someone else asked about it?"

Jane strained to hear the voice on the other end and her heart sank as she heard Bette's response.

"Mike Grey?" Jane could see Bette's mind working. "Look, we haven't had a chance to compare notes. Do me a favour. Don't tell anyone I rang, doesn't look good with the boss if I forgot he was doing this bit."

Jane was alert when Bette turned back to her.

"We got trouble. Central kept the number from the call you made, and Mike knows you rang. He'll put two and two together. It's good you're not going home tonight. Maybe we can have this interview with Mike and then you leave for a while. I'll drive you to and from the appointment. He won't dare do anything if I'm there. There's no reason for you to stay around, you're not a suspect or a witness to anything. I can let you know when it's safe to return."

Jane's eyes widened at every word.

"I thought you said this was all really very boring!" She said in an accusing tone.

"Well, it just stepped up a couple of gears, past interesting to concerning," replied Bette.

It was decided Jane would stay at Bette's that night, after some discussion. It was too risky to involve the others and neither of them thought Jane should go home alone. If Bette went home with Jane, then anyone watching Jane's house would know she was involved. The hope no one had followed Jane to Bette's went unspoken.

Jane rang Marion to let them know she'd be at Bette's that night and despite a slight smile she could hear in Marion's voice, nothing suggestive was said. Jane was very pleased the arrangement wasn't to ring Liz.

With some awkwardness, the two of them made up the bed in the second bedroom, and Bette found a T-shirt as pyjamas for Jane.

Staying the night was what Jane had been increasingly thinking about for the past hour. In her fantasy, however, she was not settling down in the spare bedroom by herself.

Bette hovered in the doorway for what seemed a long-time saying goodnight and Jane had to content herself with Bette's silhouette in the doorway.

Jane tossed and turned for hours. Images alternated between a naked Bette coming into the room and the house being broken into by the bad guys. Somewhat guiltily, Jane focussed on the more enticing image of a naked Bette and settled herself in a way that resulted in a far more satisfying sleep.

Chapter Fifteen

Jane's mysterious recovery continued with morning finding her almost pain-free and in a very good mood.

Bette glowered at Jane over her coffee. "How on earth can you be so good after yesterday and with all we've got to tackle today? I hardly slept last night thinking about you... er... I mean, thinking about Mike talking to you."

Jane found the stumble encouraging. "Yeah, I had trouble sleeping too. I spent a while imagining us being attacked by guys with guns, but I concentrated on something more... positive, yeah, positive and fell asleep," she hurriedly finished, immediately regretting the reply. She was relieved to see Bette had not noticed her comments as she continued to focus on the upcoming meeting with Mike Grey.

"You're going to have to convince him you didn't act on the phone call, admit to the call first, then say you went back to sleep and went for your usual jog in the morning."

Jane laughed ruefully. "Well, let's say I went for my new 'get fit' routine morning jog. He'll never believe I run regularly. But that might explain how I stumbled and fell in!"

"Look," Bette had an impatient tone, "Two things: one - this is serious, and you'd better be good, Mike's a damn good cop; and two - will you stop referring to yourself as if you're huge or something! It bugs me when women do that. You've got a fine body. You did some really physical things yesterday. You're not a lost case. You just need toning up! Okay?"

Jane sat back in surprise. "Well, thank you, I think, and yes, you're right. I know this is serious. It's just... I don't know... I'm just in a good mood for the first time in ages and it feels great! You really mean I just need to tone up?"

Bette looked a bit sheepish. "Sorry, I'm really worried about Mike; but it does bug me how women talk about themselves. You did really well last night by the sound of it, running, climbing, swimming, dealt with nerves. Your shape is fine, there's not much you need to do. If you want I'd be happy to help you, but let's just stick to Mike for the moment, eh?"

"Sure." Jane was feeling even better after Bette's comments.

Jane's mood did return to a more sombre level when Bette went over all she'd have to say and do for the interview. It was about fine judgements: act annoyed but not angry, show some doubts about what you remember, but don't be too vague, and don't look to Bette for sympathy.

"How will I remember all of what the story is and do all the acting as well?" Jane was getting really worried now.

Bette wanted her to be a bit anxious, but not too much or she'd look like she had something to hide.

"How about you just think and act as if it's all true. You had a bad night's sleep, went for a jog, fell in the harbour, you get mugged and here's this guy sounding like he doesn't believe you!"

Jane was happier.

"That I can do, I think. It sounds so easy now, but when he's there..."

Bette decided it was time to get the morning under way. She'd follow Jane home and ensure she got in and all was okay, then she'd ring Mike to let him know the meeting time. Bette would then head off to work. Jane agreed not to open the door again to anyone but Bette.

Jane drove home feeling as if she was being watched all the way, and not just by Bette. What if they had followed her to Bette's? Well, she'd soon find out, she rationalised, no use getting flustered.

Jane was enjoying this new side of her. She was getting on with what she could and dealing with anything else later. She didn't know when she made that decision. It was either practical or fatalistic, she couldn't decide which one, or even if there was a difference.

Parking the car, Jane unlocked her front door almost defiantly, and strode into her house. Once inside, she was confronted by the knowledge she was alone. Nervously, Jane did a quick look around, checking that all the doors and windows were still locked and there were no signs of attempted entry. All was fine so she messaged Bette. She decided to ground herself with some housework and put some clothes in the wash.

It was all going very well. She felt it was the perfect build-up to Mike Grey's visit early afternoon. She'd be found in the midst of normal house chores and this would be a great base to build her act upon. She even started vacuuming and looked anew at her surrounds.

It was time to get rid of some of the items she'd held onto after the separation. She was ready to let go of things, including past dreams. Her mind went to the 'treasures' on the kitchen windowsill, mostly stones and water polished glass. She needed to sort out which were hers and which she and Sally had found together. Time to start her own collection, her own life, again. This led to a mental process of sorting through the furniture as well. This took more time than she anticipated as each piece had its own history. Some decisions were quickly made, but others required revisiting memories and negotiating any emotions connected. In the end she was quite pleased with how much she was ready to move on.

A few hours passed and Jane returned to the kitchen to get a quick snack before Mike Grey and Bette arrived, when a sudden high-pitched whine followed by beeps announced that the washing was finished. Jane put the wet clothes in the washing basket and opened the back door.

She was only as few steps into the yard when she noticed the broken pot with the dirt spread over the path.

"Damn cat," she frowned. It wasn't the first time the neighbour's cat had created a mess in her garden.

It was a second or two before she recognised the outline of footprints in the dirt; human footprints. As Jane turned to run back inside, a hand was placed over her face and she was firmly grabbed around the waist. She kicked and struggled but to no avail.

"Forget it, bitch. You've got no chance this time," the voice hissed at her. "We're going inside to see what you've got hidden in there. You know what I'm after and you'd better find it quick. You can show me, or I'll take my time looking later… after you're dead."

Jane was unable to think of anything, except that either way she would be dead.

He dragged Jane back through the house to the front room.

"Let's start here, shall we?"

He pushed her in front of him and she turned to see his eyes staring at her from inside the balaclava he was wearing.

Angry, furious eyes. Her shaking legs were hard to stand on, but she didn't dare move. He took a look at her bookcase and nodded toward it.

"Am I getting warm?" he asked sarcastically.

Jane could only shake her head and try to delay him.

"What do you want?"

She assumed he wanted the cigarette case and the paper, both at Bette's. He wouldn't like that.

"You or the old witch must have it. I can't find her, so it's you."

He swept the books and everything else off the two middle shelves while looking at her. He spoke quietly which was all the more terrifying,

"I told you, you can show me where the case is or I'll look myself." He paused and then emphasised, "Afterwards!"

"What case? I don't have any case!"

A glimpse at the clock showed it was only a couple of minutes before Bette and Mike Grey should arrive.

The man, seeing the fleeting look, grabbed the clock and ripped off the back. Jane cried out in horror. It was her parent's wedding present from her mother's family. It had been passed onto her. It was the only bit of her family history she had. In disgust he threw it down.

He was advancing on her when the doorbell rang and Jane was able to shriek, "Help!" before he hit her across the face and grabbed her again.

He pulled her back through the house into the backyard. Jane fighting him all the way as the taste of blood in her mouth broke through her fears. A man climbed over the fence and yelled at him to let her go. Bette came over the fence a short time later. Both had guns drawn.

"I told you to stay out front!" The man who must be Mike Grey snarled at Bette.

"She's got a deadlock." Bette threw back.

They never moved their gaze from Jane and the man holding her.

The man tightened his grip on her and stood up straighter.

"Move towards the house."

Jane was annoyed when they both obeyed him. There were two of them! They had guns! Why didn't they do something?

The two police moved slowly around toward the back door as he circled backward toward the fence.

"Now put down your guns. Slowly. Move back a bit. Good."

Jane was stunned. Why weren't they doing something? She felt the man tense, heard Marjorie yell, *"Duck!"* and sagged as low in his arms as she could. There was a blow to her head, and she was pushed to the ground. Again, there was yelling, and the sound of running feet followed by arms around her.

Jane looked around while putting a hand tentatively to her head. Bette was holding her as they sat in the compost heap.

"Grey's gone after him but took a couple of attempts to get over the fence. Just enough for him to get away."

The anger in Bette's voice was obvious.

Jane gently touched her head.

"Why is it always me? I want to save you for once!"

Bette smiled tightly.

"Little damage done, with your hard head anyway! Actually, you missed most of the blow. You started to move just before he hit you with his gun and ..."

"He had a gun?" Jane's stomach flipped.

Jane felt Bette's grasp on her tightened fleetingly.

"Why else would we..." Bette corrected herself, "...I, back off? But even if he didn't have a gun, we had to keep you safe."

Jane shut her eyes again, trying to make sense of her life in the past two days and gave up. She was only aware that her head hurt, the compost smelt, and that it felt good in Bette's arms.

Chapter Sixteen

Bette didn't let Jane rest long before insisting Jane move out of the compost and into the house.

Reaching the kitchen, Bette steered Jane into a chair and pulled out her mobile, "Sorry, need to update the station."

Over Jane's protests Bette also requested an ambulance.

"The deadlock wasn't on by the way," Jane said apologetically after Bette had finished her call.

"I don't care. It was an excuse so I could follow Mike. I didn't think I should leave you with two bad guys." Bette gave a weak smile

Jane heard the sadness in Bette's voice.

"You sure he's in on it?"

"Yes, he just seemed annoyed when you called out, as if the other guy shouldn't have been here, and then the fence thing..."

Bette trailed off and Jane didn't pursue the topic.

"Is the interview off?" Jane asked hopefully.

Bette wasn't sure. "I don't know, this could make it more difficult. What happened?"

Jane shuddered. "I won't have to act with this. He wanted the cigarette case, asked for the 'case' directly. He must want the map back. He said he'd kill me if I didn't give it to him. I was too scared to say anything other than I didn't know what he was talking about. He was waiting for me when I went outside to hang the laundry… oh, the washing! It's still outside."

Bette again moved to Jane and helped her stand.

"Leave it for the minute. Let's get you into a more comfortable chair."

Jane thought she could stand by herself but liked the feel of Bette's arms supporting her. She must be falling for Bette if that was what she was thinking after a near death experience, she mused.

They reached the front room and Jane watched Bette as she surveyed the mess. "Your usual chair?" Bette asked with a rueful smile.

Jane didn't answer as her eyes went to the smashed clock

on the floor. She went over to it, bent to pick it up and immediately felt dizzy.

Bette was quickly at her side and helped her back into the chair. She then returned to get the clock and gave it Jane who hugged it to her chest crying again.

'I know a good clock maker who's still in business.' Marjorie sounded sympathetic.

Bette gave Jane's shoulder a supportive squeeze and moved towards the doorway.

"I'll go out the back, collect the washing and lock the back door."

Jane felt a surge of fear and started to rise.

"Don't worry, I'll be quick." Bette quickly reassured her.

A short time later she returned at speed, heading to the front door as someone thumped on it.

"Who is it?" Bette called out.

Jane was unable to hear the response but did hear the front door open.

"One visit and you notice the deadlock. Very observant." Grey's voice had a sarcastic tone.

Bette's reply was harder to hear, "It wasn't actually. Jane mentioned it when I asked her if she'd feel safe here alone."

"Jane eh? You sure that you're totally on the ball with this one?"

Jane was straining to hear but could sense the edge to Bette's response. "I beg your pardon, Sir. I'm not sure I understand what you mean."

Jane was unsure what she could do but understood Grey's implication. He was accusing Bette of being on her side. Jane took a deep breath, stopped her tears and shook her head in disbelief at what was happening. She had become a 'side' to be on.

Grey continued, his tone changed. "Sorry, that was out of line. I'm damn frustrated and need to be sure we all are working together, that's all."

"When have I ever not worked with you?" Bette questioned.

Jane heard footsteps and quickly sunk back into her chair, just as Grey entered the room.

After the exchange in the hall Jane had wondered what their entrance would bring. Grey's angry face was expected, but not the relieved look on Bette's face. Jane looked from one to the other. Grey scowled as she had obviously heard them.

Bette was formal, "Ms Woods, this is Detective Grey. I'm afraid we've been caught out, to be honest. We hadn't thought you might be in ongoing danger. It's rattled us both, it seems."

Grey gave Bette a fleeting look, nodded and followed her lead.

"Yes, this looks like it's more than just a random mugging. Did you recognise him from the other day?"

Jane faltered slightly as she started to answer, and she stared at Grey while he looked around the room. It was with some difficulty that she recovered herself before he looked back at her.

"No, I didn't get a look at him then, and today he had that balaclava on." she shuddered at the memory.

Grey followed up on his point.

"The assault was unusual to start off with, but now it seems you have something that he wants. Do you have any idea what that is, and did he get it?"

Jane was struggling to keep her voice steady. Seeing Mike Grey at close quarters she thought he could be the man who had looked into Marjorie's reserve after the two watchmen had left, but that man was called Paul. The same man who also appeared to be in charge on the wharf.

Jane was unsure how to answer his question. Her thoughts were spinning, when she suddenly thought there might be a way out of at least part of this increasingly scary situation.

"Well..." she hesitated and looked at Bette. "I'm sorry Officer Logan... I haven't told you the whole truth."

Jane could see Bette's eyes widen then narrow as Jane diverted from the agreed story.

"I did find a piece of paper in the street, just before he grabbed me the first time... It might not even be connected, but it's the only thing I can think of... It was just a lot of squiggles really, some kid's treasure map or something... I... I must have dropped it when he grabbed me."

Jane didn't mention the cigarette case.

Bette was obviously having some difficulty measuring her words.

"Why didn't you tell us at the time?"

Grey glanced at Bette with an almost sympathetic look.

Jane was aware that it was crucial that Mike believed her story and was delighted with what she had come up with.

"Well, at first I just didn't connect the two things. I mean how could a kid's treasure map and being mugged be linked? Then I started to wonder and was embarrassed and worried that I hadn't told you to start with, and I even got worried I'd littered. I mean you get to feel so guilty about everything; eating fatty foods, the environment, earthquake victims... anyway, until Detective Grey mentioned it again, well... I... I'm sorry. Is it important?"

Grey answered through gritted teeth.

"It could be very important. Where exactly did you find the paper?"

Jane had already thought about this.

"I think it was just below the little reserve opposite from here, I would have picked it up, walked a couple of steps, then he grabbed me, probably all outside the house on the low side of the reserve."

Without any attempt at acting, Jane's voice faltered.

The sound of a police siren growing louder seemed to unsettle Grey, who appeared impatient to look for the paper.

"Officer Logan, can I have a word with you?"

He and Bette went back into the hall, this time Grey closed the door behind them.

Jane got up and ran quietly to listen at the door.

She felt a familiar approach, *'I can help you with this.'*

The initially muffled words became clearer. She sent a quick thanks to Marjorie who stayed to listen as well.

She could hear Grey, "... so it seems she may have found something important. I want you to get her to try to draw what she saw on the paper. I'll go over the road and check if it's there. It's unlikely though. Damn it, stupid woman, worried about littering!"

"See, I told you, people get nervous around us so they hold back information on ridiculous grounds. She's just been in the wrong place at the wrong time."

Jane was delighted Bette had realised what she was trying to do and smiled.

Grey was sounding agreeable, "Yes, I think you're right.

Geez, what on earth have fatty foods and earthquake victims got to do with anything?"

Jane heard Bette open the front door and Grey step outside as the police car came to a stop and switched off its siren.

Jane's smile widened, then her mouth set into a determined line. It had worked. He thought she was just some unlucky, dumb woman. How wrong he was.

Chapter Seventeen

Standing in the doorway Bette recognised Detectives Shields and McMahon, or S & M as they were commonly nicknamed, as they got out of the car. Shields was taller, but McMahon seemed the bigger because of his bulk. She'd had little to do with them but knew they had good reputations and were on the wharf murder case. They were both grim faced and headed straight for Grey.

"G'day guys," Grey started, but he got no further.

Detective Shields was not in a friendly mood.

"What the hell are you doing here Grey? You've been warned off this case! The Inspector's pissed off and wants you in his office pronto!"

Grey turned to Bette with a sneer.

"Didn't think we could handle it?"

She feigned puzzlement at his tone.

"We had a potential siege *Sir*, so no, I didn't think we should do it alone. I called for backup immediately we heard the scream."

The contempt in Mike's voice was unmistakable.

"My, we are all formal. That's a dyke in there, but I suppose you'd already noticed."

Bette tensed with shock, then anger, but Detective McMahon cut off any chance she had for a retort.

"That's enough, Mike! Officer Logan, I'm sure Detective Grey regrets those comments. It's best we all forget them."

He then turned to Grey, "What the hell's going on, Mike? This is stupid! You're in a big enough hole already. This isn't helping."

While McMahon talked to Grey, Shields suggested Bette go inside and wait for them there. Bette nodded and went inside shutting the door behind her. As it closed, she leant against it, shaking. The situation with Grey was now clear. There was something very wrong. It was nasty and was getting personal.

Bette was interested to hear he had been reprimanded or warned previously. This had been kept very quiet, or else it had just happened. She hadn't heard any rumours at the station and keeping secrets there was near to impossible.

Why had he been 'warned off' the wharf case? Did others have their suspicions too? He could be suspended, if the previous warning had been serious enough. If he was suspended, things could get worse. At least she could keep track of him at work. It was a shaken Bette that returned into the room with Jane.

Jane got up from the chair to meet her, but Bette went around her to cautiously look through the window. Grey was pushing his finger into Shields' chest until McMahon pushed between them. Grey then turned and stormed off down the street, and, ignoring their gaze, he searched in front of the house where Jane said she had dropped the paper.

A dog suddenly threw itself at the fence next to him, causing him to jump. He thumped the fence and the dog's barking could be heard inside the room.

Bette couldn't help herself. "Good dog!"

Jane too was looking out the window.

"That's Tosca. He's the one from the other night. Got a loud bark and a nasty streak."

Speaking fast and low Bette told Jane of her concerns, surprising herself with the trust she put in Jane so instinctively.

"The two detectives out there, they're the ones investigating the murder. Grey's in some trouble, but he's also implied that I'm involved with you! They'll have some questions. I don't know what they'll be after. You'll have to see yourself through this one. Buy some time if you can."

Bette said the last bit over her shoulder as the doorbell had sounded and she went to open the door.

***

Jane was more concerned by Bette's sudden loss of confidence than the idea of new detectives and more questions. She only had time to get back in her chair and hope she looked sufficiently upset and confused, she certainly felt it, before the two came in.

Bette again started off by formally introducing them to 'Ms Woods'.

Jane forced a smile.

"I feel like I'm meeting the entire station the last two days. Please call me Jane. I've nearly got Officer Logan doing it!"

The two detectives smiled, and Shields started by

explaining that they understood that the last two days had been hard.

Jane interrupted, "Look, I'm not coping particularly well. I reckon I'll only last another few minutes before I start crying." Indeed, as she said it, she found herself trembling and her eyes filling again. "Sorry. Can we do this later? I'll be happy to talk to you later. I've just about had it right now!" The wobble in her voice was no act.

Detective Shields nodded and said, "That's fine for giving a formal statement, but we still need to ask a couple of questions right now."

He hesitated and Jane nodded, so he continued, "Thanks, we do appreciate it. Right now, we need to know everything you just told Detective Grey and anything else you think could be important or that was unusual about either assault. We'll be sending the forensic guys in to see if the attacker left any fingerprints or anything else to identify him."

Jane looked at Bette who seemed surprised that the questions included Mike Grey. Jane also thought Shields sounded genuinely concerned for her, and so she really did think hard before repeating what she had told Grey.

Bette coughed once Jane had finished and interrupted.

"He had gloves on, so no fingerprints, but he did leave footprints in some dirt out there. There might be more around the fence. Detective Grey asked me to get Ms Woods to draw what was on the piece of paper for him."

At this the two men looked at each other. McMahon then dropped his gaze and shook his head as if disappointed. Jane wondered if Bette had just confirmed something for them. Something McMahon hadn't wanted to believe.

Jane suddenly recalled a memory.

"I do remember something weird. It wasn't really clear the first time, but today it was. He smelt of disinfectant, you know the type used in government places, hospitals and schools. He smelt of it, or his clothes did, and a musty smell, like damp earth… I didn't see him the first time and this time he had a balaclava on."

She shut her eyes to try to recall more about the smell but only saw his eyes looking out of the balaclava. She shuddered and opened her eyes.

"Sorry, he said he'd kill me if I didn't give him what he wanted, and I don't know what that is!" Jane trailed off as tears came back to her eyes.

Bette moved forward.

"It's okay. Now we know we need to protect you."

The two men conferred softly for a few moments before Shields said, "That's enough for now. Logan, can you stay with Ms... er... Jane and bring her to the station around five p.m.? If possible, we'd like a copy of what was on the paper. We'll let the Sergeant know the situation, that we've got you watching Jane here and we'll get a couple of officers to drive past the house every so often until then, okay? One last thing. I'm afraid we have to ask both of you not to pass on any further information to Detective Grey. If he approaches either of you, please let us know as soon as possible."

Jane nodded her thanks and Bette let the men out of the front door.

Much to Jane's surprise Bette returned to the room with a worried look. Jane had thought it was working out fine. Mike was off their backs; she had remembered something that tied in with the hospital; and they had pointed the right people in the right direction without drawing attention to themselves. That was good, wasn't it?

However, Bette wasn't thinking in those terms.

"What you said was wonderful, and really fast thinking. But we've still got problems."

Bette was sitting on the arm of Jane's chair and Jane was more interested in the problem of how to get closer without being too obvious. She casually put her arm on the back of the chair.

"They were very open and definite about Mike just then; that's really unusual. Normally you'd try to keep that sort of thing quiet. If Mike's suspended, he'll be free to watch us."

Meanwhile, Jane had succeeded in putting her arm behind Bette's back.

Bette continued. "Mike's now aware you have seen the map. He might want to ensure you don't remember it, or you don't have the opportunity to draw it for someone else."

Jane placed one hand behind Bette, and casually turned so she could look at Bette while she spoke. This meant her other hand could 'naturally' rest on Bette's knee.

Bette's voice stumbled as she looked at Jane's hand.

"Oh, this is not a good idea. I'm a policewo…"

Bette stopped, trembling as Jane surprised herself by running her hand up Bette's thigh and squeezed.

"Right now, you being a policewoman is the furthest thing from my mind. I've been thinking about this since your place."

Bette took Jane's hand off her knee with a shaking one.

"Me too, but…"

"No buts."

Jane was amazed at what she was hearing herself say. She pulled Bette towards her and their lips met as Bette landed in Jane's lap.

Bette pulled away.

"This is not a good idea." But it was her hands that pulled Jane back to her lips.

Chapter Eighteen

They kissed again, tentative movements rapidly becoming more confident, more urgent.

"I think you know the way to my bedroom?" Jane murmured.

She left the rest unsaid and, taking Bette's hand, she led her towards the stairs.

They were only part way up the stairs when Bette started to undo Jane's shirt. They were halfway up by the time Jane had her hands down the back of Bette's pants. They were at the top of the stairs when they lay down, oblivious to anything but their own breathing, the softness of the other and the need to feel skin on skin.

Jane had never been so overwhelmed by passion. Her desire for Bette had been building since they met and its release flooded through her.

They disconnected briefly a couple of times to shed more clothes, Jane eager to touch all the places she had fantasized about. Bette was groaning as Jane's mouth teased and sucked her nipples. Jane could hear her own answering moans as Bette's hand explored her breasts, stomach curves, thighs, and down into the soft curls.

The fingers hesitated, then pushed around further and slide into wetness. They both gasped.

"Slow down."

Jane wanted the moment to last as long as possible.

Jane kissed Bette's ear and ran her hands over Bette's body. She withdrew Bette's hand, placing it in her mouth sucking and kissing the fingers. Bette moved closer and Jane swung her leg over Bette's hips, moving to lie on top of her.

Jane wanted to feel every fold, every inch of Bette's skin without breaking the bodily contact they had. Kissing and touching was no longer enough. Jane wanted and needed, to touch, taste, explore and smell every part of Bette.

Surrendering herself to Jane's eagerness, Bette allowed herself the pleasure of focussing on the sensations that Jane's hands, tongue and body were producing. It was too soon that she felt herself slipping away, slipping toward the edge of an orgasm. Jane's breathing was loud in Bette's ear as Jane kissed her neck, her tongue flicking the earlobe. But it was the sensation growing from where Jane's fingers were exploring: initially teasing and caressing, then probing for the right place, then a thrusting motion that was increasingly taking Bette's attention.

Her breath was coming in more and more ragged gasps and Bette recognised the signs of her body racing towards the edge of no return. Her hips tilting to allow even deeper access, Bette heard Jane moan and felt the next thrust go deep. Bette could hold back no longer. Head and back arching as Jane pushed deep into her again, Bette gasped and waves of convulsions rolled through her body. Her hips and legs jumped in spasms of pleasure as Jane kept her fingers moving gently inside, Bette let the spasms fade and lay quietly recovering her breath.

Bette could feel Jane's mouth on her shoulder, lazily kissing the skin. Bette let her tongue flirt with Jane's neck and felt a shudder run through Jane at the touch. She pushed up onto her elbow, rolled Jane over and moved to lay between her legs. Bette looked at Jane's face from above and smiled. There was no need to speak. She felt their skin, slick from sweat, meet across stomach and groin, and, slowly, started moving her mound against Jane's. She felt the tangles of wet hair meet and Jane react by placing her legs around her buttocks and pulling Bette down harder onto her.

***

In her mind's eye, Jane was looking down at the two of them and imagined the view of the curve of Bette's back and buttocks as she moved around Jane's body. The image in itself was enough to bring her legs up and around Bette, but when she focussed on the sensations Bette was causing and the sounds Bette was making, Jane found herself swiftly moving towards her own orgasm.

To Jane's frustration, Bette slowed things down. She felt Bette shift above her, bringing their faces together. A long, slow kiss was exchanged with Bette pulling away too soon. Jane tried to move to follow Bette's mouth, but Bette ignored her to suck hard on a nipple and Jane sunk back onto the carpet with a gasp.

As Bette journeyed south on her body, Jane tried to capture, and hold, Bette's buttocks, back, breasts, face, even her hair. However, Bette's progress down Jane's body was unstoppable, deliciously slow and steady. Jane tried to move to make the journey easier, but Bette wanted Jane to only concentrate on herself. She moved Jane's feet so they were resting on the second stair, which placed her hips on the top stair.

Jane felt a sudden loss of contact and heard Bette groan. Her knees were pushed further apart, then felt full on contact returned as Bette pushed her face, mouth open, into her. Jane felt herself respond physically and heard a roar come from her mouth and the tongue thrust further in. Jane thrust herself at Bette's tongue, throwing her own legs as far apart as she could. Jane felt Bette's tongue and her fingers inside her and was soon lost in the myriad of sensations that came from them. She could feel Bette's mouth on her clitoris, her hands on her hips, her breasts... everywhere.

All the sensations could only be held for too short a time before Jane's senses were overwhelmed. She was suddenly aware of nothing other than Bette's tongue. One of her hands grasping the baluster; the other grabbing Bette's hair; and the fact that she was going to explode. She heard herself call out and tightened her grip on both the baluster and Bette.

She came with a rush and a cry, but Bette continued to enjoy Jane's body drawing more shudders and groans, until Jane's hands pulled Bette away. Jane's body eventually quietened, and Bette, herself still breathing heavily stayed where she was, her head resting on Jane's thigh.

It was not long before Jane pulled Bette up. Bette kissed her way back to Jane's face and they lay together and kissed a while longer before Jane, almost reluctantly, suggested it might be more comfortable in bed.

As Bette helped her up, Jane stumbled and fell against the wall with Bette landing against her. They stayed there a few seconds with their hips pushed together and kissed again. Jane wanted to start again but Bette said no. Jane needed sleep, Jane reluctantly agreed and led them into the bedroom.

Jane was soon asleep, but Bette lay awake, initially enjoying the closeness, but with an increasing feeling of unease. Once Jane's breathing indicated a deep sleep, Bette untangled herself, gently, got up and quickly showered. After checking Jane was still sleeping, she went downstairs, collecting her clothes and redressing as she went.

Cursing herself, she made a quick circuit of the house to reassure herself that all the windows and doors were locked. She was angry at not doing it before they went upstairs. Her frown deepened: what was she thinking, taking a vulnerable woman, a victim of assault, and someone she was supposed to be protecting, to bed? She knew Jane had initiated it, but it should never have happened. The shudder of arousal that went through her at the recollection of their journey up the stairs made her anger stronger.

In her training they'd been told about the Four F's of Stress – Freeze, Flight, Fight and Fuck – but had thought the last was just an excuse for bad behaviour. Maybe she was wrong. Maybe surviving a near death experience did set off a primitive need for sex. She pushed the thought away. There was no excuse for her actions.

Bette found the clothes horse, hung up the washing and put the kettle on. She was hardly aware of what she was doing physically. Her mind was busy trying to decide what she should do. Should she tell someone? Who? No, she would have to take a step back from Jane. Perhaps ask to be given another assignment? Tell Jane it was a mistake… but she liked Jane. At any other time… she had been thinking about sex with Jane since the night she turned up at her door. She should have controlled herself. Why, oh why hadn't she?

It was as she pushed the plunger down for her coffee and wondered what would happen next that she heard a faint voice.

'She's a big girl; she knew what she was doing. Stay close, she's going to need you.'

Bette looked around the room and shook herself.

"Great! Now I'm hearing voices." She then checked the room again to ensure no one was there.

Chapter Nineteen

Jane woke to the sound of Bette calling her name, smiled sleepily and slowly stretched. She shivered in anticipation of a hug, and hopefully, more. However, Bette had moved away and was staring out the window.

"There's coffee on the bedside table, milk with no sugar. Hope that's okay?"

Confused at Bette's tone, Jane sat up, and, not knowing whether or not to cover herself, blushed. It was so much easier when you didn't have time to think about being naked and just did it.

"Well, that's the way of things isn't it?"

Jane started at Marjorie's reappearance and grabbed her t-shirt.

"What's up?" Bette had seen Jane jump and looked around for the cause.

"Nothing..."

Jane was thrown by Marjorie's comment. How long had she been there?

"What? You think I'd do that! I'm a spirit, not a pervert! I've lived too, you know!"

"It's okay."

Jane had responded to reassure Marjorie but spoke aloud.
"Good," said Bette,

"Just as well!" Marjorie still sounded annoyed.

Jane was sure she couldn't keep up two conversations at once and gently asked Marjorie to either go or be quiet. Marjorie decided to listen now and comment later.

Jane looked up to find Bette frowning at her.

Jane's stomach sank, "Are you okay? Are you worried about... you know... us?"

Bette turned back to look out the window.

"What happened... it was a mistake. A mistake I should not have made, and one I regret, I'm sorry."

She paused, sighed, licked her lips, then turned to face Jane.

"You're a nice woman, really nice. I like you, but I'm a policewoman. Maybe at another time... but I'm here on duty.

I'm supposed to be protecting you, not fucking you! It can't..."
Bette changed position and continued in a firmer tone,
"...won't happen again. You get ready and I'll be downstairs.
We need to talk about the interview and have to leave soon."

Jane had felt her mouth drop in shock as Bette spoke.

"But it was great wasn't it? We both wanted it to happen!
What's the problem? We're both adults, or at least I am."

Bette kept her silence.

Right now, Jane just wanted Bette to leave so she could
think things through.

She started to mumble agreement, "Okay, you go
downstairs..."

An unexpected surge of anger pulsed through her. Didn't
she have a say in this? She stood.

"No, wait! You can leave and I'll sort this out myself. I don't
want you involved if you feel guilty or forced to be here."

Jane blinked back tears and continued, "No one will be the
wiser. Think about it; you can tell me what you decide when I
get downstairs."

Jane turned towards the bathroom feeling some satisfaction
in having the last word. She waited for Bette to leave the room
before she let the shower hide her tears.

Later as she stood at the top of the stairs taking a few deep
breaths, Jane felt what could only be described as a cuddle
from inside.

*"Well... not what you had hoped for my dear... but she is
right. As lovely as it likely was, it was wrong... well, at the
wrong time. Maybe later..."* Marjorie sounded tentative

Jane was quick to interrupt.

*"No, she made it clear. I have to accept it; I have to see
myself through this... whatever it is. Thank goodness I have
you with me. I do, don't I?"*

There was a gentle chuckle.

*"Of course. I've never had so much fun. I'm not going
anywhere."*

Jane sent a hug back and started down the stairs.

***

Bette was talking.

"Don't tell everything, just what they need to know to get
them looking in the right places. Draw the map for them so

they start looking at the hospital. They needn't know you were there watching them recover the second body."

Jane blinked and tried to refocus on what Bette was saying. On Jane's arriving downstairs Bette had wasted no time saying she intended to stay involved; she wanted to find out who the corrupt police were and expose them. Staying with Jane was her best chance. Jane had missed the next few minutes as she strove to contain the hurt. Was that all she was to Bette? An opportunity? Emotions rolled through her: anger, embarrassment, sadness, self-doubt, confusion, even arousal were there, as her face grew hot, then cold, her stomach dropped, and her hands formed tight fists. It took all she had to not burst into tears and run from the room.

Jane interrupted Bette, resisting the urge to scream at her. She had hoped to maintain her icy and detached manner but settled for the polite voice she heard coming from her mouth.

"Sorry I was distracted. I'm listening now, what did you say again?"

Bette sighed, "It's okay, I know this afternoon's not been the best... for either of us. With all that's happened to you, you're doing well. Surprisingly well. You just need to keep it up."

Once Bette had repeated herself, Jane agreed she would draw a map to let the detectives know about a second body and, hopefully, check the hospital.

She had read lots of detective novels and often imagined being involved but she wasn't enjoying the real thing. She couldn't believe she'd been mugged and had a gun pulled on her. Unconsciously, she moved her hand towards the bruise above her ear and saw Bette start towards her, then stop.

"Is it too much? If you can't do it, we could try to delay the interview."

Jane shook her head, determined to prove to Bette that she could cope. That she was someone that Bette would regret not getting involved with. As soon as she thought it, Jane threw that idea out. This was about so much more than a relationship with Bette.

"Look, I'm fine." She sighed, "It's just that, well, I suppose it's all a bit of a shock. First, the events in the park, Marjorie, the assaults, and then our... er... misunderstanding."

She paused as Bette looked uncomfortably around the

room, anywhere but at her.

"Don't worry I will keep going for as long as I need to. You'll catch your corrupt cops" She couldn't help the bitter edge to her words and was pleased to see Bette react with a wince.

In fact, Jane thought she was recovering too well. She suspected Marjorie's was doing something to help, but she wasn't going to share that with Bette.

Bette said she'd try to ensure that the interview was as short as possible. She'd ask Shields and McMahon to ensure regular patrols checked in on Jane throughout the night. Jane quickly agreed, she needed time alone to think about what had happened. She also wanted to find and warn Alice that a thug was looking for her and ask about Marjorie. This would be better without Bette.

"Why not ask me? I'm dead, not deaf!"

Jane sighed again. She was either very bad at communicating with the dead, or Marjorie was in a particularly grumpy mood.

Driving to the station, Jane could feel Bette tense as they got closer. Her language and the tone began to change, and Jane thought she could even detect postural changes. Bette was sitting straighter and her hands were gripping the steering wheel tighter as she told Jane what to expect at the station, who would be there and what she needed to say.

Jane sat silently, sneaking glimpses of Bette and reflecting about their time together. She could already see Bette loved being a policewoman and was probably very good at it. What had gone wrong between them? Bette had said their going to bed was a mistake. How could that be? They were both adults…

Bette shifted in her seat and became more definite in her manner and speech. Jane focussed on this. Happy to find something about Bette that grated with her; it would drive her crazy if Bette was like that all the time. Maybe it was just as well Bette thought it was a mistake? Yes. It was just a one off; never to be repeated and that was for the best.

"Oh, stop obsessing about your sex life, you've got far more to be worried about! She's nervous about you, and about her career. I could take a little look around her head and let you know what she's thinking?" Marjorie chuckled

Jane suddenly sat upright in her seat.

"Don't you dare!" she angrily sent back.

Marjorie laughed.

Bette stopped in mid-sentence, misinterpreting Jane's sudden movement.

"I don't think it's anything to be worried about, but if you see Mike it's best to be civil but hurry past."

Mike! Was he the man in the park and possibly the boss? Jane had forgotten to tell Bette she thought she'd seen Mike that night. Should she tell Bette now? Jane realised that Bette did seem nervous, now that Marjorie had commented on it. Did Bette need to know this just before an important interview? A nasty inner voice suggested it would serve her right if Jane did tell her but that wouldn't really help and Jane was aware she really did need to get out of whatever she had ended up in... and fast.

Therefore, Jane said the first thing that came to mind,

"It's not that, I'm concerned that you love being a cop, and all this – corrupt cops and our... mistake, might put that in jeopardy."

"No, I'm fine." Bette blurted out. She bit her lip nervously, which contradicted the denial. "Why would you think that? Did Marjorie get in my head? She's wrong!"

"Whoa! You hit a sore point there," Marjorie chuckled.

Jane threw an angry accusation at Marjorie, *"Did you?"*

"Sorry." Bette sounded as if she were struggling to remain calm. "I shouldn't suggest Marjorie would do that and my career's fine." She looked at Jane defiantly. "Nothing for you to worry about."

The sentence had started off evenly but ended quite sharply. Jane felt what was left of the connection between them lessen with Bette's words.

Marjorie indignantly interrupted Jane's thoughts.

"See! Hardly knows me and trusts me! I was just teasing. As if I would! You should know me better than that!"

Jane felt Marjorie's departure, this time with a hint of a slamming door. She had started to enjoy Marjorie's commentary and Marjorie was right, Jane did trust her and knew she wouldn't go uninvited into people's personal thoughts. She sent out an apology and felt it echo around in her mind. It seemed she was the only one there.

Jane slumped in her seat and closed her eyes. Marjorie had sounded hurt and angry. Jane felt a real loss. She wanted to talk to Marjorie about her life: what Balmain was like when she was growing up and why the fire had happened. If Marjorie had any relatives perhaps, she could look them up? On top of the loss of the possibility of a relationship with Bette, the loss of Marjorie was hard to contemplate.

Jane felt a movement and found Bette shaking her arm to get her attention.

"Get your act together, we're here."

Chapter Twenty

Bette stepped ahead to open the station door for Jane and directed her across the public area. Bette nodded to the officer on the desk and indicated Jane should go through the door next to the front desk.

Bette's business-like demeanour increased Jane's feelings of being abandoned and under threat. However, it was somewhat relieved by two young men in uniform making teasing remarks to Bette about her new protective-duties role. Her terse reply surprised them... and Jane. It was a measure of Bette's tension level Jane thought.

"Right again, Marjorie. Marjorie?"

Jane gave up trying to reach her and tried to focus.

Bette opened a door into a big office where a few men looked up from desks and computer screens. Jane recognised Detective Shields and noticed the complete absence of women. They had passed a few women in other rooms, but they were in uniform or doing administrative duties. This must be the room where the detectives hung out. Jane had an insight into why Bette was so driven. She could have a hard job breaking in here. She'd need a lot of determination and hard work.

Shields got up.

"Room three, Logan. We'll be along shortly."

"Yes, sir."

Bette spun around towards the door and the day-dreaming Jane. They were suddenly face to face, with breasts touching. Bette jumped back so fast she fell over a wastepaper basket grabbing a chair to steady herself. Its wheels carried her a few more feet before she regained her balance.

One of the men quipped, "Yes Logan, get rolling!"

Amid laughter from the others, a red-faced Bette grabbed Jane by the elbow and walked out.

Bette let go of Jane's arm when they entered Interview Room three.

Jane apologised.

"Sorry! I was lost in thought. I'm so sorry!"

Through clenched teeth Bette hissed, "Leave it. Just leave

it!"

Jane went in and sunk down onto a chair by the table.

Bette stood silently next to the door and Jane took the cue for silence from that. Jane checked her phone, to give herself something to do. Nothing much, a couple of missed calls and texts from Marion and Liz. She put the phone back. They would have to wait. No doubt they'd be wanting to know how the night at Bette's went. A conversation she wasn't looking forward to.

She sighed and looked around the room. Light was coming in through a frosted window, so no outside view. Other than the two empty identical chairs, and the well-used table, there was little to see and distract her. She assumed a camera was pointed at her but resisted the urge to look for it. Was she looking innocent? What did innocent look like? Jane sighed again and focussed on the scratches etched onto the top of the table.

Shields turned up with McMahon very shortly. They had a third man with them who wasn't introduced, carried a pen, notebook and a small recorder. Shields explained that as it was a formal interview, it would be recorded if she agreed. Otherwise handwritten notes would be taken, she would then have to wait for it to be printed before reading through it and signing. Jane agreed to handwritten notes, as they seemed less threatening. While Shields and the other man sat at the table, McMahon stood a way behind them leaning on the wall.

The interview started very low-key with general questions about the first assault. Jane had to remind herself to keep her guard up as they started more detailed questioning about that morning's assault. Had it really only been that morning? So much had happened. Her life was accelerating; she needed to find a way to slow everything down. Things were happening faster than she could deal with them.

The interview was going well with Jane answering the questions as honestly as possible but along the lines she and Bette had rehearsed. So far, Bette had predicted every line of inquiry they would take. She'd even got a couple of the questions almost word for word.

In the end it wasn't the questions that got her heart pounding and gave her a dry mouth. It was the entrance of a fourth man. He glared at Shields and McMahon, then looked at Jane. Once again, she locked eyes with Brian. This time she wasn't in a tree; this time he could see her.

He frowned thoughtfully at her but turned to face Shields.

"Forgive my lateness. I only just found out about the interview."

Jane was happy the dispute was between Brian and Shields. She was busy trying to convince herself that he didn't see her that night and so he couldn't recognise her now.

The tense interaction continued without her.

"We did look for you, but you must've been upstairs with your friends. We had to proceed as Ms Woods is tired and we can only question her for a short time. Doctor's orders," Shields replied.

Jane was puzzled. Shields was protecting her from Brian. The man with the recorder turned it off, put his pen down and looked at the floor. There were definitely big things happening here. She looked briefly at Bette, but she was studiously looking out the frosted window… at nothing.

Brian broke off from Shields and looked at Jane.

"Again, sorry for my late arrival Jane, but I have some important questions for you and they may take some time. Doctor's orders or not."

Jane was scared at his tone but annoyed at the assumed familiarity.

"And who are you? I was under the impression that my case was being handled by Detectives Shields and McMahon. I'm happy with them and want to continue with them, thank you."

She noted a smile, quickly smothered, break across McMahon's impassive expression.

Shields did the introductions.

"Ms Woods, this is Detective Files. He's just been assigned to... ah... assist my partner and me with the recent events around the body found off the Darling Street Wharf. We are concerned the assaults might be connected."

Brian had positioned himself on the edge of the desk nearest Jane. This meant she had to turn her head and look up quite awkwardly. She assumed he was trying to intimidate her. Jane leant back in the chair, hoping she looked calm, relaxed and unintimidated.

Detective Files rattled off three questions without pause before McMahon interrupted him.

"We've covered all that. Why don't you relax back here with me and let Shields continue? He is the more senior and experienced officer. By the way, congratulations on your recent promotion."

Files glared at him and stood, turning to Jane.

"I'm now in charge of the investigation. I'm sure you'll get used to my style."

He then faced the two very angry detectives.

"I had hoped to have your co-operation, but it seems not. You are both off this case at the order of the Chief Inspector. He felt a new approach was needed."

Shields was now on his feet and McMahon also moved forward angrily.

Files continued, "It's probably better if you both leave. You too, Logan. I have someone here to keep an eye on Jane."

A smiling Files turned his head to the door.

"Wallace! Come in will you!"

It was no surprise that Jane recognised Wallace as the other man in Marjorie's reserve that night with Brian. This time he was in uniform.

Jane felt the blood drain from her face. Shields asked to see the paperwork and Files handed him some folded sheets. Jane caught Bette looking at her with concern and Jane could only hope she was signalling her fear of these new men to Bette. Bette seemed to understand as her eyes narrowed as she looked from Files to Wallace.

In the back of her mind Jane felt a familiar approach. Marjorie was back.

"What is the matter? You're giving off vibes loud enough to wake the dead. Come to think of it, they did, didn't they?" Marjorie chuckled but was soon on task. *"Hey, aren't they the ones from my house? They're police? You're in trouble, girl!"*

Jane watched appalled as Shields shook his head.

"It's correct, but we'll be challenging it."

Files was relaxed and confident.

"Go ahead, it'll do no good. The Chief Inspector wants someone who will get the job done. You can leave now."

Marjorie whispered, *"On the count of three, grab Bette and the two good cops. Get out of here."*

Jane mentally questioned the need to whisper, but Marjorie ignored her.

"One, two,"

Jane crouched,

"three!"

Jane jumped up at the same time that the window exploded inwards and showered the room with glass. Jane stepped around the falling Files; grabbed Shields; pushed a stunned and stumbling Wallace out of the way and pulled Bette out of the room into the corridor.

McMahon was on their heels.

"Outside," he ordered.

Bette started towards the front, but McMahon directed her to a side exit. There were alarms sounding; people everywhere but, as yet, no Files or Wallace. Jane was wondering what Marjorie had done as she followed behind Shields.

They left the building through a fire exit, which locked behind them. The din from inside was muted. Shields looked at McMahon and they seemed to agree on something.

Jane opened the conversation, innocently asking: "What happened? And who's that rude man?"

Bette spoke at the same time, "What was that?"

No one answered them. Shields looked at Jane suspiciously and said that whatever it was, it was extremely good timing.

After a quick glance at McMahon, he went on to explain to Jane and Bette why they had tried to protect her. A few of them feared there was corruption at high levels. After the body was found in the water, things started happening behind the scenes that had them concerned but they could find no solid evidence of anything untoward. One event raising suspicions was Files' recent promotion to detective, ahead of time and with a dubious history. The other was the body from the wharf being stolen from the morgue, only to be recovered later with all identifying parts removed.

"What! Teeth and fingers?" Jane was horrified.

"Actually, whole head and hands," came the response from

McMahon.

"Quicker, I suppose." suggested Bette.

Shields nodded.

Jane felt ill.

Bette continued, "There's more. Jane's sitting on information - well, we both are."

She squared her shoulders.

"Jane told me what she knows, and I advised her not to tell anyone else until I could figure out who's in this. I think Mike Grey is. The man who assaulted Jane the first time, and probably today as well, is Joe Small. I identified him in the mug shots, and I've seen him with Mike."

McMahon raised his eyebrows and said, "Okay, we've been trying to figure that out too. Look, we'd better arrange to meet somewhere else. Files will be looking, and those orders are real."

Shields smiled. "He doesn't have them just now."

He pulled a crumpled piece of paper out of his pocket.

McMahon also grinned. "Well, if it's confession time..."

He bought out the notebook from the interview room and the small recording device. The door was pushed open and McMahon hurriedly replaced them in his pocket and an officer looked out, eyes wide and hands shaking.

"It's okay, Riley, we're just letting the witness gather her breath, nothing to report out here." Shields spoke firmly.

"Yes, Sir." The young woman trembled the response and shut the door again.

McMahon grinned. "Poor devil's so scared, she'll never remember anyone was out here, let alone who."

While the others decided to meet at Bette's later that night, Jane also made a decision.

"I was at the wharf the night before the first assault." She had the men's attention. "That's when I got the map. They recovered a body. Brian Files and Wallace were two of the guys keeping watch. I can identify maybe another one. I think it's probably Mike Grey. I saw him from a distance under a streetlight, so I can't be one hundred percent certain. They know I know something, but not what. Oh, yes, I overheard them call someone Paul. He seemed to be the boss."

The others stood silent for a second then they all got

agitated. Shields let out a low whistle.

Bette said, "Shit! You didn't tell me a Paul was involved!"

McMahon actually appeared ruffled.

"That explains those orders. You definitely have to go now. We'll go back and see what's happened. I think we'd better take your address off the database, Bette. Does Mike know it?"

Bette nodded.

McMahon continued, "You know I'm not sure about Mike. It looks like he's in on it, but I've known him so long... it seems impossible."

Bette agreed. This wasn't the Mike she knew.

Shields was in a hurry to move.

"We can't take chances. We can check out any links he might have to Files and Wallace. We'll move you both from Bette's later. Be careful. God, this stinks!"

They all went to the front of the building where they let Jane and Bette out via a locked gate, and they went back inside. Jane was wondering why finding out 'Paul' was involved had caused such a fuss.

Bette's reply was quick and to the point.

"Chief Inspector Paul Dramont, that's why. He transferred Files to the station, supposed to be some mentoring scheme, but none of us had ever heard of it. Now I know why."

Chapter Twenty-One

Bette left Jane in a shop up the street and returned to the station to get her car. She was expecting a lot of unwelcome questions, but she needed to know what was happening.

There were two ambulances out front with police tape being placed around the station. The media were already arriving. Bette went in and told the sergeant she had orders to take Jane home.

He nodded. "Shields said as much. You getting a taste for plain clothes with all this?"

Bette could only smile grimly and say it was more action than she was used to.

He glanced behind, towards the back offices and shook his head.

"You're not wrong there."

He was still shaking his head as she headed for her car.

There was basically nothing wrong in the back office, just a lot of broken glass and blood in Interview Room three. Paramedics were attending to the three men inside. The note-taker was walking with help towards the front entrance and talking. The other two were in a worse state, being treated by ambulance officers on the floor of the room. Both appeared unconscious and bleeding from a lot of cuts.

Remarkably, Bette was uninterrupted as she went out to the parking area. Most people were out here - a lot were smoking, all were talking. No one seemed to know what had actually happened. She was surprised and relieved to pass through without being questioned. After her memorable entrance, all present must have known she had been in the room when it exploded.

A part of her was annoyed; another part concerned. This place thrived on gossip and rumour. She had been at the centre of the explosion! It was a rare chance for her to show her abilities under pressure. And no one wanted to talk to her? That was wrong. Something was off.

Bette got into her car and turned on the radio as she drove out the back gates. Jane got in relieved the radio was on. They sat in silence as Bette negotiated the traffic.

The first reports were exaggerated claims of 'severe damage'; 'several police officers injured'; and a fire having broken out. Bette flicked to a news station, hoping it would be more accurate. The announcer was standing by to go to the reporter on the spot.

Bette finally spoke to Jane in measured tones.

"Why do I get the feeling you are responsible for the explosion in there? I mean I don't think you're an explosives expert, but I could be wrong. Was it the way you seemed to expect it? Was it that you started moving immediately before it happened, while us trained sods just stood there stunned? It fits. I can't believe it, but I know you did it. Who, or what are you?"

Jane quietly replied, "It wasn't me. It was Marjorie. She gave me a warning, counted to three and I did what she told me."

Bette pulled the car to the side of the road, bringing it to a sudden halt.

"You mean she talked to you?" Bette sounded sceptical.

"Talks actually," Jane felt almost defiant.

"You mean you and she..."

Bette was struggling.

"She blew up the room...?"

Jane meet Bette's confused look and decided she needed to take charge, unsuccessfully resisting the rush of pleasure this gave her.

"Do you want me to drive? I'm more used to the idea of it than you."

Bette shook her head, faced forward, took a deep breath but made no move.

Jane decided to be practical.

"The guys are assuming I'll be staying with you, at least tonight. Is that okay?"

At Bette's nod she continued, "We'd better go to my place to get some clothes and stuff. Is that all right?"

Bette started the car and pulled back into the traffic. Jane sat facing forward trying not to look smug but did enjoy the occasional bewildered looks Bette warily gave her.

Bette had recovered from her muteness by the time they arrived at Jane's house.

"Why didn't you tell me?" She grumbled at Jane, then answered the question herself. "Because I would have thought you were a loony. A loony who talks to dead people!"

Jane laughed and headed for the door. Bette pushed in front.

"Let me go in first and check. We'd better not rely on Marjorie."

Bette led the way into the hall, first checked the front room and then quickly moved through the downstairs. Jane went into the front room and turned on the TV to the news channel.

While listening to Bette moving upstairs, Jane noticed the blinking answering machine and listened to the messages. There were two messages from Marion and Jo, and another two from Liz and Bronwyn. With each message her friends had sounded more anxious, why wasn't she returning their calls? There was a message from Jane's mother doing her weekly check in - that could wait. There were also two hang-ups.

Bette had returned downstairs and joined Jane in time to hear the hang-ups.

Jane knew they weren't unusual but just now they seemed to have more meaning and menace. Jane looked at Bette.

"I don't often get those…" she left the rest unspoken as her stomach turned.

Bette remained silent so Jane turned back to the machine, erased the messages and unplugged it.

"Good idea. Others could hear the messages and get family and friends names and numbers."

Bette sounded distant, as if she were repeating a well-rehearsed phrase.

Jane sighed and felt the threads of hope they might salvage a relationship or even friendship fray a little more. The feeling surprised her, she thought she'd already cut those threads.

The news started and they turned to watch. Unsurprisingly, the bombing was the lead item. The reporter confirmed three people injured, reporting that all were in hospital. Three police officers had unspecified injuries, one a newly promoted detective working on his first case.

The station then cut to a press conference by the Premier and Police Commissioner. The Premier said he spoke on behalf of the people of New South Wales and wished the officers a speedy recovery.

Jane snorted. "Well one certainly, but the other two? I wonder what Marjorie did to them?"

The Police Commissioner then spoke about previous attacks on police, their bravery and the dangerous nature of the job they did. Bette turned the sound off.

"It's really hard to hear that. The vast majority of us do a good job. It is dangerous and hard work. Then these corrupt shits come along. They don't deserve any sympathy, not just for what they've done to you, but to the rest of us."

Bette's voice trailed off and she sat in silence. This didn't last long. Jane could feel anger radiating from Bette. It wasn't a surprise when Bette suddenly stood.

"I believed the corrupt cops were gone. We could be proud; people were starting to trust us... Now, even I don't even trust us!"

She paused and her voice lowered.

"I think I'm mainly upset about Mike. I really looked up to him. I can't believe he'd be in on this! But if he is, I'll nail him and the others!"

She turned to face Jane.

"With Shields and McMahon, we might just do it, and let's not forget Marjorie! Christ! What on earth did she do in there?"

Bette went silent again, deep in thought.

While she was relieved there was less tension between them since the explosion, Jane was determined to keep Bette at a distance. She couldn't let any thoughts of a relationship, or even a friendship distracts her. The situation had escalated and was extremely dangerous and to keep herself safe, Jane knew she had to be alert and focussed. She would try to look out for Bette as well, but she trusted Bette could do that for herself. If she were honest, she was probably the greatest threat to Bette - not doing as told or not reacting fast enough.

Marjorie's show at the station had strengthened Jane's resolve to act and follow through on what she had unintentionally started.

Jane recognised she had two motives - she did hope that Bette would stay involved as working through what was happening would be a lot easier of she did; and maybe, just maybe, they could revisit the idea of a relationship. Jane was angry with herself at the thought. Why did she persevere with that? She didn't need the distraction.

Jane hesitantly ventured, "We just have to expose all of this, clear it up and show that not all cops are like that. They won't turn a blind eye like they used to."

A familiar voice sounded.

"They never should have in the first place! My life certainly would've been different if the corruption had been fought. In case you're interested the one who was taking notes is fine, just concussion with a mild loss of memory."

Marjorie's tone hardened.

"The other two are another matter, you won't have to worry about them for a while. Such a pity to have to act, but I couldn't see any other option. I don't think I'll be in much trouble; no one was badly hurt and there's no evidence of our tampering. I'm sure the committee will accept I was acting in your best interest."

Marjorie's voice then faded as if she too were lost in thought.

"A committee? You're in trouble? What's happening there… wherever there is? You can give my name as a character witness if you want. You're not in trouble with me!"

Conversations with Marjorie raised so many questions. Jane sent warm gratitude for Marjorie's actions and felt a sense of great regret, tinged with some anxiety, flow back as Marjorie left.

She glanced at Bette who had taken up position at the window. That brought Jane back to her task. Get clothes and anything else needed for a few days; lock up and go!

Jane first packed a few precious and important items, such as her insurance documents, her laptop, the backup drive, her favourite camera and passport, just in case, she told herself. On impulse, her old, much loved teddy bear, Tigger, was collected as well.

She then turned her attention to clothing; comfortable and easy washing items were best. She was determined to pack without impressing Bette in mind. Casual and practical it would be. A quick visit to the bathroom took care of toiletries. Once finished, Jane did one last look around the room and went out to find Bette coming up the stairs.

They passed at the top of the stairs briefly stopping for an awkward moment. Jane had a memory flash of the last time they were here together, which she quickly closed down. Bette reported she had double-checked the ground floor doors and windows and was just coming upstairs to do the same. Jane briefly wondered if Bette was justifying following her upstairs.

On leaving the house, Jane was sad, worried, and guilty. She silently apologised to the house and contents. She was expecting her house, her beautiful home, would be broken into and ransacked. The front room hadn't been cleaned properly since the second assault, she hadn't vacuumed, dust was on the shelves and the kitchen had dishes in the sink. It looked as if she didn't care. She felt traitorous as she closed the door and left the house to look after itself.

"Don't worry, they may search, but they'll not destroy. I won't see another home destroyed as mine was."

Marjorie's voice was gentle and reassuring.

On the way, Jane remembered the state of Bette's refrigerator. They stopped at a supermarket and bought supplies, mostly essentials, but Jane put in some treats. If she had to be stuck in an awkward situation, she would at least have some of her favourite comfort food.

The dangerous nature of their situation was further bought home when Bette suggested getting cash out, as much as they were allowed in one withdrawal. If they had to cover their tracks, it was best not to leave a trail of regular withdrawals.

Bette received a call from Shields, as they arrived, and she put it on speaker. He was ringing after being excused to get something to eat. It wasn't safe to talk in the station. Little was directly said, but a lot implied.

Shields quickly listed the developments: there was no news of Mike's whereabouts; confusion surrounded the explosion, a bomb had been discounted, but no one could explain what had happened; Files and Wallace were in hospital, still unconscious, but the note taker had been discharged. He suffered an unusual memory loss, just of the interview itself. Shields and McMahon themselves were saying that they could only recall telling Logan to get Ms Woods to safety and no more.

The Chief Inspector, this Paul, was furious at Jane's disappearance and was blaming Shields and McMahon, but they were still on the case, now Files and Wallace had been injured.

Shields said that he and McMahon were being delayed and were unlikely to get away for hours. Jane and Bette looked at each other as he rang off. That meant that they would have to look after themselves tonight.

There had been no trace of emotion in Shield's voice. Jane had thought that he was the softer.

Bette smiled, "Everyone thinks that; McMahon's the softy. That's why Shields does all the interviews. McMahon lets people off the hook too easily, but his big hulking silence in interviews is great for intimidation."

Given the situation, they decided it wasn't overreacting to organise a few defences. The kitchen table, a heavy hardwood, went against the back door. The front door would be the safest exit. Bette checked all the windows were locked, except the one onto a side path that led to the front garden. This was wedged shut with a length of wood, allowing a quick exit if needed.

Bette then suggested they eat dinner and settle in for the night. There would be no looking for Alice tonight, but Jane was determined to find her once it was safe to do so.

Chapter Twenty-Two

Bette started dinner, and Jane poured them both a glass of beer.

Bette toasted, "To nailing the bastards!"

"Safely," added Jane.

They clinked glasses and sipped in thoughtful silence.

Jane broke the mood when she put her glass down.

"Before we eat, I should ring the girls and let them know we're… I'm okay. Should I use my phone, or do you think it might be tapped?"

Bette ignored the correction and nodded towards the phone.

"Use the landline, it's safer. It's unlikely they've tapped my phone, if they are doing it at all. Keep each call short and be careful about how much you say though. The less your friends know the better"

Bette let the implication hang unspoken in the air. Jane didn't need to be reminded and had already gone over in her head what to say. She needed to reassure them while also telling them nothing about what was happening. All this was so removed from her usual life it seemed like a dream; increasingly a nightmare.

Jane rang Liz first, hoping she would be busy in the shop. It went to messages, as hoped, so Jane avoided the questions Liz would definitely ask about Bette. She gave the day and time and stated that she and Bette were safe, but things were more serious and complex than they had thought. Liz was to tell anyone who asked that she hadn't spoken to Jane since the first assault. Jane finished by saying that Liz should erase the message immediately and that they would keep in contact when possible.

Hanging up, Jane felt both scared and frustrated. When would this be over? Agitated, she called out to Bette and asked how the message had sounded. She was depressed to hear Bette say it was good - precise and clear. Jane had hoped to be told she was being melodramatic and to ring back and leave a more positive message.

Bette put her head around the door and told her to hurry up

and ring Marion and Jo as the meal was nearly ready. Jane looked at the phone. She thought she hadn't wanted to talk but didn't feel better after leaving a message; she had wanted a familiar voice on which to anchor herself. Someone to tell her she was being silly and to go home.

She punched out the numbers not knowing whether she wanted to leave a message or not. Jo picked up the phone on the second ring, and on hearing Jane's voice immediately started throwing questions at her without waiting for any answers.

It was after her third question that Jo slowed down and asked quietly, "Are you okay?"

Despite the mental rehearsals Jane couldn't keep a quiver out of her voice.

"I can only say a few things at the moment. It's serious stuff. I'm with Bette, and we're both all right. If anyone asks after me you haven't seen me since the first assault..."

Jo interrupted, "First! You mean there's been a second? Where are you? We're coming over!"

Jane could hear Marion's worried voice questioning Jo in the background, but she spoke over the top of them both.

"Jo! Listen, there's no time. I hope I'm being a drama queen, but the good guys are worried, so am I too. Whatever this is, it's big and nasty. I'll contact you again as soon as I can. Just take good care of yourselves and Bette and I will do the same."

Marion was suddenly on the phone.

"Hey Jane, this isn't funny. Tell me it's a joke!"

Jane's voice thickened.

"God Marion, I wish it was a joke"

Jane felt Bette's hand on her shoulder, as she took the handset from Jane.

"Marion? It's Bette... yes, Bette Logan the policewoman, sorry to meet you this way. We're fine, but it's really important Jane stays low for a while. She won't be home until it's over. Hopefully not too long. She left a message on Liz's machine, could you ensure Liz wipes the message? You guys haven't seen her for a few days. It's unlikely you'll be asked but you never know... Yes, I will... Yes, I'll look after her for you. We are probably overreacting... Yeah, the bombing is related...

No, I can't say any more other than none of the good guys got hurt. Okay? Bye… Thanks."

Bette ignored Jane's outstretched hand and hung up.

"They send their love and will send us golden light, whatever that is. What's that look for?"

Jane felt emotionally bruised. She had wanted to talk with a friend about all that had happened and get some sympathy. Instead it felt like she had just said her final farewells, and now Bette was making decisions for her.

"I wanted to talk to them again, you ignored me and hung up! I'm an adult and can make my own decisions. I wanted to chat to a real friend for a while."

She almost hated herself for emphasising the term 'real', but her anger brushed the feeling aside.

Bette looked uncomfortable.

"Sorry, but I need to keep you under the radar. I told you it had to be it a short call." She stood looking at the floor for a moment before continuing, "Maybe I should have passed the phone back. As you said, you need your 'real' friends now."

She emphasised the word real as well and Jane felt a wave of remorse flow through her. Bette turned towards the kitchen.

"I hope you're hungry. There's lots of food."

As they sat, Jane tried to recover the situation with a conciliatory tone.

"The light's a spiritual thing. Marion and Jo belong to a spiritual meditation and healing group. They meet weekly and send golden light to those who need healing, help and courage."

Bette stayed focussed on her food.

"Good. We are in great need of all three."

The meal was eaten in silence.

Once dinner had been eaten and dishes cleaned, Jane was desperate to leave the tension of the room but felt unable to with the awkwardness between them. Bette had put on a musical and they were sitting in silence when Jane got the courage to speak.

"Look, I'm sorry. I'm scared and confused, and I didn't handle that well. I'm sorry. You were right to make the call short and I shouldn't have implied you weren't a real friend."

She was interrupted by a knock on the door.

Bette jumped up and grabbed the hockey stick she'd placed beside the couch, but turned to face Jane with a very serious expression,

"There's no need to apologise. You're right, I'm not a friend. I'm police officer guarding you. We both need to accept that. Anything else might get us killed."

She carefully moved down the hall to stand to one side of the door.

"Who is it?"

Jane couldn't hear the reply but Bette moved back, quickly opened the door and McMahon came in.

He glanced at the television as he came into the lounge.

"Oklahoma! I did it in High School. Still know every song. Unfortunately, I was a natural for Jed. Oh well!"

He turned to Bette and Jane.

"Things have settled down, except for forensics who are going crazy trying to work out what happened in that room."

He looked at Jane.

"You have to tell me how you managed that."

Jane started to protest but held her silence as McMahon was already back to business.

"There's a roster to watch Dramont. He's not happy. Rob and I..."

"Shields." Bette mouthed to Jane.

McMahon continued, "...are to report directly to him about the investigation. He doesn't like it but he has no choice. Logan, you have to report as usual tomorrow and no doubt he'll be into you the minute you arrive. You know where Jane is! Rob's wife's best friend has a house in the Blue Mountains at Leura. They're away and Rob's wife has the key..."

Jane interrupted, "I'm not going up there! I want to be somewhere I know!"

McMahon laughed.

"That's the point. We agree that you need to know your surroundings. Logan, you'll tell the C.I. that you took Jane there to stay with friends at this address."

He handed a small scrap of paper to Bette.

"There's a few of the lads rostered to be there for the next day or so. If someone does come after Jane, well... they'll get a surprise. The aim is to grab one and get him to talk. If he does, this could be all over soon... Well, that's the plan."

He frowned as if reconsidering the plan. Bette thought it could work and it would steer them away from Jane, at least in the short term.

Jane too was frowning.

"What about the wife's best friend? Does she know what her house is being used for?"

McMahon winced.

"God no, and neither does Rob's wife! Everyone's under strict instructions to take as much care as possible; not shoot if at all possible; and to leave it clean! We hope we've thought of everything. The quicker this is over the better. The less explaining Rob has to do, the less I have to hear his complaining about it!"

Jane began to get a small glimpse at the affection McMahon had for his partner before he asked Bette to see him out.

The two stood talking in the hall for a while before McMahon handed Bette a small parcel, waved to Jane, and was out the door surprisingly fast for such a big man.

Bette returned to the lounge and put the parcel down. Jane moved to pick it up and was surprised at its weight.

"Put it down please. It's my gun and ammo." Bette explained as she sat and started to unwrap it. "McMahon snuck it out for me for tonight. I'll just tell them I grabbed it amid the confusion today and forgot to sign it out." Bette started to load the gun. "There's still no word of Mike."

Intrigued, Jane watched Bette finish loading the gun and put the safety on. Bette explained what she was doing as she went. Jane thought about asking for lessons in using the gun but decided not to. She didn't know if she would be able to use a gun if the need arose. If she did manage to pull the trigger, she felt it was more likely she'd shoot herself than any attacker. She'd just run. It was safer.

Her gaze went to the television. Singing cowboys suddenly held no interest. Bette was checking her gun, so Jane turned channels finding a k.d. lang concert instead.

Chapter Twenty-Three

Jane had said goodnight early, to avoid further awkwardness, and headed straight to the spare room. Closing the door behind her, she sadly looked around the room and tried unsuccessfully not to think about what the night might have offered at another time.

The bed was still made from her previous stay so she unpacked a few things, set up her chargers and turned on her favourite music hoping it would help her relax. Undressing quickly, she started to check her social media and emails then realised she couldn't comment or post. This reminded her to turn off all the location apps she could find. Should she turn off the phone completely? Should she ask Bette what else she should do? In a fit of pique, she decided not to. Sighing, she looked around the room. She wanted to be in her own room, in her own house. She hoped her home was safe. The feelings of displacement and isolation increased as she settled down. She picked Tigger up from the bedside table and held the bear tight. Once this was over she'd get a dog or cat, something she could cuddle, something who'd love her, and she'd love it, no matter what. She turned off the music and picked up a book. It would be a long night.

***

Despite her lack of sleep, Jane heard Bette get out of bed at seven the next morning. She lay in bed listening to the shower run, then heard Bette head back to her room. Shedding a few more self-indulgent tears at what might have been, Jane knew she had to get on with whatever the day would bring and so grabbed her towel to get it started.

There was coffee and toast going when Jane entered the kitchen. Bette was standing at the table with her back to Jane. She was in her uniform. This was the first time Jane had seen her dressed for duty and was somewhat taken aback.

Bette turned at Jane's entry and noted the reaction but seemed ready for it.

"Everyone I know from outside the force reacts when they first see me. Still react myself sometimes. It's been a dream of mine for years. Some old friends don't speak to me since I joined, others were so awkward about it I just stopped seeing them. Mind you, they didn't follow me up either."

Bette stood silently for a second.

"It's a pity really, the reactions keep cops closer together, making it less likely to socialise outside the force." She hesitated. "So how are you feeling? I mean, yesterday was a tough one."

To Jane it seemed the tone behind the question was tentative. She wondered at the feeling behind it and she also wondered if there were a right way to answer. She decided on honesty.

"If you mean assaults, explosions and corrupt police, then I'm scared, but also angry. I should be in my house, not hiding."

Jane had to work to do it, but she held Bette's gaze as she continued, "If you mean us... I'm sad, but I think I understand. I was sort of under your protection and we... well, we crossed a line for you. But I wasn't... you didn't take advantage of me. It feels a little weird being together now, but I reckon it's okay. I'll get used to it. I have to, and you have to. I hope it's manageable for you as well."

Bette remained by the table regarding her silently before suddenly moving to the bench to pour them both a coffee.

"Thanks," was all she said.

She gave Jane a cup as she made her way to the table.

Over breakfast, Bette ran a suggestion from McMahon past Jane.

"How would you feel about taking a train trip to the Blue Mountains? McMahon wants you to go to Leura, make a withdrawal from the bank, and use your credit card on a purchase or two. Make your presence known."

Jane was aware of Bette watching her as she continued, "I think it's a good idea, but it could be dangerous. I'm not happy about you going, but it does make sense. The decision is up to you. You could ask one of your friends to go with you... but that would involve them. Marjorie might be better, and safer, company."

Jane's answer was quick.

"I'd rather be doing something than sitting here waiting for them to come for me. If I'm quick, I may be on my way back before they arrive up there. I'll ask Marjorie to come with me."

Jane silently wondered if Marjorie could travel that far away from her home. A familiar approach signalled Marjorie joining the conversation.

"I can travel to Leura. I'll keep an eye out for you."

Marjorie sounded excited, and Jane smiled at her eagerness for the trip.

Bette nodded as if it was the answer she had expected.

"I'll be giving the C.I. the address this morning. I'll try to delay but I reckon he'll be after me quick smart once he knows I'm at work."

They ate in silence for a few moments before Bette continued, "I'll let McMahon know what train you're on. He'll ensure someone from the house will wait for you and keep an eye on you while you're up there in case they get there early. He asked that you wear my red backpack, so they'll recognise you. They can't risk being seen themselves so they will be watching from a distance."

Jane nodded. "Another benefit of this is that it may clear you of involvement if they believe I'm up there. You could be in more danger at work. You have to obey orders and they know where you are. I can move around with more freedom"

Jane noticed a quickly smothered frown cross Bette's face as she spoke, and realised she'd hit a nerve, so the curt reply wasn't unexpected.

"I'll be fine. Please don't worry. You'll need to concentrate on what you're doing. We both have to be very careful from now on. Take nothing for granted."

Bette had gone online and found out the times of the trains stopping at Leura, and so aimed to get to Central with only a few minutes to spare. She had convinced Jane of the need for her to get into the back seat of the car unseen, and to remain hidden until they got to Central Rail Station. She went out to the car whilst Jane, feeling silly, crept out of the front door and through the garden. Bette put the backpack in the back of the car, leaving the door open and returned to lock the front door. She passed close to Jane on her return before suddenly waving towards an imaginary person the other side of the road and starting off as if to cross. This was Jane's cue; she launched herself head first into the back seat. Bette returned giving one last puzzled look across the street, shutting the car door, getting into the front and driving off.

"Was all that necessary?" Jane asked from the back seat,

"Not sure, but it was fun!" came the reply with the hint of a smirk.

After four sudden turns and a complete circuit of a roundabout Jane declared that she had had enough of being squashed and tossed around.

"For heaven's sake, can I get up? I'm going to throw up if you do another roundabout!"

Bette agreed and Jane untangled herself to discover they were heading for Central Rail Station through Redfern via Cleveland St. On arrival Bette pulled over to let Jane out and gave final instructions about remaining inconspicuous.

Jane interrupted, "Yes, I've got all that. Now I want the 433 bus from Railway Square, or the Light Rail from Eddy St. Is that right?"

"Yes. With all you're doing today I'm amazed it's catching the bus that has you worried. You actually like the cloak and dagger routine, don't you?" Bette shook her head in disbelief.

Jane was still preoccupied with the uncertainties of bus travel, a transport mode she rarely used.

"Just hope I don't get on the wrong bus."

They exchanged best wishes for their tasks that day. Jane jumped out of the car, squared her shoulders and headed into the station.

As they planned, Jane got onto the train with only seconds to spare. The doors closed just behind her and she was certain no one could have got on after her.

Despite initial nerves every time the train stopped, and more people got on, Jane gradually settled and accepted that any problems were more likely to occur in Leura, or on her way home.

The train journey went from the centre of Sydney, past the small terraces of inner-city suburbs like Newtown, Stanmore and Petersham. The urban sprawl with its large town centres and shopping malls were next, past the large backyards of the outer suburbs with their clotheslines, pools and sheds. Finally, the train entered the Blue Mountains region with its extended sections of bush. As they climbed, glimpses of the city skyline could be seen between the trees.

Jane tried to recall her last trip to Leura. It was two years ago when she and Sally had acted as tour guides for friends up from Melbourne for the Gay and Lesbian Mardi Gras. The mountains had been a cool relief from the hot and humid February conditions.

Although early in the season, this summer was also shaping into a sultry one. Jane smiled wryly, every summer was a hot and humid one in Sydney! She turned back to look through the window at the brief but tantalising views of the distant city.

Although not a frequent visitor to the mountains, Jane treasured the fact they were there. The closeness of the bush was one of the things she most loved about Sydney. National parks surrounded it and there were surf beaches in the suburbs. Nature was always close.

Getting out for walks and bike rides had been Jane's favourite pastimes and certainly kept her fit. Sally had hated exercise, so Jane had stopped to avoid conflict, but was now determined to get back into exercise and regain her previous fitness level. She started mentally listing a few easier rides she could start with, then remembered her old bike was in need of a service, if not replacement. Another thing she'd lost in that relationship.

Smiling, Jane recalled that one of the things she most enjoyed about bike riding was that you earned, or felt you did, the right to eat well. No ice cream ever tasted as good as the one at the end of a long ride.

It was with surprise that she realised they were pulling into Faulconbridge, well into the Blue Mountains, and only a few stops from Leura. It may have been hunger that caused her stomach to turn at the thought, but Jane decided not. She actually felt quite nervous.

Chapter Twenty-Four

Jane took a deep breath taking in the smell of eucalyptus she associated with the Australian bush. She had missed that distinctive smell whilst cycling the trails in the Blue Mountains. They were called the Blue Mountains because the oily eucalyptus vapour given off by the trees gave the mountains a blue hue, when looking at them from Sydney,

Jane bought her attention back to her current situation and checked the time. It was ten a.m. It was probable that the C.I. would know by now about the Leura house. If so, men could already be heading up the M4 to search for her. She looked around for any sign of the people McMahon had said were supposed to be watching her but saw no one likely. A young skateboarder was practising jumps in the car park; two old men sat on the other platform; and a mother with a pram was struggling up the stairs but waving away the offer of help from an older man in a suit.

She ruled out the two old men and the skateboarder but would keep an eye out for the other two as she went about her tasks. She set off up the stairs aiming to head for the bank first, then to one of the many gift shops that lined the steep main street of Leura.

Jane surveyed the wide and sloping street after retrieving a substantial sum of money from the bank. There was no sign of either the woman with the pram or the older man. Someone would be watching her, she reassured herself and looked again at the village of Leura.

She had forgotten how pretty Leura was. The main street went down a hill overlooking the Megalong Valley, with verandas on either side providing shade. Flowers were on display in large planter pots and hanging baskets were in front of every shop. The many trees in bloom added to its village charm.

Marjorie, apparently, had also not seen Leura for some time.

"*Well, this is strange. Lots of new things but basically still the same as when I was last here.*"

Jane smiled and silently asked when that was.

"Oh, probably in the late sixties. It was a small village then with a few holiday houses, but not somewhere you'd live if you worked in Sydney. Coming to the Blue Mountains was a real undertaking back then. You usually didn't come just for the day."

Jane decided to walk down the street on one side and up the other. Marjorie was delighted and wanted to look in each window so Jane suggested that she go ahead to a shop she'd noticed, and Marjorie could follow at her own pace.

This amused Marjorie a great deal.

"Sorry dear, I go where you go, I see what you see - well sort of."

Jane was intrigued.

"So, you're in my head when you... er... visit me? I thought you were sort of... well... free floating."

Marjorie laughed.

"I can do the Casper the Ghost float - that's how I met you. It's hard work though. To be closer to you, and more in tune with your thoughts and feelings, it's easier to travel with you, so to speak."

They came to a halt outside the window of the shop Jane was interested in.

"You mentioned before that you can hear people's thoughts and enter minds to check things out. I know you wouldn't unless it was crucial, but can you actually do that? How do you home in on one mind? Don't everyone's thoughts confuse you? And..."

Marjorie cut Jane off. "These are really complex issues that we'd be better off discussing in detail another time. Basically, everyone has his or her own thought pattern, which we can feel or see. You'd call it different 'vibes' today, I think. I just aim for the one that interests me. You have to be very gentle of course. It can shock or even damage people if you're not careful. I could enter anyone's mind, but I just don't - a sort of moral code I suppose. Most minds are focussed on very boring things, the rent, love problems, work and so on. Your problems gave your vibes a sort of loud volume and such a distinct pattern that quite a few of us were drawn to you. I got first choice as you were in my territory and had specifically used my name." Marjorie paused. "You'd better go in, the *shopkeeper is starting to look at you strangely. You've been standing here staring at the window for ages!"*

Jane refocused and could see the woman inside looking out at her. They smiled at each other and Jane quickly moved towards the door. As she went in, she was still wondering who else inhabited Marjorie's world and who else might she be talking to.

"Don't worry girl, you were lucky to get me." Marjorie's voice went to a whisper. *"Some of the others are very stuffy, no fun at all."*

In this shop and another two it was easy to find items for the credit card. A silk scarf for Marion; a wonderful clear crystal for Jo; a special no chemical lens cleaning cloth for Liz; and a box of handmade chocolates and fudge for Liz and Bronwyn.

Bette was much harder as Jane really hardly knew her. A non-personal gift would be best, she thought, and so she finally settled on some fancy jams for the near empty refrigerator. For herself, she chose an aromatherapy oil burner, and let Marjorie chose the oil.

"I'd love the orange blossom oil, please!" came the quick response *"one grew near the house. I loved the fragrance, so fresh and bright!"*

Jane completed her purchases and was very pleased she'd bought the backpack. Swinging it onto her back she left the shop and turned to head back up the hill to the station.

Marjorie had other ideas.

"Oh, come on. You can't come to the Blue Mountains and not have a Devonshire tea! I'll let you know if there's anything to worry about. I'd love to visit the old teahouse, if it's still there. Harry would buy me one for a treat..."

Marjorie's voice trembled with emotion at the recollection. She didn't talk much about her former life, so Jane let Marjorie and her own appetite guide her further down the street. To Marjorie's delight the cafe was still there but there had been changes.

"Oh, they've gotten rid of the fireplace, and where's the old counter?"

Jane ordered coffee, to Marjorie's disdain, with carrot cake and let her mind drift listening to Marjorie's reminiscing about

Harry and her life.

***

"Jane, quick! Listen, it's time to go! Oh dear... Bad vibes driving down the main street!"

Marjorie's urgent tone bought Jane back from her musings with a jolt. Her coffee and cake finished, she quickly paid for them.

With the backpack weighing heavily against her, Jane cautiously left the cafe and, at Marjorie's direction, went up a back street instead of the main thoroughfare.

"They're parking down the bottom of the street so head directly for the station, you'll be fine." Marjorie sounded confident.

Jane was crossing over the road and starting up the stairs at the station when Marjorie reported the two men had split up and were searching each side of the road. They had photos of her. Where did they get photos?

Jane was on the platform when Marjorie spoke again.

"Oh dear. The shopkeeper of that first shop is being a little more helpful than we'd like. She's sent that man back down the hill. Ah, when do you think the next train is due?"

Jane silently swore, though of course, Marjorie heard and tut-tutted.

The next ten minutes were the longest Jane could remember. She sat on the platform trying not to look agitated while Marjorie gave regular updates on the men's progress.

"They're back together again outside the cafe. They think you went back to the house. They did look at it before but decided to check the township first."

Jane commented that she hoped the men were already in the house so they could ambush and capture anyone searching for her. Marjorie reluctantly agreed to leave Jane and check on the ambush. She didn't like leaving Jane alone, but Jane insisted.

Jane looked around the platform again. No one was in sight. No one to stop the searchers from acting if they did find her. She couldn't sit still any longer and took a brisk walk along the platform.

Marjorie's return was signalled by a snort of disgust.

"They were dozing! I woke one in the house and he's

waking the others. Some ambush!"

It was at that point the sound of fireworks came from very close to the station.

"Did I tell you the house is only a couple of doors from the station?"

Marjorie's tone was calm, but there was a hint of tension. Jane was still staring towards the noise when two men burst out of the bushes behind a wire fence near the end of her platform.

"Oops!" said Marjorie.

Jane forced herself to turn and walk slowly back towards the station building. The men were still a distance away and not looking for her at that moment. There was the sound of a train horn and the city train came around the corner and started slowing down.

She was still out in the open when she heard a yell, and three others burst out of the bush giving chase to the first two. Jane assumed they were part of the ambush. The sight of them gave her some relief.

The train had come to a halt and Jane got into the door nearest to her, the second last carriage. The speakers were loudly announcing Central as the destination as Jane went up the stairs to the top section as it would give the better view and make her harder to see.

The two men ran up the stairs from the car park, they raced across the bridge and were starting down the stairs to the platform, with the men giving chase closing in on them.

Jane's heart was in her mouth as she silently pleaded for the train to move. She had nowhere to go, her carriage was near the end of the train but the men chasing her could get on any carriage and hunt for her through the train. The loudspeaker gave warning of impending departure and the doors shut with the first man still metres away from the train, he was running with his hand in his jacket. He spun around to check on those chasing him and his jacket was thrown open. Jane could see his hand was covering a grey metal object in a holster. Jane released a long breath she hadn't realised she was holding. The man ran alongside the train looking in at passengers for a short time, before giving up as the second man joined him.

Jane was watching carefully as her carriage went past the men on the platform. Both men had their backs to the train and were facing the three approaching them. Jane hoped there would be no guns fired in such a public space. It was more likely to be an uncomfortable stand-off. At least the police officers who had been waiting there would get to see who had come for her.

The trip down was nerve-wracking. Marjorie was apologising every few minutes and, with every stop, Jane expected gunmen to enter the carriage. She couldn't think of an alternative plan so decided to head for Central and get a taxi to Bette's instead of the dreaded bus.

Uncertain how best to contact Bette, she text to let her know what had happened. She got a quick reply, Bette agreeing Jane should get a taxi but to ring next time. Bette would try to meet the train at Central, but the boss was keeping a very close eye on her. Bette would let Shields and McMahon know, but assumed the men at the house had already passed on that the plan had failed.

Jane tried not to think about the implications of the trap being sprung without anyone being caught. Surely the C.I. or whoever was the boss would realise the good police were aware of something wrong? It would be clearer who was on which side. Would they quit or just get more violent? She sat uneasily for the long journey back to Sydney.

Chapter Twenty-Five

Central was, as usual, full of people, so Jane was able to hide in the crowd as she moved along. Marjorie assured her she would 'spot' anyone with bad intentions. Jane enquired how the men had gotten so close in Leura.

Marjorie was embarrassed.

"I was distracted. I didn't notice them until their vibes were too strong to miss. Leura holds wonderful memories for me. Central doesn't. They won't get so close next time!"

Jane was coming off the Blue Mountains platform when Marjorie suddenly exclaimed.

"To your right! Man, in the garish jersey, what team is that? And what a horrible design! Maroon and yellow, who chose those colours?"

Jane tartly informed Marjorie that it was an old Brisbane Bronco's jersey, an extremely successful Rugby League team.

Marjorie was not impressed.

"Well, successful or not, fashion wise I prefer the Sydney Swans jersey. Bold, simple, yet capturing the spirit of Sydney with the Opera House design…"

Jane bought Marjorie back on track.

"Will you leave the fashion analysis for later? And the Swans are from a different football code, Aussie Rules."

"It's still ugly! Anyway, he's been waiting for the train, and he's looking for the red backpack! There's definitely a mole in the network. He's not seen you so far."

Jane quickly stripped off the backpack, wrapped her arms around it and held it in front of her. The crowd was leading her away from the man but also away from the main exits. They were heading towards the corridors under the suburban line platforms.

"How about I go up one of these and wait for him to pass?" Jane asked.

Marjorie wanted Jane to continue with the crowd and double back later when the underground passage split in two. A shout behind her decided Jane; she swung the pack back over her shoulders and headed up the platform opening next to her.

Marjorie scolded her, *"That wasn't about you!"*
Another shout was heard, this time more urgent.
"That is! Run!"

Jane ran, but with no idea of where she was going. The stairs led up to the platform, so she headed towards the other end. Maybe she could turn down the stairs there and get lost in the crowd again. She turned briefly and saw Bronco Man pushing towards her; his eyes fixed on her.

She never had any particular feelings towards the team, but she was now feeling an active dislike. He knew she'd seen him, so all pretence of normal behaviour was dropped. He shoved a man out of his way, and she jumped around people as she ran. Running around a group of teenagers cost her the opportunity to go down the second set of stairs. The stream of abuse as he pushed people grew louder behind her.

"Any ideas?" Jane threw at Marjorie.

Marjorie's reply was quick.

"No trains coming. Jump off the end of the platform and head left, under the arches of the overpass. There's lots of cover and places to hide over there."

Not believing she was actually doing it, Jane leapt off the platform and cleared the tracks. She stumbled slightly as she landed in thick gravel, recovered and ran hard. A woman screamed behind her. A loud bang sounded, and gravel kicked up on her left. Bloody Hell! He was shooting at her!

Jane jumped across the three sets of tracks. There was more yelling and screaming behind her. She could see cover ahead and headed for it as fast as she could. It still felt very slow. As she ran, she made what she hoped were unpredictable changes of direction. She reassured herself that in all the western and war movies she'd ever seen, the hero never got hit while dodging bullets.

Jane ran down a slight slope into an area where brick pillars and arches supported the raised rail lines that climbed to the upper Central platforms. She'd seen this area before en-route to Newtown.

The rumble of a train passing above her covered the sound of her footsteps crunching over the gravel. She slowed to cross two shiny tracks. The lines were active down here too, she reminded herself.

"No, they're not! It's overhead power! Keep moving! Less thinking, more action!"

Marjorie's urgent tone stopped Jane in mid-step. How close was he? Struggling to hear over her own breathing, Jane listened for any sounds of pursuit. She hoped her pursuer was as unfit as she was.

He was a big man, so it was possible. She briefly leant against an arch. If being chased was to feature in her life she'd better start training.

"It'd do you good too!" Marjorie chided.

Jane was about to use some nasty language when she heard voices approaching. The echoes made it impossible to tell whom it was, and from which direction they were coming.

It occurred to Jane that the arrival of the police was not necessarily a good thing. There could be good or bad cops on their way. She could only trust Bette, Shields and McMahon and what if they weren't the first to arrive?

After moving further into the maze of arches and archways, Jane stopped and strained to hear any hint of her pursuer. There was a light crunch off to her left, so she moved to her right. A metre-long length of wood lay on the ground so she picked it up as a possible weapon.

In a flash of inspiration, she judged the wood to be nearly as wide as the gap between the tracks. She lay the wood down and balanced on it. As she hoped, avoiding the gravel meant there was no noise. She could move without him hearing what direction she was taking. She then picked the wood up and hid behind another arch. She was able to rest briefly as she heard the crunch of footsteps in the gravel moving further away.

As she was considering her options, there was a sudden rumble and Jane saw the tracks in front of her vibrate. The backpack pushed her out too far so took it off and set it down next to her. She crouched sideways, pressing herself hard against the arch, still holding the piece of wood.

There was a blast of wind, the sound increased until it was almost unbearable and then Jane saw the flash of the train's light as it sped past her.

The noise was incredible, and the wind whipped up dirt but Jane kept her eyes open, focussing on the ground in the archway ahead of her, hoping the man wasn't in the archway behind her.

It seemed impossible for anything to exist in the whirlwind of noise, wind and vibration so Jane was stunned to see the toe of a boot poke out past the brickwork of the archway less than a metre in front of her. She tightened her grip on the wood, raised it above her head, stood shakily upright waiting for the inevitable discovery.

As the end of the train passed, Bronco Man's arms came around the arch in a sudden motion, the gun held firmly in both hands, but before he could get any further, Jane swung the wood down across his forearms as hard as she could.

The gun swung down, went off and a howl of pain erupted from behind the arch. Jane stepped forward into the archway swinging the wood again, this time at chest height. It connected with something, the howl abruptly stopped and there was the sound of a heavy fall.

Holding the wood like a baseball bat, Jane crept around the corner. Bronco Man lay across a track, gun still in hand, with blood oozing out of his rapidly staining shoe and flowing from a cut to his head.

"Well done, Jane! You really are good at this. Whammo! He's out cold. Maybe you were an assassin in a past life, or a spy. Stop shaking, you won!"

Marjorie was excited and full of praise for Jane's quick actions.

There was no time for Jane to respond, as the tracks Bronco man laid on started to vibrate and he groaned. The rumble was growing louder as Jane dropped the wood and grabbed his shoulders.

"Help me, you dumb bastard! Get up!"

As she tried to pull his heavy weight off the rail and the noise grew, his eyes suddenly opened and widened in appreciation of the situation and he pushed himself up as she pulled. The train raced by as they fell backwards in a heap; he landed on top of her.

He managed a weak, "I owe you!" before passing out again; pinning Jane under him. She lay still a few seconds, her eyes squeezed shut, and her body shaking before she managed to calm her body and started to wiggle out from under him.

There were still others around, and she didn't know who they were. She had to get up and get away. The gravel dug into her back and she resigned herself to the inevitability of more aches and bruises.

She was nearly free when Shields and McMahon, guns drawn, emerged from behind an arch a distance from where Jane lay. They ran towards Jane at full pace, yelling at the man to stop fighting and move away from her.

Jane later conceded that with her struggling under him it probably looked like an assault in progress, but at the time she rose to her elbows and shouted back at them,

"Don't be stupid, he's out cold! Get him off me!"

Jane couldn't remember who started laughing first but she knew that it was Shields who pulled her up and slapped her on the back with obvious relief, and McMahon who put his arm around her when her laughter turned to tears.

The men were quickly back to business. Shields checking Jane for any injuries while McMahon stood watch.

Shields shook his head in disbelief.

"You're fine, just a few scratches and bruises – again. Devil only knows how you manage that."

He then did a quick check of Bronco Man... besides a likely concussion, his only other injury was the foot. Jane was quick to defend herself.

"I just hit him! He shot himself!"

Shields looked first at Jane.

"It's okay. We believe you." He turned to McMahon, "That's Peterson, a nasty sort. He's wanted for that Paddington assault, amongst other things."

McMahon smiled at Jane.

"You've got to stop mixing with these bad guys." He remarked wryly.

Shields made a decision.

"Mac, I'll take Jane to Bette's, you wait for backup. Say I went off to try to catch up with whomever Peterson was chasing. We'll say we found him where he is, with no sign of the person he was after."

McMahon nodded.

"I'll ensure he knows to agree with whatever I say. He'll want to save his skin now. He'll probably need hospital. You want me to organise a guard?" McMahon dismissively gestured at the now groaning man on the ground.

"Yes, please. He's the only link to all this that we have."

He grinned at Jane.

"Well, thanks to you the plan wasn't a total bust! We had to let the ones at Leura go as it was too public for a fight. We did identify one... a retired cop... Bastard! We'll be visiting him soon, and now we've got this one..."

Jane interrupted.

"After I pulled him off the track, he said he owed me. Remind him of that too."

Shields was incredulous. "Don't tell me it was that train that just passed us!"

Jane nodded.

McMahon laughed aloud.

"You are unbelievable!" He then added grimly, "Don't worry, I'll make sure he remembers."

Chapter Twenty-Six

Shields and Jane walked at a brisk pace over two more sets of tracks and then up onto a platform. Shields showed his badge so they could exit to Eddie St where the car was parked with lights flashing on top. Shields opened the passenger door without speaking and had started the engine almost before Jane had fastened her seat belt.

When she had closed the door, he let out a sigh.

"Sorry. We really stuffed up. They were onto you much quicker than we anticipated. Bette managed to avoid meeting with the Chief Inspector for nearly an hour. We think they knew about the set-up."

Jane's reply was direct.

"They did. They knew about the red backpack. Have you had any sleep? You look like I feel, and that ain't good!"

That got a wry smile from him.

"I've been up cashing in a few favours so I could look at the records on our main players. It seems some new police at our station may not have existed prior to their joining us. Wallace, for instance, transferred from interstate but the Wallace they know retired sick and died a few months later. Our Wallace looks remarkably well for a dead man. He's just one part of it. Things seem to have started around six months ago. I've put the info in a safe place, McMahon knows where."

Jane stated the obvious. "We're all in danger now, I take it?"

Shields nodded in response.

"So where to now?" she asked.

"Bette's waiting for you at her place. I've told the Sergeant I need her to do some work for me that'll take a few days. You need to move to a safer place. Holiday homes? Friends or relatives you could stay with?"

Marjorie arrived. *"Stay at Jo and Marion's! Right under their noses! You'll be able to sneak around to see what that map was about. You do that well… sneak, that is."*

Jane mentally rolled her eyes.

"I do not sneak!" - but she did like the idea.

She would have to convince her friends to leave, as she

couldn't bear for them to be in danger because of her. Jo's mother lived on the coast near Wollongong, south of Sydney - maybe they could visit her?

"How about we move right next to the bad guys?"

Shields raised his eyebrows in interest, so Jane continued, "Two of my friends live next to Rozelle hospital. I'm certain the gang, bad guys or whatever they are, are based at a cottage there. It's just down the road from my friend's place! We could watch them from the house."

Shields shook his head. "They know you, they know we're onto them, so they'll be on guard. It's out of the question. I'll ask Gabby if you can stay with us for a few days. Tonight, it's Bette's. We've organised some extra security that should keep you safe – for tonight at least."

Jane looked down at her hands and hoped Shields took this as her accepting his decision. She knew he had when she heard him quietly let go a long breath. He'd probably expected her to argue with him.

She was determined to follow Marjorie's suggestion. Those at the cottage might be on guard, but how could they know she was so close, watching them? She'd ask Bette if she wanted to join her, but regardless of Bette's answer she would be contacting Jo and Marion as soon as possible to start organising. They drove to Bette's in silence. Let Shields think she was upset or sulking - Jane was busy planning.

'I must check the records! She's taking to this cops and robbers world a little too well. What's her family history? I just have to convince that pedant of a librarian to let me have a look at the records...' Marjorie too was planning.

As Shields pulled into Bette's driveway Bette had come outside to greet them, sucking at one of her fingertips. Jane nearly laughed aloud. Despite only knowing her a short while, Jane had noticed Bette had a habit of picking at her cuticles when nervous or flustered. Jane could see a few of Bette's fingernails had bloodied patches. Had Bette been worried about her? More likely the leaks in the plan, she decided as she got out of the car. Bette went to speak to her but hesitated, so Jane walked past her into the house.

Shields briefed Bette on what had happened at Central after Jane left the room, but she hovered in the hall to listen.

Shields warned Bette that Jane was grumpy as he'd told her she couldn't move into her friends' house near the cottage. Jane heard Bette give a neutral, "Mmm" in response before Shields excused himself to join McMahon at the hospital.

Jane helped Bette prepare dinner hoping to assess Bette's mood. Jane thought Bette's "Mmm" was one of disbelief. Had Bette guessed Jane had no intention of following his directions?

Jane raised Marjorie's idea after dinner. To her delight Bette didn't reject it outright. It would be so much easier to do it with her co-operation. They could inform Shields later, after they'd moved in. Surely, he'd accept it then.

Bette's major concern was how they might watch the cottage in the hospital grounds from Jo and Marion's house. She agreed it was possible stay there without being noticed, but pointless if they couldn't see the cottage. They got a map of the area up on the laptop, 'Street View' gave them a good idea of the view they would have. It was likely they could watch the road down to the cottage and into its driveway from Jo and Marion's house, but not the cottage itself.

"Well, to start with we just watch to see if they have a routine. Then, when we know there's no one around, we can explore the garden and set up a place we can sit and watch from the garden. It's really overgrown so it should be easy." Jane was trying to sound more confident than she felt.

"You had a quick glance at an overgrown front garden and know we'll be able to set up some sort of observation hide at the back?" Bette's tone was sceptical, and she raised her eyebrows as she spoke.

Jane felt a flush spread up her face from her neck.

"I wouldn't say it if I wasn't certain!" she pointed to the laptop screen, "Go On! Check it out on Street View"

Bette's head had jerked back, and Jane realised she had rather dramatically leant forward to press her point.

Still expressing doubt and, to Jane's annoyance, looking amused as well, Bette moved the screen image. The cottage clearly had a very overgrown front garden. Bette switched to Google Earth and a recent image came up of a very tangled back garden behind a small out-building. There were one or two patches of clearer ground, but plenty of possible areas, from the aerial view anyway, that you could hide and watch the back of the cottage. Jane let out a small breath in relief. She had seen the front garden and thought the back would be the same. The assumption was based on a hunch that bad guys wouldn't have the time, or inclination, to do the gardening.

Bette quickly accepted Jane had been right while maintaining the look of amusement. Jane thought there was smugness in the look as well but couldn't work out what Bette had to be smug about.

Bette bought Jane back to the topic by asking what reasoning Jane thought they might use to convince Shields not to come and bundle them into a Police van for disobeying him.

Jane had been thinking about it too.

"Can we use the angle that we don't want the mole finding out? The network can be told we're hiding somewhere else."

Bette nodded. "That's a reason he'll be open to. He's really pissed off someone he thought was okay is passing on information. It might even be a way to see who it is." She ended up sounding more convinced than she did at the start.

Jane wanted the network to be told she was in a safe house in the opposite direction to Wollongong if Jo and Marion agreed to move there. Bette suggested the outer suburb of Hornsby, but Jane thought it should be further out, Gosford or Woy Woy on the Central Coast. If the mole passed on the location and they acted on it, the cottage might be left empty and then they could check it out, and maybe set up in the back garden. The journey to the central coast was at least two hours from Rozelle, double that in traffic. Plenty of time to have a good look around.

The discussion of possible problems continued for a short time, but with Jane refusing to go into hiding, no matter what, Bette finally gave up and agreed to the plan.

Jane rang her friends and put the call on speaker. Jo and Marion were delighted to hear from them, but unhappy with the few details they were told. They could see it was a dangerous situation and the less they knew the better, but they wanted to know more.

As Jane expected, they were thrilled to have Jane and

Bette stay, but reacted angrily to the request that they move out. Jo was particularly adamant about staying, having started a self-defence course since Jane had been assaulted the first time. When Bette quizzed her, she was rather sheepishly admitted she'd only had the one class.

Bette tersely told them she had enough to deal with looking after Jane, without worrying about them as well. She was rather blunt about the potential consequences if her attention was split looking after all of them. Jane started protesting the need to protect her, but quickly realised it was true.

Reluctantly Jo and Marion agreed. They rang back later to say they'd be leaving the house in 2 hours, and where they would leave the key. To appease them, Bette suggested they could return on Saturday and have a short visit to catch up.

Marion was sure nothing would've happened in those few days, but Jane was becoming all too aware of how much could happen in a short space of time.

A few hours later Jo and Marion rang back, they were packed and on their way. Soon after, Jane and Bette drove their hire car into their driveway. They had a backpack each for clothes, and quite a large box of food that Jane had packed. She was anxious about being around Bette when things were so strained and nice food seemed a distraction. Bette had a different opinion as she unpacked the food Jane had bought.

"Wine? I'm not sure you have your priorities right."

Bette paused and moved across the kitchen to stand in front of Jane who felt the need to cross her arms.

"This is a dangerous place to be… next to them. It's not some weekend away together. We won't be drinking while we are here… it's just too dangerous. If we go and do some investigating, I want to be clear-headed and sure-footed!"

Jane knew Bette was right but upset at the implied motivation.

"You're right, but also very wrong. I'm finding this difficult. It's not easy being so close to you after you made it clear you're not interested in me! I am not treating it like a romantic getaway! I would prefer to get out on my bike to burn off some of this agitation, but since that's not going to happen, nice food is my solution. I've no intention of getting you drunk and forcing myself on you!"

Bette had returned to unpacking but turned at Jane's words.

"I never said you'd do that! And it's not that I'm not interested in you... I think you're... It's just bad timing." She pointed at a bottle of red wine, "Look, if nothing's happening, a glass with dinner tonight would be nice."

She picked up two of the bottles of champagne and held them out in front of her.

"We can drink these after it's all over. I'll put it at the bottom of the refrigerator in case." She looked past Jane and smiled, "There's a cat looking at us from the door. You could cuddle that."

Jane was relieved Bette's tone was playful, rather than dismissive.

"Oscar is to be seen but never touched. He tolerates an occasional pat from Jo, but that's all. A few of us have the scars to prove it. I'll feed him later."

It was late afternoon by the time they had set up in the lounge. From the main window they could see down the road, and, if they moved to the next window, they could see the entry to the driveway. They set up a spot at the second window.

Bette then made the call to Shields. She started to explain where they were, hesitated and then held the phone away from her ear. Jane could clearly hear his raised voice and winced in support.

After what seemed a long time, Shields calmed down enough to hear their reasoning and ended up agreeing that if there was a mole, then maybe it was safer to have them in one of the last places expected and, yes, it could help identify who the mole was.

He would tell the others that Jane was in Gosford. He'd ensure the address he gave was an empty block or something. Only he and McMahon would know where Jane and Bette were. If someone pushed to know where they actually were, that would make it easy. He rung off telling them to be careful and stay out of sight. He was going to go on, but Bette said goodbye and hung up.

Chapter Twenty-Seven

The moon rose while Jane was in the kitchen, first feeding Oscar, then making coffee. She could see it from the window, a huge yellow full moon, hanging low in a clear sky. She called Bette to come and look at it. Bette agreed it was a lovely sight, then hurried back to the window after grabbing a couple of chocolate biscuits. Jane sighed. What a waste of a romantic full moon! She stood silently looking at it, blinking back tears, and berated herself for being pathetic. Bette had made it clear and she was right, there could be no relationship right now... but, and Jane shook her head in disbelief as her heart skipped a beat what happened if Bette didn't say anything about after this was over.

Coming back to the present situation, Jane recalled the forecast she'd seen as they waited to drive over to the Jo and Marion's place. The full moon tonight was coinciding with a king tide as well.

Jane had always enjoyed watching and learning about the weather and it's signs. She'd become quite good at predicting the weather from clouds and animals' behaviour. She'd once told friends there was going to be heavy rain and they should move the boxes of books off the garage floor. They had laughed and asked if she was channelling Steve Irwin as she explained her reasoning by described the line of processionary caterpillars climbing the wall of their house. She had laughed along with the joke and explained that it meant heavy rain, possibly flooding. When they called her two days later complaining about the smell of wet books drying, she hoped it hadn't shown, but there was a great deal of satisfaction at being right.

Tonight, the clouds were racing, and she went out the back door to watch them. Standing very still, she looked - first up at the clouds, then at the tree's around. By the speed with which the clouds were moving, there was quite a wind up there. The trees were swaying around as well. The wind was picking up, an onshore wind too. With a full moon, king tide and now the wind as well, it would be a very high, full tide tonight.

It was later as Bette napped next to her on the couch and

Jane kept watch that she felt the now familiar sensation of Marjorie's return.

"Where have you been?" Jane asked.

"I've had some checking to do," came the reply. *"You have a very interesting family history, young woman!"*

Marjorie sounded triumphant.

"I knew you were too comfortable with all this. You just don't get over being assaulted twice in a couple of days."

Jane was puzzled.

"I thought you were helping with the healing and tiredness?"

"No… well, yes, I was. But the mental recovery, getting back into the fight, the willingness to take risks, accepting me… that's you; not me. That's not normal."

"What? Are you saying I'm not normal? What family history?" Jane was now fully awake, attending but sceptical.

"There's a long history! Your great grandmother and your great, great grandparents are particularly interesting."

Jane's memory of her great grandmother was very hazy. She had died when Jane was a teenager, and her mother wasn't that close to her. Of her great, great grandmother she knew almost nothing. Both had travelled a lot which was unusual for women at the time. Jane did recall seeing photos taken in Europe around the time of both world wars.

She had been told her great grandmother had escaped Paris, just before the Nazi's occupied it in World War Two. Her mother had occasionally referred to her grandmother's adventures and bravery. Jane had thought it was attached to cycling holidays and working in unusual places like Morocco and the Balkans. Maybe there was more…

Her grandmother was clearer in Jane's mind, though she had never seen her. Jane knew very little other than she was driving until very old, and was spoken of by Jane's mother rarely, but with a mix of respect and hurt. Jane now wished she had the box of family effects that were stored in her roof space. The family photos were all in there. Her mother hadn't wanted them when her sister, Beatrice, Jane's aunt had died.

It seemed her risk-adverse mother had the uncommon anxious gene from her family gene pool. Jane had a flashback of climbing high in the next-door neighbour's tree as a storm approached and clinging to the trunk as the winds blew the tree and her hair around... She was laughing aloud until she looked down and saw her mother's horrified face at the window. She hadn't needed to be told to get down and come inside.

"*Your great, great grandmother; great grandmother... it's all too many greats...*" Marjorie complained but continued, "*grandmother, and your mother as well! They are all very interesting. Your maternal side is, to say the least, very unusual - adventures, burglary and espionage. You should see if the secret service or Interpol have files on them!*"

Jane was literally dumbstruck... Her mother? The worrywart? For a moment she just sat stunned.

It was only Bette, who had woken up, pulling at her arm that bought her back to the room.

"Where were you?"

Bette looked somewhere between worried and amused.

"Marjorie had some news about my family tree..."

"*...and I haven't mentioned your maternal great, great grandmother, she met your great, great grandfather... er... on the job so to speak.... and there are a few relatives on your father's side with unusual jobs as well; but it's your mother's side that has a sort of family business. You were born for this!*" Marjorie was excited.

"Apparently I have generations of adventurers in my blood."

Jane decided to keep the burglary and espionage part to herself.

Bette was quiet for a moment then asked, "Do you know where they adventured and what they did?"

Jane started to answer but hesitated. She realised she knew absolutely nothing about her family after this revelation, and she had known little to start with. Who were they? What were they doing? Why didn't her mother tell her?

"Not yet. There's more for me to learn"

Spies, thieves, heroes or criminals... or all of them. She had thought her family were normal, boring even... The next visit to her mother was going to be an interesting one.

Bette took over her watch early as Jane was distracted by Marjorie's news and was mentally reviewing all she knew about her family history. So, it was Bette who saw the van driving away from the cottage. It was eleven p.m. and Bette wrote the time down, hoping to get some idea of any routine or schedule those in the cottage were keeping.

Jane stirred, sat up with some discomfort and groaned.

"I think we'd better pull out a mattress for tomorrow night! Who do you think is at the cottage? And with all the fuss, why would they stay?"

Bette nodded and spoke while still watching the road.

"I've been thinking that too... they must know they are being checked out, so yes, why haven't they cut their losses and run? We'd never have known without your involvement. They know whatever they are doing is in danger of being discovered. It must involve a lot of money for them to stay around." Bette stretched, "It means we might catch them and see who's behind it all, but it also shows it is very dangerous. They must be desperate if they are willing to take such risks."

Jane was biting into a biscuit.

"You think it's drugs?"

"Most likely... "Bette suddenly sat up. "Wow! That was quick."

Jane jumped onto the couch for a better view. The van was back and travelling fast. Bette wrote down the time.

"Fifteen minutes, not enough time to go anywhere, hardly enough to get milk... they must've had a call and returned."

Bette sent Shields a text.

Shields immediately rang back, saying that he had just told the group that Jane was in Gosford and had 'accidentally' mentioned where the safe house was.

The van reappeared, again at speed, heading out.

Bette was passing the news onto Shields when Jane excitedly interrupted,

"Tell them to get here! It's our chance to check out the cottage!"

Bette motioned Jane to be quiet as she sat silently holding the phone. Jane was standing and fidgeting impatiently, they had a minimum four hours before the van returned. Why not meet to have a little look around the cottage and see if they could find the 'door' on indicated on the map? Surely, they could see what a good opportunity this was?

From Bette's change of posture, Jane assumed Shields

was back on the line and had agreed to come over. Bette confirmed Jane's thoughts by hanging up and telling her to get ready to go as soon as Shields and McMahon arrived.

It was only thirty minutes or so later when Shields and McMahon drove up. Jane and Bette went outside to meet them. All wore similar dark colours. Jane was restless, she was ready to go. As she found on that first night in the park, action was far easier than waiting.

Jane felt quite brave as she walked towards the cottage with three police officers. She glanced around wondering if anyone would see them. She thought they looked suspiciously like burglars. Maybe four people dressed in dark clothing would look less suspicious if they were using their phones. She asked for numbers and made herself busy putting in them in.

They all checked that their phones were on silent and agreed to text each other if needed. At Jane's suggestion they set off at a jog hoping that this would help them look less like burglars. As they turned onto the street that ran parallel with the hospital drive, Shields made the call to the network. When he finished, he noted that they should have at least two hours, but to be safe they would use ninety minutes to explore then meet back at the house.

They had all looked at the scrap of paper with the map on it and agreed McMahon would go with Jane to look for the 'door' near the water. Bette and Shields would check out the cottage and see if it were being used as a hideout. If it was, then determine if there were there any places in the garden from which they could watch the cottage more directly.

They split up as they reached the lane that lead down to the water. Jane and McMahon headed down the lane while Bette and Shields had a quick look around and climbed over the fence. Recalling her lack of climbing ability displayed the other night, Jane smiled to herself. She was glad that she didn't have to do any climbing this time.

There was a chill to the air as she quickened her pace to catch up with, then match McMahon's long strides. He turned as she caught up and nodded but quickly turned back towards the water.

Chapter Twenty-Eight

The harbour... this was getting repetitive. Jane's adventure had started at the harbour's edge and she was back there again. The silvery light of the full moon highlighted features of the park in very different ways. Jane had been to the park often with friends but now it felt totally different. She was paying far more attention now to her surrounds, the sights, sounds and smells than she had ever done before. Was this Marjorie's influence? The sound of the water splashing over the seawall; the wind in the branches of the trees near the cliff; the feel of the stones and pebbles under the soles of her feet; even the faint smell of diesel. She felt alive and connected to her surrounds. At another time she would have removed her shoes and sat quietly trying to take it all in, trying to understand what was happening to her - but not tonight.

She was moving quickly along the seawall, looking over it at regular intervals to see if there was anything that might qualify as a door. It didn't help that they didn't know how big a door they were looking for: person sized, or a door to a small niche used to hide a little object like a key or memory stick.

Jane paused and looked towards the cliff face where McMahon was working his way along the cliff face under the hospital. She turned back to her task. With the full moon and king tide still rising, there was little space between the top of the wall and the water. She stopped a couple of times to inspect likely holes in the wall and concluded that, if there were a hole in the wall, the entrance would be under water. It would have to angle sharply upwards so it did not flood, which would mean that it would be at the surface. Not possible. Any hole had to be in the cliff itself, not down by the water's edge.

There was an area of parkland at the water's edge, but the parkland here had the hospital on a cliff top above it. This park was relatively recently reclaimed land; the water had been lapping at the cliff when the hospital was built over a century ago. Jane almost called out to McMahon in her excitement but managed to stop herself. The map could be referring to the time before the land was reclaimed! They could be looking for a much older door than they had originally thought, possibly a hidden entry to the hospital. It would be quite an important historical find, if nothing else.

Jane started towards the cliff face to find McMahon but took a few moments to take a wider view of where the cottage was located in relation to the hospital, the cliff and the park. Jane had been walking along the path following the sea wall which led to a playground. In the middle was the sports field. Just behind the field, near the cliff face, there was a building site with a large sand heap and a small fenced off area with a storage shed in it. Masking her torch light to a minimum, Jane looked at a sign on the fence. They were building changing rooms and toilets. The building site reached closely up to the cliff face, near the cottage fence.

She wondered how old the cottage was and if it dated back to the same era as the hospital. The cottage was also above the park but to one side and on a level lower than the hospital itself. The cottage couldn't be seen but Jane was assuming the fence and greenery that she could see were the back of it. Her eyes followed a narrow ledge of dark material, possibly rock, between the fence and the cliff. There was, she estimated, a three-metre drop to the building site in the park below.

McMahon was waving at her, so she stopped her perusal of the site and quickly hurried up to him. The council workers hadn't bothered to clear the land between the playing fields and the cliff face. Straggly trees, scrub and tangled, undergrowth remained along the base. McMahon was sweating and covered with twigs and leaves. He had worked about halfway along and was just approaching a small patch of lantana, right against the cliff face.

She shook her head at his raised eyebrows.

"Nothing I could see at the water's edge, but all this is reclaimed land. The map could be referring to a door from before the park existed, when the water reached to the cliff. It could be really historic if it's related to the hospital."

McMahon wasn't interested in the potential historical worth of any discovery as he ignored her observation. "Nothing here so far. I started below the hospital where this lot of scrub began. We've got another forty-five minutes or so. Let's just keep working towards cottage."

Jane didn't fancy dealing with the lantana – nasty stuff, strong, prickly and fast- spreading. She had long sleeves and pants, but they'd need much tougher material to cope with that stuff. McMahon didn't wait for an answer but pushed back in through the weeds and bushes to get as close to the cliff as possible. He turned and added,

"Try not to disturb it too much. We don't want them noticing someone's been looking around."

Jane needed no reminder that it was better not to be noticed. They were making slow progress but were quite near the lantana when McMahon suddenly stopped, grabbed Jane and pulled her closer to him and the cliff face.

Initially Jane could hear nothing and wondered what McMahon was reacting to, but then she heard a strange popping noise. She looked at McMahon.

"Silencers," he said grimly and pulled a gun from under his jacket.

Jane thought she knew fear, but this was another level. Where was Bette? What was going on? She reached out to Marjorie.

"What's happening?"

"Shields down... doing what I can..."

Jane froze. Marjorie sounded tense. She would be helping protect Bette and Shields.

"Mac! Shields has been shot - they need help!" Jane hissed urgently.

McMahon didn't ask how she knew. He took one look at her face, grabbed her by the wrist and started pushing his way out of the scrub, heedless of the obvious path he was creating. Once on clear ground he took off at a run.

Jane did her best to keep up but waved him on when he looked back at her. She was nowhere near as fit as he was. She stopped to get her breath and decide what was best to do. She didn't have a gun but had to do something. At this point anything was better than nothing.

She had reached the small car park where the lane ended and pressed herself into the small patch of shadow along the fence. She could feel Marjorie near, but Jane didn't want to distract her focus on helping Bette and Shields.

The popping noises had stopped but she could hear raised

voices in the distance, and then nearer, the quieter sounds of someone pushing through bushes behind the cottage fence. There was a brief moment when Jane wondered if she had imagined it. Was the night magnifying the noises or was Marjorie helping expand her senses?

Jane stared at the fence of the cottage. The noises were coming from behind it, surely it must be Bette and Shields. A few seconds later she stood with her back against the fence, straining to hear any confirmation it was them, or, and her heart sank at the thought, just one of them.

There were a couple of sudden pops, a distance away, and a muffled groan close to her. Jane made her decision, ran a couple of steps and jumped up taking hold of the top of the fence. This time there was no hesitation, she swung her leg up and over. The rest of her followed with the momentum.

Jane landed as lightly as possible, crouched down and listened. There were no sounds of any searching, so she moved towards the area from where moan had sounded. She found a small tunnel formed under some straggly hydrangeas growing wild against the fence. It was likely a tended garden at some stage. Her dealings with Marjorie had made her more sensitive to the possible histories of places. She wondered if there was a ghost here to help as well.

The ground under the hydrangeas was full of rubbish and old masonry. Nonetheless she got down on her hands and knees and made her way, quietly but as fast as possible, towards the groans.

It made sense that the person moaning would be Shields, who else would be hiding? How badly hurt was he? She could only hope Bette was with him. She didn't want to think about what she'd do once she got to him, but maybe they could get back over the fence…?

Jane soon became aware of a soft glow and headed towards that. To her great relief she heard Bette's voice, but the relief soon gave way to anxiety.

"Shields?" Bette was speaking in a tense whisper.

Jane was about to barge in when she caught sight of them, both had guns drawn, Shields was hunched over to one side and was breathing hard. It would be a bad idea to go any nearer without warning. Bette was using her phone to provide light to look at Shields injury, the glow Jane had seen.

Jane got her own phone out and sent a brief text to Bette, saying that she was very close and didn't want to be shot. Bette read the text and immediately sat up looking around. Jane then moved to join them.

There was no joyous reunion, only Bette squeezing her arm and asking where McMahon was. Jane could only say she was unsure but that said he had run ahead.

Bette quickly updated Jane. The van had returned much sooner than expected and they had been caught in its headlights, as it turned into the drive. One person had fired immediately from the cottage. They must have been watching. Shields had managed to move a bit closer to hear what was being said but Jane saw that he was pressing a cloth against his side. It was clear that vaulting the fence was out of the question.

There was a sudden flurry of noise, a loud shot and the pops of the silencers. It seemed McMahon had joined them on the property. Jane whispered that surely someone would hear and call the police? But Bette reminded Jane they were well away from houses and people near the harbour were used to fireworks going off regularly so the pops of the silenced shots would not be remarkable.

Shields asked if they could help bind his wound. He thought his belt could be used to press some wadding against his side so he could move more easily. Jane helped him sit up and pulled off his belt while Bette removed her tee shirt to act as wadding, replacing her jumper. McMahon went pale as he raised his arms so they could remove his top. Jane could hear him swearing quietly but then beads of sweat appeared on his forehead and he went very quiet.

While Bette was sorting out the wadding, Jane decided to try to distract Shields by discussing her thoughts about the 'door' being an entrance to the hospital from the cliff.

"There's this weird patch of lantana…"

She came to a stop. It was obvious that Shields was in a lot of pain as Bette pulled the belt hard to get it onto the first hole. It just fitted around his chest with her tee shirt folded over the wound. They then pulled his shirt and jumper back down and he fell back against the fence, very white, with his head back and eyes shut.

"Thought the belt would work. Lucky I've lost some weight, eh?"

Bette pressed Jane's hand.

"We have to get Shields away or draw them off. We have to consider Mac too; he seems to have drawn them away for the moment, but he might need help." Bette seemed torn about what to do.

Jane was silent for a second and, reluctantly, came to a decision. "We can't help both Shields and McMahon. I think it has to be Shields. I'll draw them off. Shields' in no state to climb the fence without help. You're stronger than me, and I know a place I can hide."

Shields had been listening and, grabbed Bette's arm, hissed,

"I'll climb the bloody fence if I have to! Go help Mac!"

Any further discussion was cut short as they heard voices coming their way.

"I got him in the body… at least once. He should've dropped then."

"He's a tough bastard. He'd keep moving. She's with him. We need them alive."

There was the sound of undergrowth being pushed aside and heavy thumps on the ground. A rat ran towards and around them. Jane squeezed Bette's hand, took off Bette's red beanie, then threw her black one in Bette's lap; smiled at them, in what she hoped was an encouraging manner, and crawled back the way she'd come.

Jane stood on the lowest rail and had a quick look over the fence. Despite the distance, she could see the tide was very high, occasional waves spilt over the wall onto the grass. The whole scene was brilliantly lit by the full moon. She had to move now and find cover fast.

Jane measured the distance mentally, took a deep breath, yelled out, "Shields? Now!" She went over the fence with the rails helping to ensure she landed with some control. She then ran a short distance along the ledge and jumped with as much energy as she could muster. She landed at the edge of the sand pile, which took most of the impact of the fall, but she still rolled over a couple of times onto the grass.

She picked herself up, struggling to get her breath, and took off towards the cliff. She heard the fence being scaled behind her but then also heard a cry... whoever it was didn't know about the drop. It sounded painful as she heard him grunt as he landed, and the swearing began.

The second man over was more careful, but by that time she was in the shadow of the cliff and nearing the lantana.

She had thought it strange the lantana covered such a small area when she first noticed it. She had once helped friends in an effort to get rid of lantana, and it was never easily contained or eliminated... yet here it was, wild, but only in a small area. Whilst discussing options with Bette, she had started thinking about the uses of it to keep people away, to hide something... something like a 'door'?

Chapter Twenty-Nine

Bette waited in the silence, hearing only her own and the heavier breathing of Shields. She was worried about Jane but had quickly realised the yell wasn't from her. One against one then, that evened the odds a bit. She smiled. Jane really was good at this - it looked like she really had inherited the adventurous side of the family genes. Bette shifted and sighed. She had to focus on what she could do. A sideway look showed Shields with eyes closed and his head against the fence. He needed medical help... and soon. She looked at her phone. Who could she trust to call?

There was a new text on the phone. Mike Grey was asking if she was okay... What? He was offering help? He had been watching the cottage, seen them and had heard the shots. He added that he was one of the good guys, but hadn't been able to tell her before... She sat back... She wanted to believe it... but was it a trick?

She looked at the very pale Shields. She decided to ring 000 and not answer Grey. She hadn't even started punching the numbers when she heard Mike Grey's voice, very close, and not on the phone.

"Come out Miss... and turn off the phone. You've played it well but it's over. Bring Shields with you or we can leave him there to bleed out. Your choice."

There was an edge to his voice she'd not heard before. It then registered he'd referred to her as 'Miss'. The beanies! She had thought Jane swapped them as a token of affection but maybe she'd wanted to cause further confusion about who was where. He must have seen the red beanie as she went over the fence. Bette needed to buy Jane as much time as she could and hope she could bring back help. It looked like she had made it away safely as there were no more shots. Trouble was, she wasn't sure how much time Shields had to offer.

Bette looked at Shields, he sighed and nodded. Bette answered, trying not to sound like herself,

"Okay! But it'll take a while to get him up."

"Don't make it too long." Grey wasn't going to let her waste time.

Bette realised that she did need to take care with Shields. He did try to help but she shook her head, whispering,

"Act worse than you are. Might be useful later."

He nodded.

Grey and friends made no effort to help but it didn't take long before they grew tired of waiting. Two men pushed in through the undergrowth to grab her and Shields, keeping their guns drawn as they did so.

Grey's eyes widened in surprise as she emerged onto the lawn and he grabbed her by the neck.

"Logan! Well, well…"

He spoke to the men with him but kept eye contact with her.

"It's okay boys, this is the policewoman. The amateur is the one we're chasing. It should be over soon, then we can bugger off! Lucky, I came for a visit, eh?"

He took Bette's and Shields' guns, shoving them in his belt. One thug, a thin edgy guy with a bad comb-over, reached out for Bette's phone but Mike snatched it from her before he could. He pocketed it before giving her a pat down while the second, a bald and sweaty man, did the same to Shields. Bette felt helpless as the man's thorough search had Shields wincing. While Grey's search of her was rough, it wasn't as thorough as she knew he usually was. He didn't even check her right sock where he knew she often kept a small knife.

Did his lack of care show he *was* a good guy? Maybe he was just nervous about her finding out he was a villain? Either gave her some hope. It might help an escape later.

With guns pointed at them, Bette half carried Shields up into the cottage. They were pushed into the lounge where the disappointing sight of an unconscious McMahon bleeding from the head and tied up on the floor greeted them. It was all up to Jane now.

Bette helped Shields sit down then moved to check McMahon. His head was cut but, despite the amount of blood, there was little damage and his breathing was regular. He'd be awake soon, no doubt with a headache and feeling very pissed off.

"You've checked your mate, now sit down and shut up" The two men guarding them were relaxed, but the way they held their guns indicated experience. Bette decided that rushing them wasn't an option – for now.

Bette was surprised at how rational she was feeling; she felt a strange calm as she sat next to Shields.

"Mac's out cold but seems okay. You?"

Shields gave a tired smile.

"I've been better. You know, they won't want us around."

"Yeah, I didn't even get a text away."

Shields smiled again and whispered,

"I did. An old friend - Ollie. He'll be here soon."

Bette tried not to react as the thin, nervous thug came towards them and told them to shut up.

Grey had left the lounge in the cottage once Bette and Shields were seated, and returned with Chief Inspector Paul Dramont, who looked at his three officers and sighed.

"What a pity. What shall we sort out for you? Missing, unexplained deaths, accidental deaths or… perhaps a policewoman gone crazy? Good headline… Murder suicide. Doesn't matter! We'll all be missing soon – I'll be missing and living it up somewhere a long way away and you three, or four when we get the other one, will be missing and dead… sad. I might stay around long enough to do your eulogies… What do you think, Grey?"

Grey looked up as if roused from deep thoughts.

"I think we'd all better disappear but yes, some sooner than others."

He turned to look at Bette, seemed about to say something, hesitated, and turned to the two thugs.

"Well let's get it done then! Let's put them down..." he paused before adding "…in the tunnels," to the thugs' amusement.

McMahon was now conscious and aware enough to swear at both Dramont and Grey, with a great deal of venom.

Dramont just smiled at him.

"Stupid thing to do. Just plain dumb to annoy a person with a gun."

He pulled a gun from his coat and pointed it at McMahon but Grey stepped in and put himself between Dramont and other three.

"Enough chat! Move it!"

He could have been talking to Dramont or the three captives. It wasn't clear. Dramont looked hard at Grey, then spat in McMahon's face and left the room, snarling,

"I'll get Joe".

Soon after, the front door slammed.

Grey grabbed Bette's arm himself and issued instructions that Shields and McMahon were to be handled with restraint as they did not want unexplained injuries and it would be easier if they could move without help.

McMahon was untied and told to help Shields. They were taken out of the lounge and through the kitchen. At another time Bette would have loved to have a closer look at the Kookaburra wood stove and the old ice chest that stood in the kitchen. The cottage had retained a lot of its old charm.

She was trying to keep an eye out for opportunities to escape and grab any possible weapons but, as they had moved through the house, she realised Grey was moving his hand on her arm… he was squeezing hard at times and loosening at others. She looked at him but he was looking ahead.

She briefly tried to wrestle free from him as they crossed through the kitchen and asked how much his loyalty cost…and a couple of other far baser comments. Not because she was angry and frustrated, though she was, but to try to get him to look at her. She wanted to see his face and make eye contact to try to judge what was going on. She got no response other than a tighter grip.

Bette tried to recall any knowledge of Morse code but couldn't remember anything other than SOS. He did seem to be squeezing in a three by three pattern. Maybe he was trying to let her know he was a good guy or maybe he had a nervous tic. It was hard to work all this out whilst being so scared.

Grey pushed her in the direction of a small building outside. Bette could see it was the old laundry and she was certain they would be shot there. It contained an old washbasin and wringer as well as a new machine but what really grabbed her attention was the open trap door to one side of the room. Tunnels! Grey had said tunnels. Her heart rate jumped as Grey pushed her towards the trapdoor. She was about to find out if the rumoured tunnels under the asylum were a myth or reality.

Grey ordered three of the four thugs down first, the thin one protesting vigorously until Grey threatened to knock him down the stairs. He then waved his gun at the prisoners.

"You can get yourselves down or I can shoot you and you can fall down. It's easier for us all if you can walk."

Bette controlled a sudden urge to lash out at Grey, to push him to show his hand. She really needed to know if he was a good guy or not? She realised that a part of her was still holding onto the hope that he was actually after Dramont. She started down the steps as ordered. At this point it was about staying alive, and in good shape, to act when an opportunity came... ignoring any hopes about Grey.

Bette stopped on the stairs to help Shields; McMahon came last. Grey moved closer as if to help but quickly backed away as McMahon went for him. He gave McMahon another whack on the head but just enough to make him sag on the stairs, not knock him out.

The man behind Grey tried to give McMahon a much heavier blow but Grey stopped him.

"We want them walking!"

He then called down to the three other men who were already in the tunnel.

"We'll meet you in the top chamber. Don't do anything until Dramont and I get there. If they aren't in one piece, you'll answer to me!"

The trap door shut above them with a loud bang. The men were now pushing their prisoners ahead of them and complaining loudly. If they were in charge, they'd just shoot the prisoners right there and then. It'd be weeks, months, even years until the bodies would be found.

Bette found herself agreeing with their logic and more hope bloomed. If Grey was ensuring they were kept alive maybe he *was* a good guy. She needed to stay alert; she needed find a way to let Shields and McMahon know about her thoughts; and that she had a knife. They might only have one chance, and all would need to be ready to act when the moment came.

As they were pushed along the dimly lit tunnel, it was becoming increasingly obvious that Shields was struggling, even with McMahon and Bette on either side of him. He was stumbling and getting heavier to support. Bette wasn't sure what, if any, of his behaviour was an act. He had been shot in the side and lost a lot of blood. Even with Marjorie's help he may not be able to do much when, or if, an opportunity did come.

Bette looked around as the group marched along. Despite the situation, she was curious about where they were. The angle of the tunnel, the surface of the floor, the aged brickwork... These must be in the mythical tunnels under the hospital – although, obviously, not such a myth after all.

Chapter Thirty

Around the time Bette was reading the text from Mike, Jane was tentatively pulling at the lantana. It was carefully tied with a rope to give it some structure, so she was right - it wasn't natural. Was it like a door or did she just have to push it aside? She knew she only had a little time, but she continued to take care not to be seen or heard. She had to admire whoever had put the door there. The lantana stem and roots were located in a pot in the ground so it could not spread far. It was a live door. This must've taken quite a while to set up. She found a bit of cloth tangled up in the branches, then realised it was shaped for a hand to grab, so she did.

Jane found the lantana door needed to be lifted a little then pulled open. It took a lot of strength to open it even the small crack she needed to push her way in, sideways. She squeezed herself around in the small opening, wincing at the scratches the lantana was giving her, unpicked her sleeve from the plant, turned into the tunnel and let out a quiet whistle. She was in the entrance to a small brick tunnel, about five foot high, but quite wide. She moved forward so the light of the full moon shining into the open doorway enabled her to see as much as she could. It was beautifully made and obviously old. It reminded her of photos she'd seen of London's tube tunnels as they were being built.

The growth of the lantana forming the doorway was very dense. There was no breeze where she was crouched in the tunnel, so the lantana door sheltered it well. Someone had taken a lot of trouble putting in and maintaining the lantana.

She took note of the direction of the tunnel and, with great effort, dragged the lantana door shut behind her. Her glimpse into the tunnel showed it offered no place to hide. She briefly worried about the second man over the fence, but hoped he'd been delayed helping the first man.

Jane thought about using her phone as a torch but quickly dismissed the idea. She wasn't sure who else might be nearby and how far into the tunnel the light would shine. She wanted to save the battery too... in case she had to call for help.

She had noted that the tunnel floor was smooth gravel and

so walking slightly bent over, she placed one hand on the brick wall and moved cautiously forward into the dark tunnel.

A short time later Jane came to a sudden halt, her heart jumped, and goose-bumps rose along her arms, but it wasn't because of the cool air. It was the smell of the tunnel, the smell of damp earth. This was what she had smelt on her attacker... he had been here as well. She felt a little nauseous.

She stood stock still a few moments, fighting the urge to run back to the lantana doorway and out into the fresh air. She forced herself to breath slowly and reminded herself that she was being hunted. She had to find somewhere to hide, wait a couple of hours and then go for help. But - who could she go to? She'd have to cross that bridge when she came to it. She felt as if she were being pushed ever closer to danger. She took a deep calming breath and moved forward, proceeding even more cautiously, if that were possible.

Eventually she realised that she was moving towards a bright light. The light increased until she had to remain still for a few moments to let her eyes adapt before edging quietly forward. Her tunnel opened onto a bigger tunnel and she was able to stand up straight and look around. This tunnel was built with the same skill as the side tunnel and was at an angle that suggested that one way was headed under the hospital, the other towards the water. It wasn't as bright as she had first thought. She could see it was rather dimly lit with a line of roughly strung electric lights, only some of which were working.

Jane moved into the main tunnel and looked both ways. As she did, she accidently kicked a small stone. It tumbled a metre or so, making a noise that briefly echoed. She stood, frozen, but there was no other noise. This would work both ways, she would be able to hear anyone coming, but she'd have to be very quiet herself.

She was trusting that the man chasing her didn't know she had found the tunnel entrance. He was likely helping the injured guy, had given up looking for her or had gone off searching elsewhere. He couldn't know she had found the tunnel entrance, let alone gone in. She was hoping that they would assume she had run out via the lane and were looking for her there, if she was lucky, or Marjorie was helping.

Jane decided to head down the tunnel, she assumed that was towards the water, and a possible exit, or if there were any good places to hide along the way. She turned left and moved quietly along the wall keeping an ear out for any hint of company. She soon saw the reflection of light on the water where the tunnel ended… sort of.

There was enough light to show that the end of the tunnel enclosed a beach area. The water was lapping high, threatening some large bags lying on the rocks to one side. Jane had saved up and bought good waterproof bags for her cameras and thought that these looked high quality ones too. She had to resist the urge to move them to a safer position.

She noticed that the rocks had bolts in them with ropes that led into the water. They could be moving drugs or money in the bags out to a boat on the harbour, she speculated.

There were a couple of large crates in the mouth of the tunnel that contained diving gear and some smaller waterproof bags. Her theory about them moving drugs, or whatever, to a boat was looking good. Whatever the ropes were being used for, they offered a possible escape route. Not one she wanted to use, she mused, as she had no idea of how long she'd have to hold her breath. The presence of the scuba gear suggested it might be a long time.

The gear was dry, so no action yet tonight.

She had an idea and took out her phone for a few photos with the flash. Not her usual quality but it would have to do. She briefly sat on the rocks and considered her options. There was no hiding place and they may be planning to use the small beach tonight. She checked her phone for reception, but, as she expected, there was none. She sighed, put the phone in the smallest of the waterproof bags and closed it up in case she had to quickly get in the water and swim out. She then quickly headed back up the tunnel.

Jane wondered where the others might be as she hurried up the tunnel. Had she been able to draw the men away long enough for Bette and Shields to escape? Where was McMahon? And where was Marjorie?

Jane stood hesitating next to the small side tunnel she had entered by. She desperately wanted to get out and back to Jo and Marion's house and meet up with Bette and the others. They'd know what to do next. This was their line of work.

However, it was unlikely to be safe to leave yet, so she continued upwards hugging the wall. Maybe Marjorie was right - despite her nerves, she was rather enjoying the feeling of adrenalin and her satisfaction with what she had managed so far.

Chapter Thirty-One

Bette went over what she knew of the hospital. Its sandstone buildings were well known in the inner suburbs and she'd done a walking tour of it only last year. She knew that it had first functioned as an asylum, opened in 1878. Callan Park Hospital for the Insane had been its welcoming name and, as with many such institutions of the time, it was not a good place to end up. It was rumoured that there were tunnels underneath the asylum with a secret water entrance for discreet admissions for use by people anxious to avoid publicity. Bette assumed this came at a price. It might be handy if you wanted to hide the fact there was a mad person in the family. It would also be handy if you had someone you wanted to get rid of - get them certified as insane and they would disappear. Just as the bad guys intended for them... Bette felt a shiver go up her spine. These tunnels must've seen some nasty stuff.

At this point in her thoughts, the tunnel opened out into a small chamber and Bette and McMahon were finally told they could put Shields down. They placed him gently on the ground and were ordered to sit next to him. Bette looked around and realised that the tunnel ended with a solid wall of dirt. It was hard to tell whether the tunnel had been filled in fully or whether part of it had just collapsed at some stage. There were boxes stacked to one side.

Two of the men watching them spoke little, and quietly when they did. However, the third man, the nervous one who hadn't wanted to go into the tunnels, was very agitated. He paced around and asked how long Grey and Dramont would be. He might as well have been talking to himself as the other two ignored him. He didn't seem to be liked; Bette began to see an opportunity. He was the only one no one spoke to... other than to give orders.

He asked again, this time a little more loudly.

"I said, how long 'til they get here?"

"Keep your shirt on! Geez, Bill. Relax! Another few hours and we'll be out of this hole."

The bald, sweaty man smiled at his own play on words. Bill

wasn't laughing.

"I hate this place... bloody shit hole!"

The two ignored him as he continued to fret and pace and turned back to their own quiet conversation.

Bette decided to see if she could unnerve him more. She turned to McMahon,

"You know, I think we're in those tunnels below the hospital, where the wealthy got rid of unwanted family members... must be a few unhappy crazy ghosts here."

McMahon looked surprised at the topic, but with Bette's eye movement towards the pacing Bill, he quickly caught on.

"Yeah, you get a real sense of the age of it... and the weight of all that dirt above us, pressing down."

One of the two guys standing together turned, but the nervy Bill spun towards them more quickly, yelling,

"Shut up!"

Bette pushed on. "Sorry, but I understand why you hate it. It's so closed in, as if the walls are pressing in. I feel really hot. It's hard to breathe."

Bill covered the distance to her in one step and hit her hard across the face.

"Shut UP!"

Bette bordered on the edge of passing out as she fell heavily back on the floor. She was aware of a short scuffle and assumed it involved McMahon; but it was McMahon who helped her sit back up.

"What happened?" she asked, tasting blood.

She carefully felt along her jaw, while checking with her tongue that all her teeth were where they were supposed to be. The punch had partly connected with her nose and split her lip. Both were bleeding.

To her surprise it was Shields who answered.

"You seemed to hit a raw nerve with that one. The others were only too happy to... er... calm him down."

He finished by pointing weakly across the room where the formerly restless Bill was now lying motionless on the floor.

Bette looked at Shields. Despite his calm voice, he was sweating in the cold air. He sat sagged against the wall, breathing heavily, and added quietly,

"You two get a chance... you go... leave me. Ollie should

be above, looking for us by now."

Both shook their heads.

"We get a chance, we all go." McMahon's tone made it a fact.

Shields shook his head and leaned back against the wall.

McMahon continued quietly to Bette.

"We need weapons."

Bette looked at the two who were debating whether or not to tie Bill up. Seeing they were occupied, she nodded towards her right foot and mouthed, "Knife."

McMahon nodded and glanced over her shoulder to her right – there was a tool kit a couple of metres away. It was open with a crowbar on top. Bette quickly looked away to see the two men taking Bill's gun off him but leaving him where he lay; baldy was saying,
"Grey can decide..."

The other disagreed.

"Dramont should decide."

Baldy continued with a dismissive snort.

"Dramont's got no balls." He then looked over at them. "You might have company on your final journey."

Chapter Thirty-Two

Jane was still making cautious progress along the tunnel. She had just reached another small tunnel coming off the main one at an angle. The electrical cord powering the lighting system came out of it.

This new tunnel wasn't as old, nor as well built, as the main one. There was still some debris where the builders had broken through into the main tunnel. Jane decided to follow it to check for places to hide. She progressed fast along the smooth floor, and in a few minutes came to a set of steps leading upwards. The electrical cord also went upwards.

Jane concluded that it was probably heading up to the cottage... this was useful to know, but she doubted it was a good place for her to linger.

She had no idea what was happening up top. She accepted that it was unlikely Bette, Shields and McMahon had gained the upper hand and captured the men at the cottage, but they might have escaped. That thought raised her spirits, but she had to focus on what she could do. Those at the cottage must now realise their operation had been compromised. Did they have plans to deal with such a situation? Surely this tunnel must be one of their escape routes. She needed to move. Now she had some information, she should escape too.

Breathing hard, Jane quickly turned back to retrace her steps. Growing more anxious as she walked, what if someone came into the tunnel now? She was out in the open with nowhere to hide. It might be best to go out via the lantana door and return to Jo and Marion's or hide in the scrub along the cliff face. It must be near daylight by now, people would be around. No one would dare attack her in public... Would they? But they already had, hadn't they?

Jane reached the main tunnel and started towards her lantana door tunnel but stopped abruptly. If the others had escaped, they would need as much information as she could gather. Feeling torn between escape and investigation, she settled herself by slowing her breathing and placing a hand on the wall to ground herself. Any extra information she could get now would be really helpful; it could save lives. Were there other entrances to the tunnels that could be used? Somewhat reluctantly, she turned, stood and faced up the tunnel, straining to hear any hint of danger before she started up the tunnel to resume her search.

She hadn't gone far when she noticed an indentation in the wall. Thinking it may be a good hiding place, she checked and found the floor went back about a metre or so, but by clambering over some rubble she could get around a slight corner. It looked like a side tunnel had collapsed at some point in the past.

Clambering over the rubble to get out again, Jane realised that there had originally been another tunnel directly across the main tunnel from where she stood. The other side was also sealed but with a brick wall. Maybe as a safety measure after the first tunnel collapse?

Jane's thoughts were shocked back to the present by a sudden explosion of noise, and her head jerked towards the sound of yelling and fighting coming from up ahead. Heart racing, she pressed back into the side tunnel and waited for the noise to die down. Once it was quiet again, Jane started up the corridor. She'd have to get closer to find out what was happening.

Jane continued until she could see a bright light ahead and heard quiet talking. The entrance to a larger chamber opened up as she got closer. She clung to the wall as she moved forward.

Jane could see half of Shields. He wasn't looking at all well. She wasn't sure he was even conscious. She craned forward a bit more and saw Bette and McMahon. They were alive! She smiled as initial relief flooded through her; but not for long as she realised Bette was bleeding from the nose and mouth, her eye was bruised and swelling; McMahon had dried blood in his hair and down his front and Shields was sunk back against the wall, eyes closed. She felt a cold anger take relief's place.

She realised Bette was looking at her. Their eyes locked briefly then Bette looked away and nudged McMahon. To McMahon's credit he didn't react other than to start talking.

"Shields is in a bad way. He needs help. Have you got a first aid kit? Tell Grey to bring one when he comes back with Dramont. They must be coming soon. There's no need to do anything drastic, just leave us and piss off. It'll take us a while to get him out. You'll be long gone."

One of the men, a stout guy in a badly fitting suit, came a few steps towards them.

"Oh, they'll be here soon and yes, you'll be staying, but he'll have no need for a medic."

Bette joined the conversation.

"Where are the bastards? Thought they'd be here gloating… and what are you doing here? Drugs?"

Baldy laughed.

"You don't know?" He slapped his mate on the back. "And all that time we thought you knew!" He laughed. "Shit! Riley thought you knew, the fucking idiot."

Jane saw McMahon react to the name. They now knew who the mole was - Senior Constable Jan Riley.

Baldy continued, waving his gun towards the boxes.

"One last shipment to make tonight, a big one, and we are done... and so are you."

Bad suit guy grabbed his mate's arm and told him to say no more.

Jane had quickly realised that Bette and McMahon were passing information to her.

She didn't need to hear much to know she needed to hide, and quickly. With a last look at Bette and, with what she hoped was an encouraging smile, Jane went back down the tunnel to hide and think. She had little option about where she could go.

Jane quickly found the collapsed tunnel entrance again. It was right under one of the working lights. She took off her jumper, folded it a few times, quickly grabbed the light bulb and turned it until it went out. She crossed over to the other side and did the same to the bulb opposite.

Putting her top back on, she quietly moved the rubble around so she could stand as far back into the side tunnel as possible. She weighed the bigger pieces of rubble in her hand, as she moved them, and she found four of a size and shape she could throw with a hefty long one she could wield as a weapon.

Jane's apprehension was growing as she waited. Why was she thinking she could rescue them? How stupid was she? Bette, Shields and McMahon were police officers, fully trained, and they had failed. She would surely freeze at a vital moment and they would die. It would be her fault. She wasn't up to this!

Shaking her head, Jane did more slow breathing and tried to be rational. Of course, she was nervous; she was in a real and very dangerous situation. However, this was different: a physical and emotional hit. She realised she was reacting to more than the situation. Her gut reaction was telling her there was something really bad here... something worse than the criminals.

Jane was anxiously moving from foot to foot when she felt the texture of the ground change under her feet. One minute she was shuffling around on dry, gravelly earth; the next it was wet! She looked down and briefly regretted turning off the light bulbs, but she could see the ground wasn't just wet, there were puddles forming. Water was seeping out of the ground and pooling. Through the dirt she could see something white emerging but there was no time to think about it. Voices were coming down the tunnel. Angry voices.

It turned out that there was actually only one angry voice. Someone was furious and Mike Grey was getting the worst of it.

"She's a bloody nothing, Grey! A damn civilian, no experience, nothing, and you can't find her! And tonight, of all nights! Are you even trying? I swear sometimes Grey, you piss me off. What are you doing here anyway? I never told you about this place!"

"You did tell me about it, and it was just as well I came to check it out. I didn't know anything was happening tonight. Your guys weren't even keeping watch. Four people got past them! It's a joke!"

Grey's reply was calm but firm.

The angry man stormed past Jane's hiding place quickly followed by a shorter second man moving fast to keep up. Despite his striding past at a fast pace, Jane was certain that the angry one was the man at the wharf, the boss. That must be the Paul who the men watching the wharf referred to as the boss: Chief Inspector Paul Dramont. She didn't recognise the second man. Behind them, Grey followed at a gentler pace, not even bothering to answer as Dramont raged on.

It was as Grey passed where Jane was hiding that he

paused, looked thoughtfully at the dark light bulbs, and glanced towards where she stood in the darkness. Jane felt her stomach churn, but he kicked at the ground and frowned at the water that pooled in the small divot he had created.

"Interesting... Nothing's really what it seems, is it?"

Grey spoke loud enough for her to hear and then suddenly moved off. Jane suspected that was in response to Dramont's swearing when he realised Mike wasn't right behind him.

Jane waited until Grey's footsteps had faded, moved out of the collapsed tunnel and leant against the wall. The dread subsided a bit once she moved, and she fought the urge to flee through the lantana door.

She did her maths. On her side, she had Bette and McMahon. Shields would do all he could she was sure, but how much that would be was uncertain. She had the benefit of surprise. She might get two hits in before they realised what was happening.

On the bad guys side - there were three in the room, and three just arrived. She assumed they all had guns. She would have to act fast and in conjunction with Bette and McMahon. Mike was an unknown. Jane was sure he'd seen her, yet not acted and said things weren't as seemed. Was he undercover? Jane decided not to hit him first. Dramont, the boss, would be best... that would even the odds.

She then got a very strange feeling in her head. Marjorie was talking to her but as if from a long way away, muffled. Jane turned her head then stopped herself. It wasn't as if she would get a better signal, but it did seem Marjorie wanted her to move and she was happy to do just that. It felt... wrong, really wrong where she was.

Jane could hear a faint murmur of voices from further up the corridor. She trusted Marjorie to keep her safe, so moved up the tunnel a few steps and stood quietly, the water deepened around her feet. What Marjorie said terrified Jane.

"Get the others! Get out! Can't... help... draining me... stay out of wards!"

Chapter Thirty-Three

In the end chamber they could hear Dramont well before he strode in. His voice got louder and the language worse as he approached,

"Mike! Where the fuck are you? Get the fuck here!"

The men guarding them grinned at each other and turned in anticipation towards the entrance.

Bette reached down to her ankle and heard McMahon whisper,

"Just let the bastard get within reach..."

She retrieved her knife and pushed it under McMahon's leg. "Let me know before you go for him, then it's all in."

Baldy shook his head as he faced the entrance,

"He'll bring the bloody place down! Fucking idiot."

Dramont came in and looked around, taking in the three prisoners sitting on the ground, and Bill lying on the ground holding his head on the other side of the room. He addressed the two standing.

"What happened?"

"Bill freaked out. Apparently, he hates tunnels and stuff. He went right off, started yelling and hit her." He pointed at Bette. "So, we hit him."

Dramont spat his reply.

"Pathetic! What else can go wrong?"

He stood and ran one hand through his hair.

"Where are the divers? Grey! You said they had gone ahead?"

Grey came in, looking relaxed.

"Probably at the water getting ready. I assume those on the boat will be keen to load fast."

Grey's relaxed demeanour was a stark contrast to Dramont's angry and agitated manner.

Dramont was frowning at Grey.

"You know a lot about the operation for someone who wasn't told anything."

Bette's attention had moved to the man who followed Dramont in. It was Joe Small. The one who attacked Jane, twice. Thankfully, Jane didn't know what he looked like as that might affect her reactions when it mattered.

It was increasingly clear to Bette that this was going to come down to some sort of fight, probably a deadly one. On their side they had a knife; the surprise of Jane being there; possibly Mike; and maybe even Marjorie. One or two of them might make it out.

If Marjorie had anything to do with it, one would be Jane, Bette thought. A warmth flooded through her which bought an involuntary smile to her face. She gave in to what she had known all along - she wanted to be with Jane. She just had to survive long enough to tell Jane that!

McMahon elbowed her in the ribs and motioned with his eyes to the men still arguing. Bette refocussed.

Dramont was still questioning Grey.

"How'd you know about the fucking boat?"

"Pretty bloody obvious. We're in a tunnel that leads to water and you have two police divers involved... I am a detective, for God's sake!"

Dramont turned away from Grey, swearing as he did.

Bette moved onto her knees, both to be in a better position to take action, but equally to stop the cramping that was affecting her. This was noted by one of the guards but his attention quickly returned to the increasingly intense exchange between Mike, Dramont and Joe Small.

"You've fucked it up!" Joe was yelling at Dramont. "One last run and we can all go home, but you go and start making demands. Of course, they're pissed off!"

Dramont leaned over him.

"They need me... us... to do this! They'll come around once they get this new delivery!"

Bette was tightening and relaxing her muscles, trying to hasten her legs through the pins and needles stage. McMahon was also surreptitiously moving his legs, and though Shields had his eyes shut, Bette could see him tensing and releasing his leg and arm muscles.

Joe was almost spitting at Dramont.

"They have more important people than you in their pockets! You're stupid to think you mean anything to them! If they want, those three won't be the only bodies found down here!" He gestured towards the prisoners.

All eyes turned towards the three on the floor and there was a brief pause. Mike entered the conversation, drawing attention back to the fight.

"You're a piece of shit, Joe! You've been pushing Dramont to try for more! If it's anyone's fault, it's yours!"

Mike suddenly pushed Joe. Joe pushed back and Dramont grabbed at the pair of them.

It was now or never, Bette launched herself at the crowbar sitting on top of the open toolbox. Grabbing it, she spun and ran at Joe. Wielding the small knife, McMahon had thrown himself at baldy, stabbing him in the side while turning his body to try to knock over the knot of pushing men as he did so.

Bette's blow landed on Joe's shoulder instead of his head as he fell with McMahon's lunge. Joe lashed out with his other arm, but she had anticipated the punch and ducked. She bought the wrench around to smash into Joe's thigh, which bought him down on top of the thug McMahon had just stabbed.

Dramont was knocked to one side but didn't go down. He took his gun out and was trying to decide where to point it when Shields hit him across the head with a plastic crate. Dramont staggered with the blow as Shields sagged to his knees.

Grey side stepped as McMahon hit the group and had his gun out but used it to hit the stout guard on the head.

Bette took a long stride towards Dramont while he remained off balance, hitting him with a glancing blow to the shoulder. He stumbled again, but didn't go down, and roared in anger and pain.

"Fuck! Enough!"

Dramont had his gun up again and, despite blood running down his face and shoulder, was aiming it at Bette and Shields.

"Dead! You're all fucking dead!"

Bette was focussed on the gun in Dramont's hand when she glimpsed movement over his shoulder. There was very little time between his last shout and him lying on the ground with Jane standing above him holding a big rock.

Joe Small had started to stand using his uninjured arm to

help himself up. Mike quickly moved to take all the guns, kicking Joe's good arm out from under him for good measure as he passed. He gave guns to Bette and McMahon, offered one to Jane but she declined; McMahon put it in Shield's pocket.

Mike was looking sheepishly at an angry Bette.

"Sorry…"

He got no further as Jane interrupted him.

"We have to go. Something bad is about to happen, we can't stay here."

"It's okay Jane, something bad was going to happen but it's okay now, thanks to you." Grey said gently.

Bette looked at Jane.

"Marjorie?"

"Yes, she's almost hysterical, something's really wrong. We must leave. Now!"

Bette turned to Grey.

"Later. We get out - now!"

Grey turned to McMahon for support, but he just shrugged.

"Don't question, just do… Jane's been right so far"

Grey looked unconvinced until Bette added,

"Marjorie did the station bomb thing."

Grey's eyebrows raised, but he just nodded and pointed his gun at the heap of bewildered and groaning bad guys on the floor.

"Okay gents… we're leaving. Bill help Dramont."

He pointed to the two thugs.

"Ryan, help John. And Joe, get the hell up!"

Jane looked at Bette. "That's Joe? The Joe?"

Joe stood looking defiantly at Jane while cradling his arm.

"You! Bloody hell! I should've fucking shot you when I had the chance!"

Grey moved between the two to protect Jane, but she pushed past him and punched Joe as hard as she could in the face. Joe staggered back a step and she stepped forward again punching him hard in his injured shoulder.

"It's easier when women don't know you're coming isn't it? Bloody coward!" a furious Jane yelled in his face.

Joe groaned and held his shoulder gingerly.

McMahon whistled in appreciation. Grey smiled and Jane

heard Bette suppress a cheer, which turned into a reminder that they had to leave and Jane remembered how distressed Marjorie had sounded.

Chapter Thirty-Four

The group started off up the tunnel. McMahon was leading the way supporting Shields, with Jane close behind them. Grey and Bette were at the back pushing the men ahead of them. Ryan was helping a complaining John, whose stretched shirt had finally burst open in the fight; whilst Joe was still telling Dramont he was an idiot and telling Grey he was going to die slowly. Dramont was walking alone after refusing Bill's help and swearing a lot. Bill limped along alone and in silence while looking nervously around.

Once the group's attention was elsewhere, Jane cradled her hand. It was a surprise how much that punch had hurt. There was no regret, however, in having delivered the punch. In fact, she felt quite good about it.

McMahon suddenly stopped and called out,

"Water!"

They were near the intersection of the cross tunnels where Jane had hidden and the water was knee deep. Jane instructed McMahon to continue,

"Keep going, there's two ways out, but the way you came in will be better, it's nearer. If the water is this high here, the way I came in will be completely under water."

Jane then raised her voice so all could hear.

"Just ahead there's the remains of a cross tunnel – move past it as quickly as you can, no stopping. One side's bricked over, the other's filled with rocks. There's something really bad there. Don't go near them."

Bill started whining but Joe just snorted whilst McMahon reacted to the fear in Jane's voice with a puzzled frown.

"Okay, but you just hit a guy holding a gun with a rock. What's the fuss about an old tunnel?"

He shook his head in disbelief. Jane could see it made no sense to him. It didn't to her either, but she trusted Marjorie. And if Marjorie was scared, so was she.

Mike came closer and looked ahead at the water.

"How deep? Can we make it to the stairs?"

Bette took a couple of steps into the water and shivered. Moving her feet ahead testing the ground, then turned back to them all,

"We know the ground is even. It'll be fine. I doubt it will get much higher than it is. I'm surprised it's this high."

Impatiently Jane entered the water and immediately felt cold surround her. It felt what she imagined evil would feel like.

"Come on! Bette get them moving, this is not good!"

Jane had a sudden connection with Marjorie, who seemed faded and weak.

'What's happening, Marjorie? Leave! Save yourself!'

'Can't... won't let me go...'

Marjorie sounded desperate.

'Who?'

Jane was looking around and could see nothing.

'Feed off fear...Get out!'

Marjorie went silent and Jane heart sank. What was going on?

"Keep a look out, something's happening but I don't know what."

She hoped that was enough to warn the group, but she didn't know what she was warning them about. Bill started whimpering again and Joe lashed out at him.

"Shut up, you idiot! The bitch is just messing with us. Ain't nothing going to happen... excepting I will kill them."

By this time, they were all knee deep in water, but something had changed. The water wasn't *feeling* like it was getting deeper, but it *looked* like it was. Where the watery air rose up and touched the walls the old bricks turned white. There were tiles along the floor. Jane realised she was now seeing through the water.

"What the hell?"

McMahon's voice trailed off and he stopped moving. Jane tried to tell him to keep going but wasn't able to find her voice. The water was over their heads... but it wasn't... she could still breathe.

The tunnel had come alive. Gas lights that hadn't existed a few moments ago, now hung from brackets high on the walls; men and women in white uniforms silently moved around and through the group.

It was the silence that was the worst part of this... The

figures around them weren't making a sound, and neither was anyone in the group.

The group was frozen in place. Jane was desperate for them to move. They were stopped right at the junction of the collapsed and bricked off tunnel... except they were both no longer blocked off, they were open.

Chapter Thirty-Five

Jane looked into the formerly collapsed tunnel and could see an old hospital ward, turn of the last century or even older.

She then turned her head to look at the tunnel with the bricked-off wall. It looked the same but, on closer inspection, the beds had restraints. The men in the beds were silently screaming and yanking at their bonds or lying seemingly unconscious.

Near the entrance to this ward, a group of four men stood. Two were in uniform, but Jane briefly wondered if they were real nurses. They were big and muscular and looked more like guards. The other two were dressed in old style police uniforms. All were watching three male 'nurses' holding a man down on a trolley. They were struggling to keep him there. He was fighting hard and yelling, though Jane couldn't hear him. A man in a white coat, a doctor Jane assumed, approached the trolley with a needle. The man on the trolley became more violent and as he fought, he turned his head and looked towards Jane. No, more than that, he looked *at* her, he *saw* her.

She saw his mouth form her name. She stared back at him in amazement and horror and he became even more desperate in his fight. He redoubled his efforts to get up and kicked the doctor who flew back against the wall. The men holding him down were losing the battle. How could he see her? How did he know her name?

Jane had to fight to turn her head away. She could feel his eyes still on her, his desire to get to her. She was terrified. With great difficulty she turned her back on him and looked for Bette. Jane repeated to herself, 'Not real, not real, not real' as she moved towards Bette.

All seemed to be in slow motion but, once she caught Bette's eye, she locked on and held her gaze until she could reach out for her hand. Their fingers touched and this simple act steadied her.

She then looked at Grey to find he'd lowered his gun in shock. As she looked, Joe grabbed for the gun and Grey reacted too slowly. Joe hit him, knocking him to the ground and took the gun with his good arm. He shot at Grey but missed.

From the corner of her eye Jane saw Bill take off, running back the way they had come. Joe grabbed Dramont and they took off into the other tunnel, the previously collapsed one, into the ward.

Jane heard Marjorie and herself yelling,

"No!"

Marjorie's voice quavered and trailed off weakly.

Once in the ward, Joe and Dramont seemed to enter the ghosts' world. The ghosts were aware of them, reacted to them. In the corridor the ghosts weren't reacting to the group, it was as if they couldn't see them. In the ward they not only saw the two intruders, they were drawn to them. Could touch them.

One female nurse reached out and touched Dramont's arm. Initially she appeared confused, but the touch became a grab, then a tug. Joe shot at the nurse, but the bullet had no effect. Dramont stood frozen as the nurses, doctors and patients all edged closer, forming a circle around the two men.

Grey started to go towards the ward, but Jane held his arm, desperately yelling at him not to follow. He stopped but called out to Joe and Dramont to get back to the group. Joe turned, looked at them and tried to break through the milling figures but the way was blocked. Dramont began screaming. The ghosts, or whatever, were moving very slowly but inexorably tightening the circle around the men.

Jane turned her head away not wanting to see any more, but she could still hear and feel both men screaming. In turning her head, Jane then looked directly into the other ward. The big man had broken free of the restraints on the trolley and was headed towards the group, still unmoving in the tunnel.

Nurses, police and doctors were fighting him, but he was throwing them off, breaking their grip and tossing their bodies aside as he attempted to fight his way to Jane. She had no doubt he was intent on getting to her. A policeman shot him, and blood spurted but he didn't go down.

Bette yelled out, dragging Jane's attention back to the group. Grey had started into the ward after Joe and Paul. Jane lunged after him and grabbed his arm. As she did, she was assaulted by pain, not just physically but mentally as well. Hurt, betrayal, fear, grief… a multitude of emotions assailed her. Some she couldn't even identify. She staggered and almost fell to the floor. She felt a quivering, weak Marjorie touching her mind, easing the chaos there. It was enough and she tugged Grey's arm again. He turned to her, white-faced and, holding each other tightly, they stumbled back into the main tunnel.

This broke the spell. Bette stepped in between the two, and, grabbing them both by the elbows, started to run, pulling them with her. Ryan grabbed John; McMahon lifted Shields off the ground; and they all ran further down the tunnel, deeper into the water.

They ran unthinking and unheeding of direction until McMahon stopped and they all stumbled to a halt next to him. They were at the 'beach' Jane had visited earlier, in calf- deep water, real water. No ghosts or wards were to be seen.

McMahon looked around,

"What the fuck just happened?"

That seemed to break the silence, and all spoke at once

"Fuck! Fuck!'

"I need a drink…"

"Where's Small and Dramont?"

"I'm going to throw up."

No one expected any answers; they were all just talking.

It was Bette who managed to say the first sensible thing. "How far back to the stairs? Where are the divers?"

Jane looked around.

"We passed the turn. We need to go back, it isn't far."

Grey answered the question about the divers.

"I dealt with them before Dramont arrived with Joe."

McMahon started back up the tunnel supporting his partner, stating simply,

"We're going back to the cottage. Shields needs an ambulance."

In silence the group, still shaking and shocked, followed McMahon cautiously back up the tunnel. There was the occasional ghost still moving around but not in their world. Grey and Bette had guns out but, after what they'd seen, it was only for comfort.

There was no need to guard Ryan and John. They were too scared to do anything other than cling to each other and follow closely.

At the junction leading to the stairs, Grey stopped and insisted on returning to find Joe and Dramont. He was sure it had all been some sort of trick

"What we saw was not real! It was something Dramont rigged up! I won't let them get away!"

Bette was willing to go with him, but stated she didn't expect to find them alive, or sane, if they found them at all. She was mostly worried about Bill who had run back towards the end chamber. She thought they would find him but wasn't sure what mental state he'd be in. She couldn't leave him there.

Jane paused with them, half listening but silently calling out to Marjorie. There was only silence. Was she gone? Was she somehow stuck in the ghost's world? Would it help Marjorie if Jane was closer to where she last heard her? Jane was scared and desperately wanting to escape the tunnels, but Marjorie might need her help.

Jane turned to Grey and said she was going too. Bette started arguing, but Grey didn't want to waste time arguing as he was keen to find Dramont and Joe. He addressed Bette and Jane,

"You can come, or you can stay and argue."

He started up the tunnel but quickly stopped and called back to McMahon.

"Mac? The divers are tied up in the kitchen larder. Can you deal with them?"

McMahon grunted in reply, but he wasn't waiting any longer and started towards the stairs with Shields. Ryan was following McMahon, dragging John with him.

"Wait! We're coming with you. I'll help with your mate. Just get us out!"

"You think Ryan and John will try anything with McMahon?"

Jane asked Bette as they jogged to catch up with Grey. Bette shook her head.

"After whatever that was, I don't think either of them are able to do anything... I'm not sure I can either."

They caught up with Grey just before the cross tunnels. Jane realised she was shaking and unconsciously reached out to touch Bette's arm. Bette jumped at her touch.

"Shit! Don't do that. I nearly had a heart attack!"

The gaslights were almost gone, fading rapidly, the string of modern lights growing more solid. The wards were nearly closed off. Jane turned to the bricked side, where a small gap remained as bricks reappeared, blocking off the doorway. The big man's hands and face filled the gap – he was still looking at Jane, his hands reaching out for her until the last brick sealed him off.

Jane cried out and fell back against Grey. He had been looking into the ward that Joe and Dramont had run into. He turned awkwardly to catch her; his pale face filled with horror. Bette was leaning against the wall of the tunnel, vomiting.

Jane instinctively looked at the tunnel and was relieved to find it again filled with debris... There was no sign of Joe or Dramont. She hadn't expected there to be.

Grey put his hand out to steady himself against the wall.

"Who is this Marjorie? Did she do this?"

"No, she is... was a good person." replied Jane.

"Was? Is?"

Grey was confused.

"Later," said Bette, wiping her mouth.

They continued up the tunnel until they reached the small end chamber, where they found Bill. He was on the ground at the far end in a foetal position. Jane thought he was dead until Bette touched him and he whimpered and curled up even tighter.

It took a long time to convince Bill that it was safe for him to uncurl, sit up, then stand and even longer to get him to walk with them back to the stairs. He broke away from them to run past the cross tunnels. Jane was happy to join him running. Grey and Bette quickly followed suit. They ran nearly all the way to the stairs before they caught up with Bill who was shaking and crying. Grey spoke to him gently, simply asking him to 'be good'. Bill could only nod. Like them, he just wanted out.

Jane was glad she had run. She thought it might help steady her. She was wrong. Once she was on the stairs, she started shaking. The adrenalin had helped her run, but shock was setting in. Now that she was safe, she was almost unable to climb. She felt Bette's hand on her back and took the first step up the ladder.

Chapter Thirty-Six

They climbed up into the cottage laundry, into a world of dazzling light. Jane shielded her eyes. It looked like late afternoon... What day was it?

Grey halted before they went into the cottage.

"I need to stay undercover, so I can't be seen with you, or here at all. I'll fill you in on as much as I can later. John, Ryan and Bill need to be told it's in their interests to forget I was ever here. We'll need to decide what we say about," he waved back towards the tunnel, "all that. Sorry to do this, but..."

Bette gave him a quick smile.

"Just pleased you're not bent... and sorry I thought you were."

Grey smiled.

"I suppose I should be pleased you thought I was. I must've been convincing."

He nodded at Jane and moved off into the overgrown garden.

"How can he think so clearly? I'm struggling to walk and think at the same time."

Jane watched Grey as he disappeared.

"Army, Special Ops." Bette answered.

Jane's surprise showed on her face as she followed Bette into the house.

Jane felt like she was in a dream. Nothing seemed real. She was aware of Bette's posture growing straighter and her stride more purposeful as Bette prepared to join her colleagues in the front of the house. Jane knew breaking this case was a huge feather in her cap. As they passed through the doorway, Bette moved faster leaving Jane behind.

Bette was greeted by a colleague in the kitchen and patted heartily on the back. He directed her towards the front of the house where flashing lights shone through the frosted glass sliding doors. Jane felt almost ignored as he merely nodded at her as she stumbled on in Bette's wake.

They kept moving through the house to the lounge where they found uniformed police, federal officers Jane thought, trying to interview Ryan. They weren't getting much out of him.

He was silently staring ahead, clearly still in shock. Bill dropped down, shaking, next to him. The two divers were looking at the silent men with concern.

"Just be glad you missed it." Bette threw at them and kept walking.

Jane followed Bette as she went out the front door. Two ambulances were in the driveway. Shields was lying in one, which was preparing to leave, John was in the other with McMahon was being patched up behind it.

McMahon broke off his animated conversation with another detective and waved to Bette and Jane. The surrounding officers started applauding, calling out congratulations and teasing comments to Bette who waved back and called out in return. Paramedics approached her, but she pushed past them to get to Shields before they corralled her and started assessing her wounds.

Jane stumbled to a halt and noticed McMahon grab a paramedic, and head quickly towards her, calling out to someone as he did. It was only then that Bette turned and looked back towards her. It was so much to take in that Jane started to stagger. She felt tears well up… they had made it! They were alive! She didn't know whose arms were around her, but she gratefully accepted their help to sit down.

Bette, Jane and McMahon were waiting to give their statements when Grey rang. He was able to let them know a few things, from which Bette and McMahon made educated guesses to fill in the gaps. They discussed the information while Jane sat and listened, cradling a weak and sweet cup of tea in her hands. Despite her interest, her attention was fading in and out. She was exhausted and worried about Marjorie. They had been given food, but she had hardly eaten anything.

Grey had agreed to go undercover about four months before. Federal Police were watching certain officers at their station they suspected had connections to criminal activities. Grey had been quietly approached and asked to infiltrate the group. He was ordered to tell no one. Files was one they were aware of, so Grey befriended him and had gradually convinced Files to let him do a few minor jobs. The finding of the body, Jane's involvement, then Files and Wallace's injuries had sped up his advance within the group.

Jane quietly got up and headed out of the room, while Bette and McMahon were discussing this. Bette noticed, excused herself and followed.

Jane was worried. Marjorie was missing. Where was she? There had been nothing from her since she had helped calm Jane's mind after she grabbed Mike in the ward. Was she hurt? Could she be hurt?

Bette caught up with Jane as she was leaning against the kitchen bench, looking out of the window. She thought she knew what the problem was.

"You heard from her yet?"

Jane shook her head and turned to lean back against the bench.

"Maybe she's tired, resting. I don't know. Do ghosts need to rest?"

Jane knew Bette was doing her best but could feel annoyance growing. Bette had been overly attentive since Jane had collapsed into Shields' friend Ollie's arms. Jane was annoyed that Bette had been striding ahead enjoying all the attention, but she immediately regretted the thought and reminded herself there was no relationship, no reason why Bette would stay with her. Why wouldn't she enjoy her moment?

Jane wasn't to know that Bette was feeling wretched. She cursed herself as she remembered seeing Jane being lowered to the ground by a stranger and McMahon being the one racing to comfort her – why hadn't it been her? Too busy being a cop, too busy looking after her career, too busy staying in control to be a friend... maybe even a lover?

They were standing awkwardly in silence when Jane recalled a conversation with Marjorie.

"Marjorie refers to herself as a spirit. Maybe there's a difference between ghosts and spirits. I get the impression spirits were more independent, not tied to repeating or existing in history."

Jane then repeated Marjorie's comment in the tunnels.

"She said they were draining her. Maybe they, whoever *they* are, killed her."

Jane had tears rolling down her face as she spoke. She had called to Marjorie every few minutes once they got out of the tunnels, cried for her, but Marjorie didn't answer. Jane had no idea what to do.

Bette moved closer and tentatively put her arm around Jane's shoulder.

"There's nothing you can do at the moment. We'll look for Alice and see if she knows anything. This might have happened before."

They stood that way for a few moments more, Bette then gently guided Jane back towards the lounge. Jane didn't know what else to do. She was uncertain about Bette's arms around her but allowed herself to enjoy being held. Eventually Bette sat her down next to McMahon and suggested that she called Jo and Marion to say it was over and they could return home.

While they were in the kitchen, a federal policeman had told McMahon that the police were conducting raids across Sydney. McMahon was almost gleeful as he passed on the new information. Federal police had become aware that drugs and money had been disappearing from police evidence storage and identified Files as one of the police officers involved. The involvement of Chief Inspector Paul Dramont had surprised everyone.

Some high-profile arrests in the state police force, and related government departments, were happening at that moment but it would take a while to unravel all the players. A yacht anchored off the hospital had been impounded and those on board arrested.

The problem for the whole enterprise had been Dramont's arrogance and Joe Small's temper. Joe's assault of Jane had put the whole scheme at risk. It started an unrelated investigation that Dramont ordered Mike to sabotage, hence linking Small to Dramont.

The whole scheme was high risk. Not only were they stealing from the police; they were stealing from a variety of crime gangs as well... biker gangs, criminal families, triads. Joe Small killed members of each of the gangs, which heightened tensions and threw suspicion for theft of drugs on other gangs. The infighting and reprisals this caused had kept the gangs busy amongst themselves.

The surfacing of the body at the wharf caused difficulties as the two bodies dumped there had been from different gangs –

if the second one were found, it would point to a common killer. Joe's dumping of both bodies off the wharf was laziness and stupidity.

At the same time the local council unexpectedly started on a long-delayed project – building new changing rooms and public toilets for the sports fields in the park below the hospital.

The chance that the side entrance to the tunnels would be discovered meant that everything had to be done a lot sooner than anticipated. While it made Grey's job easier, he also had to balance maintaining his cover while protecting first Jane, and then Bette, Shields and McMahon as they got involved investigating Joe's two botched assaults.

Three hours later they were sitting in Jo and Marion's lounge room with Jo and Marion fussing around them. On hearing the ordeal was over, Jo and Marion had taken it on themselves to rush home via a quick stop at a bottle shop. It was nearly dark outside and the table had the remnants of Jane's comfort food and packs of half eaten snacks on it. Empty bottles were on the floor with a half empty champagne bottle on the table.

Basic statements had been taken at the cottage with appointments made for more detailed questioning and debriefing later. McMahon had returned from the hospital with news that Shields had stabilised after surgery, and his wife was with him, but he would be out of action for at least a month.

Jane had been torn. She was desperate to find Marjorie, but the need to hear what others had gone through and get the whole picture, to understand it all, was strong. The story had been told in detail from all perspectives. Jo and Marion had insisted on hearing about it all.

McMahon felt the worst bit was walking into the tunnels from the cottage. He was certain they'd be shot there and was surprised they were given a chance to make a fight of it. He'd not doubted Shields would do his bit but was delighted how well Jane had handled it all. Bette had been more optimistic. She knew they'd be a fight and admitted that she had expected one or more of them might die in the fight. There was some debate about Grey's role. McMahon felt he should've acted sooner, Bette thought he'd played it well.

Jane's story had McMahon shaking his head in wonder.

"You notice the lantana, and think there *might* be a door? Then, when you found a door, you went in and explored? Amazing. But I'm bloody pleased you did. You hitting Dramont…"

At the mention of Dramont, he fell silent. Jo pressed him to continue but he just said Jane had done really well and had saved them. By unspoken consensus the ghosts and the old wards weren't mentioned. Bette just told Jo and Marion that some weird things happened but wouldn't elaborate. Jane knew that each of them would have to come to their own understanding of what happened. Then they might talk about it.

Not long after, Jane called a halt to the evening. She wanted to go home and get closer to Marjorie's park to see if that helped contact her. Jane also needed time alone to think about it all, especially the fighting man in the ward. How did he know her? She knew she wouldn't sleep but she wanted to be somewhere familiar and safe.

She stood and hesitated. How would she get home? Bette looked at her, stood slowly and said she'd get their bags. Jane was pleased, but too tired to speculate. She just wanted home. If Bette dropped her off or stayed, she didn't care… although, not being alone would be good.

Chapter Thirty-Seven

Jane dozed as Bette drove to her house. Despite her head racing to make sense of what had happened and her worries about Marjorie, Jane was having trouble keeping her eyes open. She managed to force them open when she heard Bette exclaim happily that there was a parking space just down from her house. Bette drove further down the road to do a U-turn and, in doing so, went past Marjorie's place. Jane suddenly sat upright.

"Stop the car! Stop!"

Bette swore in shock at Jane's unexpected outburst and slammed on the brake. Jane had the door open before Bette came to a stop.

"Alice? Alice! You okay?"

Jane was out and running through the gate. Bette quickly followed her, leaving the car in the middle of the road as she ran after Jane. Jane threw herself down next to an old woman lying face up a metre or so inside the fence. Bette dropped down on the other side of the woman and felt for a pulse. She detected a faint one and Alice moaned as Jane placed her jumper under Alice's head.

Alice opened her eyes as Bette took her phone out of her pocket,

"No!"

Both Jane and Bette jumped.

"No."

Alice repeated weakly and looked up at Jane.

"I'll be fine, but she needs help. There's not much more I can give, and she won't take any more in case she hurts me."

"Marjorie? She okay?"

"No, she's in a bad way. Says they drained her, and she's sort of faded. I gave her enough to slow it down, but she needs more to stop it and recharge."

Alice closed her eyes again.

Jane didn't hesitate.

"What do I need to do?"

Bette looked at Jane with concern.

"You? You need to rest!"

Jane looked at Bette and snorted with indignation.

"I can make my own decisions!"

Bette ignored her protest and addressed Alice.

"What about me? Can she use me?"

Alice shook her head.

"She needs an existing connection. I talk with her. Jane talks with her."

Jane again asked, "What do I need to do?"

"Just get comfy, open your mind and trust her, she takes energy, life energy. At your age, you're able to renew your energy relatively easily, but, being dead, she can only do it very slowly. Not as fast as she needs, so she could fade away soon. They nearly killed her."

Bette was looking thoughtful.

"Who nearly killed her?"

"She didn't say much other than it was in the tunnels. They felt her there and sort of leached onto her. She could've escaped when it first happened but stayed to help you escape."

While the two talked, Jane lay down and closed her eyes. Soon after Alice, nodded to Bette and did the same.

***

Letting out a frustrated sigh, all Bette could do was make herself comfortable, and watch over the two women lying next to her and wait. She didn't even dare to leave them long enough move her car.

Bette looked closely at Jane, while she waited. Jane had often been asleep or resting in the time they'd known each other. It was a surprise to realise it was still only a few days. So much had happened.

She looked around at the park that marked where Marjorie's house had been, marvelling at Jane's bravery and the sheer stupidity of that first visit here to get evidence. Thankfully Marjorie was there to help her. She turned back to see Jane still breathing deeply and smiled. What guts! Jane was constantly impressing Bette with her resilience and stubbornness.

This train of thoughts led to the memory of their meeting at the first assault, and then to the time they made love in Jane's house. Bette recalled her own surprise at how quickly it all happened, the immediate attraction.

She also recalled her shame at letting it happen. She had to talk to Jane to explain. She knew now how much she wanted to get to know Jane better. She had to let Jane know that she really liked her, wanted to go out with her, wanted to get back into bed with her. Bette's stomach churned at the thought of taking such a risk. She prided herself on taking on all the physical challenges her job, and some of her colleagues, threw at her. She had tackled knife-wielding thugs and broken up pub fights. But this was different. How much did she want to be with Jane? Enough to open up about her feelings? She knew very little about Jane. Despite sharing a few incredibly tense days with both of them struggling at times to keep up with what was happening. Jane had coped – more than coped, she triumphed – grew with the challenges, and Bette was highly attracted to her. Did she need to know anything else?

The thought was a reminder of her earlier realisation in the chamber, about her feelings for Jane. She was usually so good at cutting off her feelings, a survival habit from childhood. Jane had manoeuvred past all her guards and her feelings could not be turned off or dismissed. She had tried. This wasn't something she could ignore. She would have to face Jane, and her feelings. She sighed deeply. Despite the situation, the fear and the stress, or maybe because of it, her mind was looking beyond the now.

Doubt niggled at the edges of her mind. Jane was angry with her over her reaction to them having sex. Did Jane reciprocate her feelings? Did Jane need her? Bette body jerked as she recalled being told to look after Jane. The morning after they had made love. That morning – she was told that Jane would need her. She'd not realised it, but it must have been Marjorie. So, she did have a connection!

Alice was sitting up and smiling at Bette when Bette came back from her thoughts.

"Marjorie *has* spoken to me… in my head, a few days ago. I didn't answer as I didn't know what or who it was. Is that enough for a connection?"

Alice thought on it for a moment and nodded.

"Reckon so; she'll say if not."

Bette gently touched Jane's face, then reached out to Marjorie in the way she imagined it might be done.

"Marjorie? Can you hear me? She's tired, we both are. You've talked to me. Stop taking from Jane. Let me take a turn. Can I give you some energy as well?"

There was a soft, tired chuckle in reply.

"Yes, I still need more. And you're right, you and Jane do need to talk. Together you make quite a team."

"Mmmphff."

Bette replied as she lay down, nodded at Alice and closed her eyes.

"Thank you," was the last thing she heard.

Chapter Thirty-Eight

Bette opened her eyes and looked up at an unfamiliar ceiling. She sat up and nearly lay back down again. She was so very tired. She could hear voices from downstairs. There was no mistaking Liz's voice. Ah, Jane's spare bedroom, she thought. It was daylight.

How had she got here? Bette's last memory was of shutting her eyes lying on the grass at Marjorie's place. Had it worked? Was Marjorie okay? Where was her car? She'd left it in the middle of the road!

"I'm fine, thanks to you, Alice and Jane. I'm nearly back to full strength, but you'd better not need help fighting bad guys for a while."

Bette had jumped at the initial shock of 'hearing' Marjorie but relaxed quickly.

"How did I get here? What happened down in the tunnels? It was horrible. I was scared. Was it real? Had it really happened in the past, or was it some projection of what we were thinking or fearing?"

Marjorie sounded thrilled.

"Such good questions! I've been waiting for you to wake before talking to the two of you about lots of things."

Bette looked around.

"Where's Jane? Is she all right?"

"You go look for yourself, lazy bones! I'll return when you're ready to sit and talk." Marjorie started to retreat but softly added, *"You will talk to Jane, won't you, about the two of you? There's a real chemistry and you are good for each other. More than either of you realise."*

Bette lay back for a few seconds then, shaking her head, she got up, and looked around for her clothes. They were nowhere to be seen, but a set of clothes had been set out. Bette grabbed the track pants and top and headed for the shower. What had happened to her life? Did she want the excitement that seemed to come with Jane? What was she going to say to her? More worrying - how would Jane respond?

Jane was downstairs, frustrated at her friends' insistence that she must sit and rest. She had tried to help a few times but Jo and Liz had firmly told her off, and continued to fuss around doing the laundry after putting her front room back together. Marion had cleaned up in the backyard but was now in the kitchen. Jane heard a cheer from Liz and looked up, and realised it was for Bette who had just come downstairs.

Marion called a greeting from the kitchen and asked if Bette wanted coffee and toast. Bette did and, guiltily, Jane also answered and asked if she could have another coffee. Jane watched Bette move closer with mixed emotions, Bette's appearance was a relief. They might get a chance to talk about what happened in the tunnel, but would Bette just want to leave as soon as possible?

Bette moved as if to sit next to Jane, but suddenly changed direction and sat in the chair opposite. Marion came in a short while later and handed Bette a tray, which was accepted with heartfelt thanks and Bette quickly focussed on eating. Marion returned to the kitchen saying she'd put together more rounds of toast and they could all sit and talk.

As Jane held the fresh hot coffee, she was watching Bette who was smiling and chatting to Liz as she ate her toast. Bette looked exhausted. Jane took the opportunity of a break in Bette and Liz's conversation and caught Bette's attention.

"It takes a while to recover it seems from donating energy. The girls have been wonderful and refused to let me do anything. They've tidied up and done both our laundry, hence you're wearing some of my things."

Liz interrupted, "Oh, that reminds me. I'll go and check on your washing, Bette".

Jane waited until Liz had left and lowered her voice to add, "And there's no need to worry about boundaries, as we slept in separate rooms. Anyway, I'm glad you're up. I'm sick of my thoughts circling around in my head. There's so much that doesn't make sense... especially in the tunnels."

She shivered at the memory.

Bette shifted and looked around, Jane thought she looked uncomfortable, but no one was close enough to hear.

"I'd like to talk. We need to talk about...us. Us, and what happened in the tunnels. I'm amazed I slept at all..."

Jane could only nod in response as the others joined them. There was some general chat about how they were all feeling, and repeated statements of disbelief about the whole thing.

Bette looked up from her second plate of toast and whispered to Jane,

"Marjorie... er... popped in when I woke to say she'd be back when we were ready to have a chat."

"Jane, I have more news of your family. You need to have an honest talk with your mother. You have important decisions to make and information will make for better choices."

Jane looked at Bette in surprise; Bette returned the look. The others just looked puzzled by their sudden silence.

Marjorie had sounded very formal and serious but added in a more relaxed tone.

"You enjoy the company of your friends and I'll rest up and recharge a bit more. See you soon."

The conversation in the room had moved to what would happen next - for Bette at work and Jane in her career. Did she have another article planned? She wondered if the others were trying to put Jane and Bette's adventures behind them. This topic, however, got Jane anxious. What *was* she going to do next? Was she safe, was it really over? And could you return to normal life after something like this?

She wanted to have a talk with Bette as soon as possible. Maybe they could salvage a friendship? Right now, it felt awkward and painful. She was desperately trying not to think about their lovemaking, and her feelings towards Bette. There was a burst of laughter, which bought Jane back to the conversation.

Bette was being told that Alice and Jane had carried her up to bed. Jane briefly pondered about Alice; she was something different again, more than just the old frail woman she pretended to be... Another question for the already long list. There was teasing about Bette sleeping in the spare room. It was a relief to Jane that Bette didn't respond and changed the topic by asking what had happened with her car.

Jane could reassure Bette that her car was safely parked in the spot they were originally heading for.

There was time to talk about other things. It was strange to think life had been continuing as normal for other people. Jo had them laughing as she gave a demonstration of her self-defence skills. Liz was delighted that the student she helped, Ross, had been selected as one of the finalists for the award and would be exhibited. Bronwyn was off on another work trip but was applying for a promotion so she could spend more time at home with Liz. To everyone's surprise and delight Liz actually blushed. Jane was finally able to give out the presents bought in Leura.

Jane requested an early dinner, then declared she needed to sleep, which surprised no one. Despite enjoying her friends' company and the normality they bought, Jane wanted to talk with Marjorie. Dishes were cleaned and put away quickly, and Bette hung back as Jane walked her three friends to the door. There were plenty of hugs all around as they took their leave.

Jane turned to find Bette standing awkwardly in the middle of the room. There was a brief silence before Jane sighed.

"Look, I do understand what you were saying about us… er… us being together. I agree it was the wrong thing to do. Hang on, no it wasn't! It was the wrong time. Just the timing was bad. We both have to accept responsibility. I was flirting and hoping something would happen." She stopped and took a deep breath. "I really like you but now's probably not the right time for us…"

Bette took the hesitation as an opportunity.

"I want to apologise. It's my fault, not yours and my responsibility. I don't understand how I let it happen and if you want to make a complaint, I'd understand…"

Jane was stunned.

"A complaint? No! It was a mistake, yes, by both of us; but I was thinking clearly, you didn't take advantage of me. I'd been thinking about you… and us, since the night I first stayed at your place. I was unsettled by everything, but I wasn't helpless. I hope we can continue to work together 'til it's formally all over. You have the outcome you wanted with the corrupt cops identified and arrested. I hate the awkwardness between us. It seems almost loud. I'm surprised the others haven't noticed."

She didn't want to continue about what might have been, so returned to a safer topic.

"I assume there'll be a court case and some police enquiry,

so we have to see each other for a while yet."

Bette nodded, "Yes, this will take a while to sort. I'm sure we can work together without it being difficult. Maybe we can talk about us again once it's all over? If you want to… because I do. I've never felt… I'm just saying…"

Bette trailed off and was shifting her weight from foot to foot and fidgeting with her shirt sleeves, in a manner that Jane found frustratingly attractive.

There was another silence before Bette recovered herself and asked whether Jane would feel safe in the house alone for the night. She was happy to stay or go.

Jane hadn't thought about it and realised she had just assumed Bette would be there.

"Oh! Well, I'd rather not be alone, not after the tunnels. Would you mind staying? You can have the spare room. You can borrow any clothes you need. Just tonight, I can ask Liz to stay tomorrow if I'm still nervous."

Jane could see tension leave Bette's shoulders and realised she probably hadn't wanted to be alone either.

Bette nodded, "Good. I was wondering if I'd be brave enough to ask if I could stay if you said no. I'm not sure I could sleep if I were alone at my place." She smiled broadly at Jane. "That's okay then. My clothes haven't dried anyway."
Bette picked up a plate that had been missed in the clean-up and headed for the kitchen. Jane hoped her reaction to Bette's smile hadn't been noticed.

Chapter Thirty-Nine

Bette returned to the lounge and looked around. Jane picked up a couple of things to put in the refrigerator then told Bette to leave the rest until tomorrow. They were both standing awkwardly when Bette broke the silence.

"Do you want me to hang around while you to talk to Marjorie? It sounded personal and important. Marjorie's tone was that you needed to know whatever it is soon. I can go to bed, stay up and be in the kitchen or stay in here. Whatever you want me to do."

Jane looked upset and bit her lip.

"To be honest I've been wondering about that myself. I'm not sure what she's going to say. I don't really know you, yet I trust you. It might be good to be discuss whatever it is with you. What if my family are criminals? Marjorie talked about espionage. What if they worked for the Nazis or something?"

Bette moved from behind the chair she was leaning on and crossed over to Jane, hesitated, then gave her a hug.

"I've seen you at your worst – wet, mugged, bruised and battered, and I've seen you at your brave and stubborn best. You saved my life! Your family's history is just that – their history, not yours. You can choose to do what you want with what Marjorie tells you. How about you hear it alone and call me in if you want? Although, I admit, I'm keen to know what she says! You stay here and chat with Marjorie. I'll go and check my clothes."

Jane sat heavily in her favourite position on the couch and wondered if she should sit somewhere else... What if the revelations ruined the couch for her? Could she sit comfortably here again if the news were bad?

She quickly gave up on that line of thought as she was too tired, as well as too comfy to move.

"Okay Marjorie! Bring it on. Do your worst! I'm ready!"

The reply came quickly,

"Goodness! I'm not going to hit you! I have news, interesting from my point of view, but I'm not sure what you'll make of it. It seems the events in the tunnels weren't just about the high tide and an awakening of the ghost world there.

I've done some research on your family history. Your presence was a major influence on things as well."

Jane was confused.

"Me? I've never been there before! I didn't know the tunnels even existed."

"That's why you need to look at the family history and have a serious talk to your mother about the family line of work... not just about the criminal and spy history."

Marjorie didn't pause even though Jane jerked in reaction to this news.

"But this is also about your great, great grandparents, Mary and Len Woods... They did work for governments, wealthy individuals and some corporate spying. They were very successful, a couple who used their, um... talents... mostly for good. They made a lot of money and invested it well... before Len disappeared."

Jane interrupted, "Disappeared? Money? Is it dirty money? I've never heard anything about this. Mum said we come from a working-class background. Comfortable, but there was never any extra money...Mum worked hard to get me to Uni. And what's 'mostly for good' mean... What did they do?"

"They were well paid for finding things and getting information. You don't need to worry, they never did things that would hurt innocent people, they had morals. The money was often not legally gained but it wasn't 'dirty' as you put it. From what I can gather, the vast bulk of their fortune was taken by your great... Mary and hidden after Len disappeared. She gave her daughter clues as to where it was hidden, who told her daughter, who told hers, but it's never been found.   If your mother hasn't told you anything about the money or your heritage, there must be some reason. Mary and Len never willingly killed anyone... well, anyone innocent... in fact they saved a lot of people, mostly by stopping bad things happening. Len was a big man, an excellent fighter, very light on his feet. He, and your great," Marjorie let out a sigh, "great grandmother excelled in martial arts, could climb anything, pick locks, and were very good shots. But above anything else they were fast thinkers, creative, clever and bold. You've inherited those qualities."

Jane was thinking hard.

"I haven't really studied the photos I got from my aunt, so I can't recall any of them and I haven't read the letters and documents. I've never been that interested. What's all this got to do with the tunnels, though?"

Marjorie's voice became gentle.

"You saw Len in the tunnels. I was too busy defending myself to realise and warn you… He saw you too, he recognised…family…"

Marjorie went quiet.

Jane began to shake.

"A big man? A fighter?"

Marjorie's voice was hardly audible.

"Yes. That was him."

"I thought he wanted to kill me…"

Jane took a cushion from the couch and hugged it to herself.

"He wanted to protect you. He might have thought you were there with him. He may have wanted to protect you from what was happening in your world."

Jane sat up.

"That really happened to him? He really was in there? Did he go crazy? Are you telling me I'm going to go crazy?"

"No! I'm telling you that he was betrayed and locked up there. He did not deserve to be there. He was seen as too dangerous. He found out something… I don't know if all that happened to him at the time or whether it happened as he fought to try to save you… You don't need to fear him."

Jane started to softly cry. Marjorie continued,

"The tunnels come alive every high tide when water reaches up into the tunnel, touches the walls. Bad, horrible things happened there, people were mistreated, died in mental and physical torment, were murdered and it was all hidden. The negative energy that exists there now was started by the fear and negativity that existed in the wards. It was leaching energy off me. If those two men from your group hadn't run into the tunnel and given their life energy, I might have been drained out of existence. I was dropped, let go, when those two entered the ward…"

Jane fought to calm herself so she could try to make sense of it.

"It was Dramont and Joe Small who ran in. We went back to look for them, but the wards were nearly closed up. I was watching that man, Len, as his ward closed over. I didn't see the other ward but from Bette and Mike Grey's reactions I'm glad I didn't. You are saying they 'gave their life energy' confirms what I thought. Dramont and Small were killed in the ward, then sealed in when the water receded."

Jane sat in thoughtful silence before continuing.

"So, there were two things happening… First, the tunnels opened up as usual with the high-water level. But the second was these… evil energy suckers, that latched onto you. You warned me before the peak of the water... so were the energy suckers active before the tunnels opened?"

"Yes, they are sort of dormant it seems, always there, but benign to humans until high tides. I followed Bette and the policemen down into the tunnels to help but the negative energy attacked me as soon as they noticed me. We knew these things existed in places where evil happened, but it never occurred to me they'd be there, and in such numbers. I won't be making that mistake again. What happened has caused a lot of fuss here I can tell you!"

That begged the question of where 'here' was and who 'we' were. Jane wondered if there were some paranormal parliament or management committee. That discussion would just have to wait. Jane gathered her thoughts and continued her line of reasoning.

"The first thing happening, the wards. It was the history of the place coming into existence with the high tide and Len being drawn to me and so setting off a re-enactment of his time there, but it included me in it… Is that right?"

"I think so. I couldn't observe much; the energy suckers were coming at me from all sides. I think he was there this time because of you… He seemed desperate to help you, to get to you…" Marjorie sounded uncertain. "I can't recall anything clearly once they started on me, and I hate being helpless. The last time I was, it got me killed!"

Jane hadn't thought about how terrifying being helpless again must have been for Marjorie.

"That must've felt awful! I'm so sorry. I had no idea. And you were helping me. Again". Jane dreaded what she felt she must do next, but she did it anyway, *"Would it be easier, better for you, if you, er, left me? I'd hate it, but I'd understand, I've put you in danger. I don't understand your world..."*

There was a longer pause than Jane wanted, and she waited anxiously for Marjorie to consider the suggestion.

She didn't have to wait long.

"Oh, for heaven's sake, Girl. I'll not be 'leaving you', as you put it! I'm having the time of my life. I had just forgotten what being helpless feels like. Having the memory forced on me at the same time I thought I'd die again. Well, it was dreadful. But here I am, and we have more adventures to come. No, I'm not leaving. Though thanks for thinking to make the offer."

Jane blinked back tears, blew out her cheeks and decided to change the topic.

"So, about Len..."

"Yes, let's focus on the problem at hand."

There was relief in Marjorie's voice. Jane was happy to do so.

"If he, Len, had escaped the ward... made it into our tunnel... would he have been in our world physically or remained in theirs?"

Jane's mind was back on track and working very fast on several different angles.

There was a long pause before Marjorie answered.

"Not physically, he's dead. But transferring spiritually? I don't know. It has been known to happen when the connection is strong enough; so in that place, with the high tide, a king tide even... you being there... he may have been able to pass across..."

Jane let that sink in. Marjorie's answers always created more questions! She decided to preserve with Len.

"Was he one of the sucker things?"

"I don't think so. We refer to them as the negative energies, and they seem to have developed differently to ghosts and ourselves. We are wondering if they develop from angry lost souls or if they are the expression of all the negative emotions that are accumulated in sad, evil places, or a mixture of both. If they are from souls, then probably they were the same type of person in life. People more willing to drain others for themselves, no matter the cost to the person being drained.

We really don't know enough about them, but there are plans afoot. Of which I can say no more! Anyway, I think your great, great... Oh heavens! Len! Len chose not to drain others so he remains a weaker spirit. Which may be why he's trapped there. In the tunnels there was a fair exchange of energy both ways... He may have also received energy, once those men ran into the ward. I did and I am sure that it saved me."

"When we gave you some of our life energy... Is that the same as they do? But without permission and without stopping."

Jane was very interested in how this worked.

"Yes, they are sort of energy vampires."

That sounded much worse than Twilight.

"Can they leach energy without the tide? Without the tunnel transforming?"

Jane was forming a plan.

Marjorie hesitated.

"I'm not sure... We don't think so, but they are certainly there in the tunnels waiting for any opportunity, possibly regardless of the tides."

"Would there be a way to protect yourself from them? Block off access to your life energy?"

"There are ways... It requires a lot of mental strength and... Why? What are you thinking?"

"Nothing... just interested. Trying to understand what happened. I never want that to happen again."

Jane was genuine in that but wanted to stop Marjorie pushing her for more information, so she asked if Bette could join them.

"Yes, of course," came the reply, but Marjorie sounded suspicious.

Jane called out for Bette to join them in the lounge. Marjorie sighed and reminded Jane that Bette could join them from where she was, but Jane said she preferred to have Bette's physical presence.

Bette came in and hesitated until Jane motioned for her to sit.

"We haven't discussed what we saw in the tunnels. Did you look at both sides?"

Bette shuddered and nodded.

"Yes, the guy fighting to get out on the bricked-up side was bad enough, but then Small and Dramont ran into the other side…"

Jane didn't ask what Bette had witnessed. She hadn't seen much of what had happened to the two men and, from Mike and Bette's reactions, she really didn't want to know.

"Well, Marjorie's just informed me that the big guy fighting was my great, great grandfather, Len Woods. He saw me and called my name. We think he was trying to get out to help me. My presence probably affected what came 'alive' in their world."

Bette sat quietly for a moment.

"So, he really spent time there? Was he there because he was crazy, or was he a prisoner?"

Jane smiled at her in appreciation.

"Thanks for suggesting there's another option to crazy! He saw something he wasn't supposed to, apparently, and a powerful person put him away… and yes, I'm from a criminal and spy family, but a moral one apparently, well mostly."

Marjorie interrupted Jane.

"One more thing you should know, and it explains a lot… One of the reasons they were so successful was that they both had psychic talent, though Mary's talent was much stronger than Len's. It runs in the female side of your family. It's strong in you, but undeveloped."

All three were silent for a while.

"What about Bette?" Jane asked, *"She's taking this all in her stride and she can hear you."*

Marjorie spoke directly to Bette.

"Sorry dear, you just have an open, curious and flexible mind. If you experience it… then you accept it. Nice way to be!"

Jane wasn't finished giving news to Bette.

"And to top it off, Marjorie says that there's some family treasure which has been hidden!"

"So, we're off on a treasure hunt!"

Bette had leant forward excitedly, then sat back and blushed,

"Sorry. Am I invited to join the hunt?"

Jane started to make a joke but recognised the tentative

note in Bette's question, so gave a considered, serious answer.

"Yes, you are invited. Who else would understand what I'm rambling on about? Okay! We have a few things on our 'to do' list then. A treasure hunt; I need to talk to my mother and research the family history; we need to talk to Alice; and, if it's alright with you Marjorie, I want to investigate the fire that killed you. Alice said it was deliberately set... that makes it murder. I want to know who killed you and why."

Marjorie was delighted, *"Yes! I'm keen to know why someone decided to kill me too!"*

Jane hesitated but added,

"... and I want to go back into the tunnels and get Len out!"

"NO!" both Bette and Marjorie replied at the same time.

Chapter Forty

The next few days were about recovery: physical and emotional - sleeping, resting and nursing the many injuries they all had sustained.

The raids and arrests had ceased but the top men were still unidentified and at large. Mike Grey would continue undercover, working at the station as normal but waiting to see if he was contacted once things had settled. He wasn't in Dramont's inner circle and wasn't supposed to be at the cottage and so it was hoped that he wouldn't be suspected.

A short press statement announced the tragic death of Chief Inspector Paul Dramont in an accident, detailed his career, then expressed the government's sympathy to family, colleagues and friends.

In an unrelated, low key press release it was reported that Ollie Warner, a retired policeman, had stumbled on a drug ring, notified police and helped capture some of the gang.

Ryan and John remained grateful that Jane and the others saved them from the tunnel and had happily accepted reduced charges in return for their silence. Bill had been admitted to a psychiatric ward and not said a word since that night.

No one could explain what had happened to Paul Dramont and Joe Small, so the agreed story was that the two had tried to escape into a side tunnel, which then collapsed and efforts to dig them out had failed.

Bette found out that the tunnels were seen as too dangerous to try to retrieve the bodies, so the entrances were to be sealed off. Engineers would give reports about the tunnel's structural safety before decisions were made on its future.

Jane asked a lot of questions at this point. She was planning an excursion at high tide to help Len escape, so she had to find out when and how the entrances were being sealed. She had said nothing about her plans to Bette, but could she hide them from Marjorie? She didn't like the idea of lying to either of the women.

A few days later, Jane was moving the first of the items

she had advertised for sale to the front room, when a very happy Bette arrived.

She'd received a phone call from Grey saying she was being given the opportunity to sit the sergeant's exam ahead of time. The new Chief Inspector had received good reports of her conduct from Grey, Shields, and McMahon. It also helped that the station was suddenly short of police.

She had a week to study for the exam. If she passed, she'd be a Detective Sergeant and partnered with Mike.

Bette was thrilled. Being a detective in Homicide was what she had wanted for so long. She was excitedly chatting about how much it meant to her to be offered the chance, and what she hoped to achieve, when she suddenly stopped.

"I'm sorry, you probably don't want to hear all this. It's strange, but after what happened, and not just in the tunnel, it feels like you're the only one I can talk to."

She stopped again, her face went red then she blurted out, "and the guys too of course."

Jane tried not to react to Bette's obvious confusion.

"I don't mind, and yes, you're right. It's hard to speak about what happened to someone who wasn't there. I know I could speak to Jo, Marion or Liz, but I don't want to explain the details. I don't want them to understand, to freak them out about what happened..." Jane's smile disappeared. "...or about me."

Bette frowned thoughtfully as she replied.

"They won't freak. You're still the Jane they've always known. There's just a new side of you to get to know."

She held Jane's gaze.

"But maybe you should keep it to yourself for a while yet, or better... we should keep it to ourselves. If you want, we can discuss it. In fact, I'd like that. Marjorie will help us get Len out I'm sure; but I think your abilities and family stuff should remain a secret for the time being."

Jane gasped; she was stunned at Bette's reply.

"Us getting Len out! How did you know I was going ahead with it?"

Bette grinned. "You went quiet immediately Marjorie and I argued against it. You never do that... Well, not in the time I've known you. You're a stubborn woman, a brave woman. I knew you'd not give up on the idea. And now I know why. Risk-taking's in your genes. You'll need a calming influence with you, that's me."

"You cheeky bugger! And I was worried about you studying for your exam."

Jane managed to get a solid whack in on Bette's arm before Bette grabbed her hands, laughing as she did.

Bette looked down and said in a quieter voice, "And I've got a confession."

Jane looked expectantly at her.

Bette continued, "I've been studying for the exam for months now. I, umm, I spend a lot of time studying for the exams ahead of me and learning any new regulations, policy and so on that are announced. I like to be prepared... I just assume I'll be sitting them."

Bette's looked embarrassed, but Jane noted that Bette had kept a hold of her wrists.

Jane started laughing.

"That's exactly the sort of thing I'd do! So you're feeling confident about passing the exam?"

Bette groaned.

"Oh! Don't say that! But yes, I'm pretty sure I'll do well enough to pass without too much study."

"You'll jinx yourself saying things like that!"

Jane grew bold and pulled her hands out of Bette's grasp to reverse the situation by grabbing Bette's hands.

Bette laughed and they struggled playfully a short while until they fell against each other. They stopped and stared at each other for a short time until Bette suddenly dropped her grip, clumsily took a step back and turned away.

"I think I should head home. I need a good night's sleep, and we have a lot to discuss if we're going back in the tunnel. Should I call back tomorrow afternoon?"

Jane could only nod in reply and watch as Bette collected her keys and headed out the door.

Chapter Forty-One

Jane sighed loudly and dramatically threw herself onto her side. Despite the sunlight streaming into her room, her mood was dark. It was no good. After a sleepless night tossing and turning, Jane admitted defeat and sat up. She could only think about two things – holding Bette close, and returning to the tunnel and ward to get Len out. Both made her heart-beat fast and her stomach churn – one with excitement, the other with fear. Putting her thoughts about Bette to one side. She hadn't come up with any clear idea of how to protect herself in the tunnel, or what she would need to do once in there. She only knew she needed to be in the tunnel at high tide, the higher the better.

When she imagined defending herself from whatever might try to leach onto her, all she could think of was based on a scene from one of the Harry Potter movies... hardly a reliable source. She would have to ask Marjorie and convince her to help. Once she had decided this, she felt more relaxed.

She felt compelled to help Len. The desperation in his face, the horror of his situation was the main memory of her hours in the tunnel. The idea of him being trapped there, reliving the horrors, was highly distressing. She couldn't live with herself if she didn't at least try to get him out.

There was a sudden intrusion.

"I'm pleased Bette will be with you. She's right, she will be a calming influence on you and you'll need that." Marjorie had an official tone. *"You need to trust her, and she trust you. I'll do what I can to help prepare you. I won't be able to do much once you are in the tunnels... but she can. You need her."*

"You knew?"

Jane was embarrassed.

"I know because whenever you think about the tunnels you think of me, what happened to me, what information I might have and how I could help you... when you think of me, you are calling me - so I listen to what you're thinking."

Marjorie was formal. She sounded upset.

"Okay, what's the matter? You sound like one of my old teachers when I hadn't studied for an exam."

Jane didn't want Marjorie to stay in this mood. The awkwardness with Bette was bad enough.

"You didn't trust me. You were going to put yourself in a dangerous situation, which would put me in a dangerous situation. I would feel obliged to try to save you, you know I would. Getting it wrong could result in your death and being trapped in the wards yourself, and the end of my existence. It was thoughtless and selfish!"

Jane was shaken by how angry and upset Marjorie sounded.

"I… I mean… I just thought…"

Jane was floundering as she realised what might result from an ill-planned journey back into the tunnels.

"That's the point. You didn't think! How could you not see how dangerous it would be? You were there, you saw what happened when those two men made a mistake. Getting Len out will be extremely risky."

Marjorie paused and her tone softened. *"For an intelligent woman you can be naïve and very stupid! Luckily for you I have been thinking about it. And have a partial plan."*

Jane recognised Marjorie's anger had blown over, but the sting of her words still hurt.

"I'm sorry, I just focussed on how horrible it must be for Len and little else. It's putting it all together, isn't it? My heart wants him out, my head will have to plan it, and my body will have to do it."

"You forgot something."

Jane could feel Marjorie waiting for her to realise what it might be, then she pushed.

"Well?"

Jane could almost hear Marjorie's foot tapping with impatience.

Marjorie could wait no longer.

"Pride, girl, pride! Get over yourself and ask for help! This is no small task you've set yourself. You need advice and help. Stop trying to do it all yourself. To a point it's admirable, but after that it's just bloody stupid!"

No one had ever spoken to her like that. Her mother had been often absent from her life and when present had been too critical, or too protective. They had little meaningful contact now. Jane had learnt to do things and apologise later if needed; it was easier than asking and being disappointed.

"I've had to do most things by myself. I suppose I just expect it to be that way…"

Marjorie was having none of it.

"Friends don't help when you don't ask. They assume you don't want or need them. As a result they stay away, then you feel isolated. It gets into a repetitive loop. Ask for help this time. Take the risk of being vulnerable, physically and emotionally. Bette accepts your new world and is willing to help. Ask her to help, accept her help and see it as a strength. If you don't…"

Marjorie let the implication hang in the air.

Both women fell silent and Jane suddenly realised it wasn't a sullen, pained silence where hurt was likely to follow. It was a thoughtful silence, an encouraging silence, albeit still uncomfortable.

"Thank you. You're right and I'll think about it. I need to ask for help and let my friends get closer… though it might take a while. I want both you and Bette in my life. She seems to be wanting that as well, but we haven't openly discussed it."

Jane was anxious to put the discussion behind them and move to the part she felt more comfortable with – Marjorie's plan.

"Can we move onto what you've been thinking about getting Len out?"

Marjorie laughed and Jane again felt an inner embrace.

"The silence felt fine on my side too. So, it's okay if I give you a kick up the backside when you need it?"

Jane laughed aloud.

"Yes, I give you permission, but hopefully not too often!"

***

Jane spent the day finding out about council and police plans for the tunnel complex. It had become an administrative mess. The police said they had to wait for council engineers to determine if the tunnels were safe and, if not, how to seal them; the council said they were waiting for the police to allow them entry to inspect; and all the heritage groups wanted a say and an inspection as well.

Currently a private security company was guarding both the

cottage and the cliff entrance. Jane and Bette decided that getting in through the cottage would be easiest way to access the tunnel without being seen.

Marjorie was excited by the planning but frustrated at how limited her role would be. She could only prepare the Jane and Bette as best as she could. All agreed she could not enter the tunnels with them again.

Marjorie said that she knew of only one way to protect against the Negative Energies – this was now their official name – that she knew of. They had to learn to shut off their emotions. All of them, especially fear, and use strong defences.

The discussions were difficult for Marjorie and Jane stopped the conversation a couple of times to check she was ok.

"I'm fine. It's actually getting easier each time I talk about it. I think if It's helpful to you, then it's worth the discomfort."

From Marjorie's experience it seemed the Negative Energies initially fed off emotions, but the real goal was the person's life force. Closing access starved the Negatives of what powered them. Jane and Bette had to focus on the rational details of what they were doing, when and how they were doing it and nothing else. The 'why' they were doing it had to be avoided, as the answer was an emotional one and therefore dangerous.

Jane thought the experience of having been in the tunnels would act in their favour. they were more prepared, knew what to expect and so be less fearful and vulnerable.

Bette was worried that Jane's attachment to Len could make her vulnerable.

"How will you hide your emotions if you're so determined to get him out? What if he can't escape, like last time? Would you go into the ward? Would he physically come into the tunnel with us or be like Marjorie? If so, would it be best if I hosted Len out?"

"I don't know. I'll have to be very controlled. I think it'd be like Marjorie..." Jane trailed off.

Marjorie had the answer to a couple of the questions.

"No Bette, he'll stay dead, no physical body... and Jane will have to do the... hosting, as you put it. He recognised her,

was drawn to her. It has to be Jane."

There was silence, then Marjorie added cautiously,

"How would you feel about another person going there with you? One who is more detached? I am concerned that if Jane is affected, Bette you could struggle with your own reactions… and that would be very dangerous for both of you. It could be very good to have someone there to drag you both out if need be. And Jane, we have to consider that it may not work or be too dangerous. You would have to accept this and get out. How long should you keep trying?"

Jane reluctantly nodded and sighed.

"You're probably right. Who'd you have in mind? McMahon or Mike? It has to be one of them, someone who knows what they'll be getting into."

"Which one of them would be willing to accept Marjorie, be trained by her and agree to go back down - all with a small chance of saving a spirit?" Bette sounded dubious.

"I was thinking of Alice." Marjorie sounded more certain.

"Was not expecting that!" said a surprised Bette.

"That could work!" Jane was excited. "She understands, is talented in… something."

Marjorie chuckled.

"Great idea!"

"That's good. She's on her way, now." Marjorie sounded smug.

"It's not fair!" wailed Bette, "That was a set up, Marjorie!"

Marjorie laughed and suggested they put the kettle on.

Chapter Forty-Two

It was two days later that Marjorie declared the three as ready as they could be. It was easier to teach them than she had thought. For different reasons all three were already experienced in closing off parts of their life and their feelings.

With Jane and Bette this was because of their sexuality and upbringing, but Bette because of her job too. Alice had a lifetime experience of shutting out people's judgements and comments. A lot of Marjorie's work was making them aware of when they did it, how they did it and how to maintain it.

Marjorie probed and used weaknesses and trigger points to try to put them off balance as had been done to her in the tunnel. With Marjorie unprepared, and so her mind unguarded, the Negative Energies were able to discover her hurts and fears and used these to confuse and weaken her. She tried to replicate the techniques that had been so successfully used on her in the tunnels. She declared them ready when they could block off her attempts to draw energy from them.

She did however warn them that in the tunnels the negative forces would not hesitate to use any deeply held fears, hurts and shame. She hadn't wanted to do that to them in the training.

"Be honest with yourselves… What are your worse fears, your darkest secrets? If you accept them now it will have less impact in the tunnels." Marjorie sounded very serious. *"They opened me up by going over when my Harry was unfaithful. It was if I was there all over again… deep pain and feelings of rejection. It took me totally by surprise. I think they would've overwhelmed me anyway but that really sped it up…"*

"I didn't know that, Marge. Sorry."

Alice was the first to comment, and then sighed.

"Think I'm okay. I may not like it, but I am fat, old and ugly. I scare people when they look at me too long… but animals love me! I wouldn't change much in my life, other than not checking on you that night Marge; that I truly and deeply regret. I felt something was wrong but I ignored the feeling."

"I forgave you years ago Alice, for anything done or not done. It wasn't you who locked me in and lit the fire! But, they

will throw guilt at you, self-pity... everything they can. You must believe, believe with certainty, that it's false."

"I know you forgave me. I need to work at forgiving myself..."

Alice's voice broke and she could not continue.

Jane and Bette were silently listening to this exchange, when to their surprise Marjorie appeared and hugged her friend. Alice did her best to put her arms around the shadowy figure in front of her. Tears flowed between them.

It wasn't long before the women moved apart and Alice wiped her eyes.

Despite the emotion of the moment, Bette couldn't hide her delight.

"I wondered what you looked like, Marjorie!"

She looked around at the women staring at her.

"Oh, sorry, not appropriate timing... but it's true..."

"I have a question." Jane addressed Alice. "What happened to the little old lady with the working-class accent routine?"

Alice laughed. "I gives people wot they expect!"

Alice had easily changed to the nasal drawl and accent Jane associated with cockney chimney sweeps or flower sellers from old musicals, but an Australian version. Alice then seamlessly returned to her usual way of speaking.

"People say anything in front of someone they consider to be stupid. I learn a lot."

Alice looked at Jane defiantly.

Jane nodded thoughtfully and returned the conversation to the topic at hand,

"I think my deepest fears are about my size, being loved etc... the usual stuff."

She ended with a self-conscious laugh.

"You will have the 'usual stuff' thrown at you early on." Marjorie sounded frustrated. *"That's the easy bit. The really difficult stuff is the deeper things. Things you may not even be aware of unless you really explore what it is that you avoid, pull away from or react too. What makes you cry and what's behind that."*

Marjorie had remained present in the room, pacing up and down. She started speaking aloud, which Jane found hard to adjust to.

"I'm sure that this will be important. You must be aware of what could hurt you the most, scare you, make you doubt or hate yourself. That's what they hit me with… I thought I'd forgotten it, forgiven him… but I found out – as Alice just said – I hadn't stopped doubting myself. I kept thinking I had done something to deserve it. That's what they pounced on."

There was a prolonged silence, with all reflecting on what might be used against them… if they relaxed the blocks in their brains. Jane thought she knew what her weak points were - her relationship with her mother, the disappearance of her father and, now, a fear of disappointing her talented ancestors.

She believed her mother either knew where her father was, or had clues, but refused to let her know. Now there was the added secret of the family history. Jane knew there was a lot of anger and feelings of loss that she was hiding, but she was just realising the depth of it.

She looked across at Bette who was deep in thought as well. Bette almost never mentioned anyone in her family. Was this her weak point too? That's the thing about family, she reflected, they could protect you or make you so very vulnerable.

The silence continued for a bit longer until Alice announced she had to leave to get to the post office in time.

"Need a stamp? I've got some spare you can have."

Bette was mindful of the walk up the hill that a visit to the Post Office required.

"Thanks, dear, but no. Just posting a few precious pieces to myself to keep them safe before we head off… just in case."

Jane couldn't stop herself.

"Why? You think we won't get back?"

"Yes. I think we'll be fine… I worry about what might happen while we're away. What happened to Marjorie taught me to keep precious things safe. They even dug up her garden after the fire…"

"*You'd best be going.*"

Marjorie had started to fade but was quick to interrupt Alice. Alice rolled her eyes at the girls and headed to the door followed by Bette.

Jane asked the now empty room.

"You're not going to tell us what that was all about are you?"

"Not yet."

Marjorie's answer was short and she left Jane to ponder on what Alice might be referring to.

The next day Alice was waiting outside her house when Jane and Bette went to collect her. Bette was more than a little surprised.

"Whoa!"

Jane could only add, "I hadn't really thought about it, but yes, not what I was expecting either."

Alice was wearing in a very fashionable, and form fitting, outfit - matching tights and top with a lightweight coat over the top. Far more practical than her usual flowing skirts.

Bette pulled the car over and gave a whistle as Alice opened the back door and got in.

"You're looking good, why don't you wear this sort of outfit more often?"

Alice gave her a long, hard stare.

"Maybe I do. You really don't know me at all… yet." She then shook her head, "You, Bette, have a lot to learn!"

"Sorry. You just look so different from when I last saw you."

Bette stumbled over her words and had blushed at Alice's scolding of her.

"Don't worry. You're assuming things about me, which I don't like anyone doing – about me or anyone else. Everyone has their own story and role. You'll improve. I'll make sure of that. Now, let's get this done."

After much discussion they had decided to enter the tunnels with the morning high tide. Bette had checked and double-checked to ensure there was no king tide.

It was nearing a full moon, but that wouldn't have any influence on the tide yet. The strong onshore wind, however, would influence the height the high tide reached. The water levels might be a bit higher than for a usual high tide.

Jane felt goose bumps rise along her arm when Bette mentioned it. She was anxious about what they were attempting to do and where they were headed, but she couldn't imagine being better prepared than they were. She felt ready.

The short trip to the waterside car park was completed in silence with Jane focussing on what she expected to happen, what she wanted to happen and what could go wrong. Bette was driving as she said it would help distract her, but now Jane suspected it was also helpful in Bette getting over her interaction with Alice.

Alice was sitting in the back and Jane could hear her softly murmuring. She noticed Bette glance at Alice in the rear-view mirror.

As they came to a halt in the car park, Bette caught Alice's eye and asked hesitantly,

"Praying?"

"No, I believe in doing the work yourself. Just an incantation or two." Alice spoke casually. "I'm getting a few tricks ready if needed."

Jane turned in her seat. "Incantation?"

Alice was out the door. "Marjorie's not told you? I'm a witch."

She watched closely as Jane and Bette joined her open-mouthed and silent outside the car.

"Ah, obviously not... well, we can discuss that with her later."

Alice took her coat off, threw it in the back seat and closed the door. She then turned to walk towards the front of the cottage, but Jane called her back.

"Alice, we were to go over the fence and get to the trap door that way."

Alice smiled.

"You two agreed, I never did... over a fence? Me? I'll take myself in the front way, thank you! I'll meet you in the laundry."

They went their separate ways with Jane and Bette quickly climbing up to the fence and getting over it. There were no sounds coming from the cottage, so they slowly made their way through the undergrowth to the back of the laundry. So far, they were unlikely to be seen from the house but to get around into the laundry they had to move to where they'd be seen by security.

"You're fine, the guard's out front. Alice passed him, using some spell I assume... and sorry I didn't tell you about her.

She's not keen on people knowing, so I left it up to her. Good luck!"

Marjorie made it sound so normal.

Bette shook her head. "Why does it seem so reasonable that I'm listening to a spirit, before I go down into tunnels with a witch to free my psychic… er… friend's dead relative from evil energy suckers? My life has definitely taken an unexpected turn."

Jane just took Bette's hand and squeezed it hard. Together they walked hand in hand through the open laundry door.

Chapter Forty-Three

Jane and Bette entered the laundry warily keeping their eyes to the cottage in case someone appeared. Once in Bette quickly shut the door behind them, then turned and jumped in fright as they saw Alice standing at the back smiling at them.

"You enjoyed that!"

Jane whispered accusingly.

Alice's smile just got wider.

Bette halted Jane as she bent over to open the trap door. She opened her backpack and took out a can of lubricant and sprayed the hinges.

"Now we just wait a few seconds and it should open without any noise."

While they waited, Jane pulled out the waterproof bag she'd taken on her last visit to the tunnel and put her phone it and held it out towards the others. Bette nodded and put her phone in it. Alice looked bemused and said that she didn't carry a phone - technology and magic weren't a good mix.

"Ah." said Jane and rolled up the bag and fixed it to her belt.

Bette took hold of the handle a few moments later and opened the door. Her eyes met Jane's above the trap door, and they shared a grim smile. Taking her courage in hand, Jane went down first, then Alice, with Bette last, pulling the hatch down behind her. Jane had her torch out and Alice was fishing hers out from the small bag at her waist.

"What, no magic flame?"

Bette asked mischievously as she joined them.

"Saving my energy. I might need to use some of my tricks later and using any energy now might alert them to our presence."

Alice's response was so overly patient that Jane wondered if it were sarcasm.

"Ah, yes… good thinking."

Bette replied somewhat sheepishly.

"We need to talk. You need educating!" Alice replied with a meaningful look.

The walk down to the main tunnel was quick. Nothing had changed from the last time they were here, other than the lights weren't turned on.

Bette checked her watch.

"The tide should be at its peak now, so if it's going to happen…"

Alice had lost any semblance of a smile.

"It's happening already. Let's get this done. Quickly. They know we're here."

Jane didn't need Alice to tell her. Subtle whispering in her head had started - Sally had dumped her because she was fat and ugly, Bette laughed at her behind her back, and could never love her. The negative ones were there.

Jane looked at Bette and saw she was frowning and shaking her head. Jane reached out and touched Bette's arm and smiled. Bette gave a brief nod in reply. Jane momentarily closed her eyes and mentally shut and locked the heavy doors she had created to protect her emotions and memories. She opened her eyes to see Bette had done the same, and Alice nodding her approval.

Jane took a deep breath and led them up the tunnel towards the cross tunnels or wards. Her stomach was churning, and she was aware of her heart pounding in her chest and ears. Again, there was the subtle change underfoot where water was pooling. Tiles were appearing as the tunnels took on the yellowish tinge of gas lighting. They had timed their entrance perfectly.

The whispering in Jane's head was getting louder and had progressed to how her mother had never loved her. Jane refocused on the task. As they reached the cross tunnels, where the wards would be, Jane heard Bette make a quiet plea that Small and Dramont's run into the ward not be replayed. She turned to Bette to warn her to stay focussed, but could see Alice looking sharply at Bette, shaking her head. Bette nodded in reply and her face set a bit harder.

As before the ghosts were moving around and through them, paying them no interest. Jane took a quick look into the collapsed tunnel to see that ward replaying what was probably a normal day. Then she saw Small run in, dragging Dramont behind him… They had become a part of the ghostly repeating loop of that ward. She quickly turned away. This spun her so she was facing the sealed off ward. There too a normal scene was playing out.

A feeling of dread went through her... What if Len didn't show up? Alice grabbed her elbow and shook her head. Jane forced herself to shut down her emotions again, but her wave of fear seemed to have caused ripples in the ghost's world as those in the ward became more agitated. She worked hard to keep herself closed off. The nurses looked towards them, but not at them and, at last, the backs of three men came into view.

Len was in the middle, being held on either side. Jane twitched with excitement and got another squeeze from Alice. Len was hunched over, but at Jane's reaction he straightened up and began to look around.

Alice had kept hold of Jane's elbow and squeezed again, hard. Jane jerked in response. She'd have a bruise at this rate. Bette also turned and gave her a 'what the fuck are you doing?' look. Jane started to panic. She must be giving off huge vibes. Nodding to the others, she closed her eyes, breathed gently a few times as they had practiced and felt the doors shutting and locks sliding firmly into place.

She opened her eyes and found herself looking directly into Len's eyes. He started to struggle, but feeling more detached and settled, Jane merely nodded at him and reached her hand out towards him. They had decided that this gesture was unmistakably offering help.

Instead of wildly fighting as he had that first time, he quietened and started flexing his hands. The men accompanying him relaxed and loosened their grip. One let go entirely to talk to the nurse at the desk. The hand-over was completed, paperwork signed off, they unlocked the shackles.

Len sprang into action immediately the shackles came off. He didn't fight this time but pushed the man still holding him aside, turned and ran directly at the women waiting in the tunnel. He ran stretching out his arm, hand open.

Jane stepped forward to take hold of his hand. Her one step changed the whole scene. Everyone in the ward reacted. They turned to look. Not at Len, but past him towards Jane and her outstretched hand. There was a moment of stillness, then a mad scramble by those in the ward to get to Jane's hand.

The whispering in her head became screams. Jane could

feel a sense of outrage at her interfering in their world, their domain. She not just heard but felt their contempt of her and all she cared for. She could never meet Len's standards. He'd just use her and laugh. She had put Bette's life at stake for nothing. She was worthless, pathetic at all she attempted. Of course, her father had loved her brother more, that's why he took him and left her. She breathed through her fear and distanced herself from the words, watched them flow past her without listening. The howls of rage increased.

Bette called out a warning that those in the ward on the other side of the tunnel, were also moving towards them.

Alice, turning towards this danger, spread her arms.

"Focus on Len! I'll try to hold this lot!" she then started an incantation. Almost immediately feelings of anger and frustration rolled over them from that side of the tunnel. Alice's incantation seemed to be working.

Having moved first, Len had an advantage, but others were scrambling behind him.

Jane distantly noted two men standing near, and moving with Len, but making no effort to get to her. One had braces, the other a big moustache, waxed at the ends. Looking determined, they were blocking and pushing away those trying to get to Len. Jane had no idea who they were, but they were obviously helping Len. She had no time to do more than note it.

Others were closing in on Len and a couple of male nurses had hold of him. Would they come through as well? Could she survive if they did?

Bette shouted for Jane to take one more step forward, then yelled at Len to free himself of those holding him. She moved closer to Jane, took hold of Jane's other hand and leant the other way. The screams in her head made thinking almost impossible, but Jane leant further forward with Bette anchoring her.

The two nurses grabbing at Len had started to fight each other, this helped Len free himself of one. Jane could see the two men she noted before were still close, then risked turning her head to check how Alice was going. Her stomach fell, Alice was swaying, was it part of the incantation or tiredness?

She turned back to see the man with braces punching and

pulling at the one remaining nurse who was holding onto Len. She started to think it wasn't going to succeed when Len roared, the last nurse let go, and he surged forward. As he did he grabbed the hand of braces man, who grabbed the hand of moustache man and, in slow motion, Len's free hand wrapped around Jane's.

Chapter Forty-Four

Len disappeared. Bette looked around quickly to see if he was with them in the tunnel. Where were the two men she'd seen helping Len? In the ward, frustrated people were becoming violent, with fights breaking out. Bette shuddered and quickly turned away from the scene to see Jane lying on the floor, shivering and blankly staring at nothing.

Before Bette could reach Jane, she heard Alice swear and turned to see Alice stagger backwards, raise her hands higher, then suddenly lower them.

"Run!"

Grabbing Jane up off the floor as if her weight were nothing, Alice raced off.

"There's going to be one hell of a backlash!"

Bette stood still feeling utterly confused. She could almost feel the cogs of her brain slowly turning trying to make sense of what was happening. What should she do?

Alice looked behind at her and yelled again,

"Run Bette! RUN!"

Despite knowing she shouldn't, Bette turned to look behind her. An impossible wave of screaming ghosts, beds, lights, bricks and dust was forming. It was pulling back up into the tunnel and growing. To Bette's disbelief, it reached up to the tunnel roof and beyond, building into tsunami proportions and then started to collapse back down, slowly at first but gaining speed.

"Shit!"

Bette's head and body were back in sync and she turned and sprinted after the others.

Bette could see, to her relief, that despite an initial stumble or two, Jane was running at full pace too. In spite of her apparent age, Alice was leading them as they raced down the tunnel - and she was able to talk.

"Head for the water! The other tunnel won't be safe."

Bette was sprinting hard on their heels and could feel the tension growing behind her. The chaotic noises in her head were no longer forming coherent words, just furious howls.

The next few seconds dragged out as if for hours, until they hit the small beach.

"The rope! Follow it out!" Jane yelled as she led them towards the rocks where the rope was anchored.

Alice wasted no time and ran straight into the water, heading towards the rope, only turning to yell,

"Take a deep breath!"

Then she plunged under the water.

Jane waited to let Bette go first, but Bette grabbed her and pushed her into the water. The noise, both inside and outside Bette's head, had reached a crescendo, with screams ringing out, as well as rocks and debris falling, crashing and scraping.

"Go! Go!" Bette yelled at Jane, her last word breaking into a cough as dust thickened the air.

"You too!" Jane replied, gulped a breath and followed the rope.

Bette took one last look to see the tsunami crash through the tunnel opening and saw eyes, furious eyes full of malice, open screeching mouths and darkness racing towards her ahead of the debris-laden dust cloud. She didn't get the full lungful of air she wanted before she too threw herself downwards.

Jane surfaced, drawing in a shaky breath. She turned around in the water to get oriented and found herself about ten metres out from the park. She could see Alice just reaching the sea wall at the edge of the park and starting her way up a metal ladder.

Jane was very disoriented, confused and close to crying. Len had arrived forcefully in her head as he disappeared from the ward. He obviously had none of Marjorie's experience or ability to be subtle about being a guest in someone's head.

Not only that, he had brought two others with him. Braces and moustache, she guessed but they were all talking at once, thanking her, asking questions, talking about the escape, and, most annoying of all, telling her what to do. Independent thought was almost impossible for her.

She was having problems just focussing on staying afloat. She yelled aloud for them to stop, to shut up. Alice was sitting on the seawall calling for her to swim over. But where was Bette?

"*Shut up! Bloody men!*" Marjorie was furious. "*You trying to* drown her? Leave her alone! I expected Len, but who are you two?"

There was a chorus of, *"Sorry... didn't mean to... just excited... Hi, I'm David... Cy here, nice to meet you,"* then silence.

Not because Marjorie yelled at them again, as she was about to, but because the water started bubbling around Jane. All attention focussed on the water.

The tsunami of wind and debris had hit the small, enclosed beach area at the mouth of the tunnel, and the pressure was pushing air into the water. The resulting turbulence was forcing sand and larger things out into the harbour and up against Jane's legs. She didn't want to know what those larger things were.

There was a huge eruption of water a metre or so from Jane. Bette surfaced, gasped once and went back under as if dragged down. Jane screamed and swam over, turning around, desperate to grab Bette when she surfaced again.

"Now I can do something!"

Marjorie left Jane and yelled at Len to go with her. There were noises of confusion and concern from David and Cy.

Bette suddenly surfaced and Jane grabbed her.

"She was being held by one of the negative ones, but Len and I got her free. One alone and cut off from the others wasn't too difficult to fight off!" Marjorie sounded triumphant. *"Len was very useful. I'll be doing some education with these three about being more respectful of your space. Just get Bette to shore, she'll be fine. She's just been drained a little."*

"It was my pleasure to help." Len had a soft voice. *"I, we, are in your debt. David and Cy were there under false pretences as well. I had promised if I got out they were coming too! You haven't any news of Mary?"*

"For heaven's sake Len. Stop!" Marjorie wasn't impressed.

Jane sent her thanks and Len apologised. One had been hard enough to cope with, but four!

Jane found those Bronze Medallion lifesaving lessons come in useful again, as she turned Bette away from her, kept her face above water, while putting an arm across Bette's chest. Jane then struck out using sidestroke and pulling Bette along behind her. Bette was now breathing regularly after some initial gasping and spluttering and kicked weakly to help Jane.

Once at the wall, Alice guided them to the ladder and helped haul Bette up. Jane followed up the ladder and, laughing aloud, plucked one of the expensive dry bags she had admired so long ago on her first visit to the cave, from the water and threw it on the grass.

She then crawled over to check on Bette who wearily smiled and reached up a hand to touch Jane's face.

"Did it work? Is he out? Are you okay?"

Jane took Bette's hand and kissed it. "Yes, he's out, with a couple of others"

Bette nodded. "I wondered; they were helping him in there, then disappeared when he did. Are you okay?" She hesitated then added, "Are we okay?"

Jane leant down and kissed Bette softly on the mouth, lingering slightly before answering.

"I'm okay, and we are more than okay I hope"

Bette raised herself up on her elbows. "Are we? Yes! We are! I thought I'd stuffed things up with you."

Bette leant in for another kiss then jerked her head around.

"Hang on, where's Alice?"

They looked around but couldn't see her.

"I told you she's fast! She disappeared on me in the park that first night."

Jane was now sitting up and looking around. There was no one to be seen. It was unusual, but welcome as there was no one to ask why they were in the harbour.

They sunk back down to lie on the warm grass, hands tightly clasped, while looking up at the blue sky above.

Jane was listening to Marjorie chatting to her visitors. David and Cy were lovers whose families had agreed to have them committed to hide them, and the shame. Marjorie was answering questions but was mostly listening to the stories of their lives.

Jane was thankful she and Bette didn't have to face the level of fear and hatred directed at David and Cy. She'd had some incidents and verbal clashes because of her sexuality, but nothing to what they had experienced.

She was dozing, taking in the warmth of the sun, when a shadow fell across her face and she felt Bette suddenly sit up.

She opened her eyes and the discussion in her head ceased.

Mike Grey and McMahon were standing looking down at the two women.

"What the fuck just happened?" Grey was not happy.

McMahon told them that he had been given an anonymous tip. A note had appeared on his desk. No one knew how it got there. It said someone had gone into the tunnels from the cottage, so he and Mike had come down to find the trap door sealed shut.

They had walked over to try the side tunnel when there was a rumbling, the earth shook, and dust had spewed from the opening.

As they evacuated the park they noticed three people sitting at the water's edge, so had come over to move them along... and found just the two of them.

"You didn't go back down, back without us?" McMahon sounded worried, but Jane caught an edge of respect in his tone as well.

Grey repeated himself. "What just happened?"

Jane sighed and pushed up on her elbows.

"Would you believe we were jogging, fell in the harbour and then got mugged?"

Bette coughed a few times and lay down again. "Or Marjorie did it. I'm too tired to explain it right now."

Marjorie chuckled and was joined by Jane's three other visitors, so Jane started as well.

Grey looked at Jane raising his eyebrows.

"I really want to meet this Marjorie."

Jane looked from Bette to Grey, McMahon, then onto the harbour and smiled. She lay back down with her head on Bette's stomach.

The wind had dropped, and the harbour was looking lovely. Blue sky with white clouds, blue water, green and yellow ferries, a blue and white catamaran and the multi coloured sails of boats, big and small, all added their colour to the harbour and river. Above their heads a flock of white cockatoos raucously announced their arrival, with the smell of a recently abandoned barbeque close by.

"Nice day for it, eh? For once we have the time to just sit and relax. Interviewing Bette and I could take the rest of the afternoon, and best to do it at the scene. What do you guys think?"

"I know what I think! I think I'd love a beer," muttered Bette.

Mike and McMahon laughed and joined the two of them on the warm grass. McMahon took out his phone.

"Beer can be ordered with pizza you know. Two family sized pizzas - Margarita and Mexican sound ok?"

"Oh, yes! We've definitely earned a good feed."

Jane realised with some surprise, just how hungry she was. She heard but ignored Cy asking what a pizza was. She had a nagging suspicion that something important had been said to her in the tunnels. Something she needed to remember, but it faded, and she focussed on the other thing she was feeling. Something she'd only experienced fleetingly in the past. But now, she felt…settled. She recognised what it was and relaxed. She was content. Not just happy or satisfied. She pushed away doubts and just accepted that right now, for the first time, she was content with her life. And that felt pretty damned good.

All four…

"*eight really,*" said Marjorie

… sat in a comfortable silence looking out over the beautiful harbour view.

About the Author

Glenys Wilson was born in Melbourne, Australia but lived in Hobart, Tasmania for ten years and Sydney, New South Wales for 20 years. While in Sydney, Glenys lived in Balmain, near the Darling St Wharf and the bustling working harbour beyond. A strange and vivid dream while living in here, led her writing Harbour View.

Following her heart, she now lives in London with her partner, Lynn. Her Australian dog, Scooter and cat, Xena, made the move with her and are also happily adjusting to a new country, and a new cat, Tim.

Working as a Clinical Psychologist has given Glenys a curiosity about what motivates and challenges people as they go about their daily lives.

Glenys continues to work on more adventures for Jane, Bette, Marjorie and friends and hopes you enjoy them as much as she does.

Take a look at Glenys' website, www.gmwilson.org, for information on her books, new releases and lots more.

Lightning Source UK Ltd.
Milton Keynes UK
UKHW011209131019
351525UK00007B/249/P